Praise for *The Ten Thousand Things*

'Immersive… an entertaining and insightful study about
the art of nature and the nature of art.'
Tan Twan Eng, author of *The Garden of Evening Mists*

'The story of Wang's career becomes an intelligent,
graceful meditation on the difficulties of reconciling spiritual
life with the material world.'
Sunday Times

'It has the sort of sensual prose that makes the reader
purr with delight and is surely destined to be
one of the books of the year.'
Daily Mail

'This is a remarkable novel that deserves to be read
slowly and savoured as one would a stunning
landscape or a beautiful painting.'
Herald Scotland

'I've never read anything like it… great feats of scholarship
and imagination have gone into making these people,
so distant from us in space and time.'
Literary Review

'This intricately wrought study of medieval Chinese
scholar-artists is wonderfully well imagined.'
Spectator

'It is ostensibly a historical novel, but Spurling
has in fact written a love letter to Chinese art.'
New Statesman

Also by the same author

PLAYS
MacRune's Guevara
In the Heart of the British Museum
Shades of Heathcliff and Death of Captain Doughty
The British Empire, Part One

NOVELS
The Ragged End
After Zenda
A Book of Liszts
The Ten Thousand Things

Arcadian Nights: Greek Myths Re-Imagined

CRITICISM
Beckett the Playwright (with John Fletcher)
Graham Greene

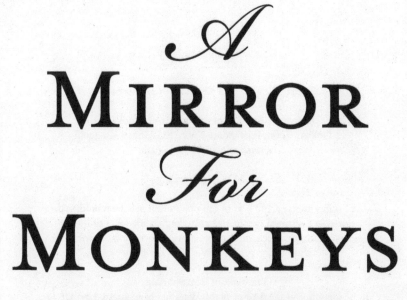

A MIRROR *For* MONKEYS

JOHN SPURLING

DUCKWORTH

First published in the United Kingdom by Duckworth in 2021

Duckworth, an imprint of Duckworth Books Ltd
1 Golden Court, Richmond, TW9 1EU, United Kingdom
www.duckworthbooks.co.uk

A catalogue record for this book is available from the British Library

Text design and typesetting by Geethik

Printed and bound in Great Britain by Clays
9780715653623

For Richard and Elizabeth Buccleuch, generous patrons
and kind hosts, to whose ancestor, Ralph, Duke of
Montagu, William Congreve dedicated his last play,
The Way of the World

CONTENTS

	Preface	xi
	Prologue	xiii
1.	The Temple of British Worthies	1
2.	The Rotondo	11
3.	The Temple of Fame	24
4.	The Queen's Theatre	39
5.	The Lake Pavilions – Western	58
6.	The Lake Pavilions – Eastern	76
7.	The Temple of Friendship	106
8.	The Temple of Ancient Virtue	122
9.	The Gothic Temple	136
10.	The Temple of Venus	154
11.	The Ladies' Temple	176
12.	The Pebble Alcove	198

So many years and months have passed away
Over that gate he fastened with a hook.
Beyond it sits the scholar day by day
Deeply immersed in writing book on book.
Those pines he planted once against the gales
Are all grown up and old with dragon scales.

Inscription on Wang Meng's painting *Writing Books Under the Pine-Trees*, 14th century

PREFACE

My friend and patron, the Russian entrepreneur Oleg Kashankomsky, was constructing a cinema and swimming pool under his garden in Chelsea when part of the row of mews houses at the bottom of his garden collapsed.

'Is nothing,' he said when he summoned me and I commiserated. 'No person hurt. We restore facades and build up-to-minute insides and sell at big profit. But we make one interesting discovery.'

He handed me an old tin cylinder, black and battered.

'From underneath old floorboards,' he said. 'You English have such historical houses. No surprise they tumble down.'

The cylinder contained a thick roll of handwritten papers.

'Is all Greek to me,' he said, as I spread them out.

'Actually it's Latin,' I said.

'Same thing. But you read?'

'It seems to be a memoir. Eighteenth-century.'

'Is interesting?'

'Oh, yes. Quite amazing, if it's genuine.'

'Valuable?'

'I should think so. If it's genuine.'

'All yours, Henry. Translate and publish! But return valuable manuscript to me.'

So this is my translation. The Latin was somewhat crabbed, tight. I have enjoyed easing it into a more modern idiom than either the author or his subject would have recognised. I cannot speak for the authenticity of the original, since so far as I know it was never shown to an expert. I handed the manuscript and its cylinder back to Mr Kashankomsky, but where it is now, heaven knows, its owner having also disappeared, leaving no address and some very angry neighbours and builders.

H.T.

London, 2017

PS. Sums of money mentioned in the text should be multiplied by about 120 to suggest today's equivalent.

PPS. Mrs, short for Mistress, was used then for both married and unmarried women.

PROLOGUE

Jeremias sum speculumque teneo. I am Jeremy and I hold a mirror. My knowledge of Latin was acquired at Oxford, where I served an old master of the language whose whim it was to speak nothing but Latin and have his manservant do the same. After his death, with the small sum of money he left me, I moved to London. My new master, at that time a young student of law at the Middle Temple and apprentice poet, was amazed and amused by my facility in a language usually reserved for the learned and only too pleased to help me improve my style. So now that he has gone to the Elysian Fields to hobnob with his literary compeers and I am spending my old age in very comfortable circumstances, I think it is incumbent on me to tell the inside story of this famous author's life. But he would not thank me for exposing him to the greedy gaze of the general public he grew to dislike, so I am taking the trouble to write it in Latin. Only the most polished people, in these days when it is no longer fashionable to write books in Latin, will be able to read it; and since Latin remains the lingua franca of all properly educated Europeans, whatever their own language, my humble but authentic biography may even reach beyond these shores.

I am not really called Jeremy, by the way, but my master made such a celebrated character out of me in his comedy *Love for Love* and gave me that name instead of my own, that I think it only quid pro quo to keep the name for this real-life comedy in which I am the author and he the character. And just as he could not help but be reflected in his own mirror, so I daresay I am in mine.

I entered Mr William Congreve's service just before his first success in the theatre, *The Old Bachelor*, when he was twenty-two years old and I was his junior by what? – a year? three years? People of his class have distinct dates of birth, while people of mine often do not. It hardly matters. I can make a good guess by looking in the mirror and frequently do so. I have a liking for mirrors, since what I see there usually pleases me, even in old age.

My mother, whom I never knew, gave me to the parish almost as soon as I was born; and my father, whom I think *she* hardly knew and whose identity nobody else ever did, must have been a handsome couple, although they came together so briefly, perhaps only the once. I like to believe that he was a landed gentleman, as Mr Congreve's grandfather was, or at least the younger son of one, perhaps a military officer, like Mr Congreve's father. Or my father could have been – if I dare say so in this irreligious age which breeds religious hypocrites – an itchy parson. He must surely have been a well-educated man or how could I have grown up so clever as to be able to learn Latin during the few years I spent in Oxford?

The truth is that I have an unusual power of memory. Consequently, although any reader of biography is wise to discredit passages of direct conversation, you may be assured that those you find here are absolutely genuine, word for word. Many of those which took place in my absence were relayed to me by Mr Congreve himself and I wrote them down immediately afterwards. So, if you suspect any embroidery or invention there, you should blame the master not the man.

Now I have cudgelled my memorious but not particularly inventive brain to discover the best method of presenting this story, and have finally settled – in deference to Mr Congreve's friend and associate Sir John Vanbrugh – on a sort of architectural and appropriately classical design. The ancient Roman rhetoricians

used to teach their pupils, especially those hoping to become
lawyers or senators, to organise and memorise their speeches
by mentally attaching the various topics or headings to some
feature of a building. Then, by visualising each feature in order
– a window, a column, a doorway – they could instantly call
to mind the topic associated with it. My system here is more
spacious: I have attached each of my topics to a single whole
edifice. Some of these structures already exist, though only two
or three of them did so in Mr Congreve's lifetime. Some may
exist in the future, some may be standing by the time you read
this, others – or indeed the whole estate – ruined or demolished.
Buildings like most things made by man go in and out of fashion.
Those I make use of here are the temples or other monuments
constructed or suggested during Mr Congreve's frequent visits
to his friend Lord Cobham at Stowe in Buckinghamshire,
together with those which have been constructed there since
Mr Congreve's death.

I accompanied my master, of course, on all his visits, when
he, his host and the other guests would regularly discuss the
improvements Lord Cobham was making and proposed making
to the garden and fields surrounding his great house. But since
my master's death I have been resident at Stowe, for Lord
Cobham, honouring a request of my master's that His Lordship
would find employment for a dead friend's faithful servant, took
me on to his own staff. At first I was merely one of his footmen,
but one day, meeting me in a corridor he kindly asked after
my welfare and remarked on how much he missed my master.
Indeed, he said, he had asked Mr Kent to construct a monument
to Mr Congreve in the grounds. I replied that I felt quite lost
without him and that I believed my only remedy was to try to
bring him back in some way.

'You want to raise his ghost? I don't think he would thank
you for that, nor do I think he would come if you called him. He
lived for this world and did not expect another.'

'Nothing of that sort, my lord. I mean only to write down my
memories of him.'

He laughed and said, 'So that's what my dear friend planned when he asked me to find you employment?'

'No, my lord. I am not even sure he would approve. It is entirely my own idea.'

'Is it wise, do you think? People have already published scurrilous things about him. Won't this give them more ammunition for their ill-aimed cannonades?'

'I have thought of that, my lord. I intend to write the book in Latin.'

'In Latin! My dear man! Is that possible?'

'I hope so, my lord. My Latin is quite serviceable.'

'Well, Mr Congreve used to surprise me with his learning and now post-mortem he surprises me even more with his learned manservant.' He paused and thought for a moment or two. 'My library is at your disposal. But you can hardly combine your literary work with your duties as a footman. I will re-employ you as my assistant archivist – you won't find that work too arduous, I think. And in future you will not take your meals with the servants, but with the family – that's to say on the same terms as the archivist and the vicar.'

'You do me too much honour, my lord. I never did eat with Mr Congreve, although he was so good as to call me his friend as well as his servant.'

'Well, you are going up in the world. And why not? We would all like to do that. But I should warn you that both Mr Vaizey [the archivist] and Mr Rand [vicar of the parish church just below the house and formerly Lord Cobham's military chaplain] make rather a display of their Latin.'

He looked at me with his fierce Field Marshal's gaze, testing me, I suppose, in case I had made a boast of my Latin which I could not sustain.

'I will endeavour to meet them on their chosen ground, my lord.'

He laughed. 'Good man!'

As for the archivist and the vicar, I may say without crowing unduly that I did not find my grasp of the language of Cicero and Caesar inferior to theirs. After a few exchanges, they were happy to converse in English and Lord Cobham was plainly delighted.

'Good man!' he said, patting me on the shoulder. 'You have quite silenced their guns, a relief to all of us. But I am sure you are tactful enough not to make enemies of them. Treat them both, please, with due respect.'

'I will do as you say, my lord. Indeed, although I may speak the language more fluently, I do respect them both as scholars and will try to enlist their help in improving my style.'

So here I am at Stowe, ideally placed not only to gather up my memories of Mr Congreve, but to set them against the constant development of Lord Cobham's grounds. I should point out that the buildings which are part of this development are not meant solely to beautify the place, though most of them are certainly handsome enough. No, they have meaning too, each an individual meaning and all together a greater meaning. I will come to the individual meanings as I pass from one section of my story to another, but the greater meaning is simply, in Mr Congreve's own words:

> *Britannia*, rise; awake O Fairest Isle,
> From Iron sleep; again thy Fortunes smile.
> Once more look up, the Mighty Man behold,
> Whose Reign renews the former Age of Gold.
> The Fates at length the blissful Web have spun,
> And bid it round in endless Circles run.
> Again, shall distant Lands confess thy Sway,
> Again, the wat'ry World thy Rule obey;
> Again, thy Martial Sons shall thirst for Fame,
> And win in foreign Fields a deathless Name.

I quote my master's and others' verses and passages of prose in their original English, not wishing to distort their style or precise meaning with my clumsy imitations. 'The Mighty Man' in these verses refers to King William III, the great hero of the Whigs. All Lord Cobham's guests, with two notable exceptions, were and are Whigs and many of them, like my master, were members of the Kit-Cat Club, which was the secret engine of Whig activity in the parliaments and governments at the end of the last century and beginning of this.

One exception was Mr Pope, a Roman Catholic and not a member of the Club, but he was invited for his poetic genius and perhaps to prevent him directing his savage satirical fire at Lord Cobham's circle. Lord Cobham, after all, gained his fame as a successful general in the Duke of Marlborough's army in Flanders and understood very well how best to neutralise an enemy's fire. Mr Pope was also himself the owner of a famous if much smaller garden at his house in Twickenham and besides an admirer of Mr Congreve, so that as long as his fellow guests were prepared to ignore his Papist background, his lack of Whig credentials and his unfortunate physical appearance – he was a misshapen dwarf – Mr Pope could be considered an asset to the company. The other exception was the Reverend Dr Swift, a clergyman of the Church of England, a Tory, and, like Mr Pope, a noted satirist.

To return to the theme of triumphant Britannia: the Whigs considered it was all their doing. They had driven out the tyrannical Catholic King James II in the Glorious Revolution of 1688 and replaced him with the Protestant Dutchman, William of Orange. They had made William sign a Bill of Rights, giving Parliament at least equal power with the King. They had achieved financial stability with the invention of the Bank of England and the National Debt. They had engineered union with Scotland, creating the United Kingdom of Great Britain and Ireland. They had defeated the armies and navies of King Louis XIV and baulked the French attempt to dominate Europe. And they had finally ensured – against Tory conspiracies to bring back the son of the exiled James II, 'the Pretender' – that the throne passed to the Protestant Elector of Hanover and his heirs. The British Navy commanded the seas, the British Army was recognised as the most formidable in Europe, and the plantations in the West Indies, the colonies in North America and the trade with Africa, India and beyond were bringing great riches to the City of London, whose merchants were mostly Whigs.

These Whigs, with their flushed, chubby English faces framed by enormous shoulder-length wigs, dressed in expensive, usually dark-coloured velvet or silk coats and breeches, and sturdy footwear, did not look much like Ancient Romans; but peering into the mirror of the past they saw themselves as a new race of Roman Republicans and when it came to statues of themselves they often preferred to bare their heads and wear togas or Roman armour. Indeed, young Mr Lancelot Brown, Lord Cobham's new head gardener, who is also proving to be something of an architect, is even now constructing on the high ground at Stowe a fluted pillar 104 feet high, to be topped by a cupola and a ten-foot statue of Lord Cobham himself, bareheaded in Roman armour, with a Roman fringe to his hair and a Roman helmet at his feet.

The Whig poets, notably Mr Congreve, translated and imitated the Ancient Greek and Roman poets; their architects and sculptors looked to the classical models of the Renaissance and the great Italian architect Signor Palladio. But Sir John Vanbrugh's architecture added another patriotic element. He mixed the classical with the Gothic, invoking the ancient Saxon ancestors of the English, whose love of political liberty, resurfacing after the Norman Conquest in *Magna Carta* and the Protestant Reformation, was thought to inspire the true Englishman's innate desire for democracy. Lord Cobham liked this idea. He commissioned statues of the seven Saxon gods after whom our days of the week are named and built a Gothic temple. Stowe is one big Whig history lesson.

Mr Congreve was an out-and-out Whig. But his grandfather, Mr Richard Congreve of Stretton Hall in Staffordshire, had been a passionate supporter of the Stuart monarchs. Following the defeat of the monarchists in the Civil War and the execution of King Charles I, Mr Congreve's grandfather helped the dead king's son to escape after losing the Battle of Worcester. Mr Richard paid for his loyalty with heavy fines to Oliver Cromwell's republican government, so he might have expected to be rewarded with at least a title and some financial recompense when Charles II was restored to the throne in the year 1660. But that unreliable king, short of money though generous enough to his many whores, did nothing for him. The Congreve family therefore remained obscure and somewhat penurious.

All this, of course, was before the days of Whigs and Tories, who only began to emerge as opposing parties during the reign of Charles II. But I have no doubt that, in spite of the king's forgetfulness, Mr Richard Congreve's sympathies were with the Tories. They were the party of the country gentry and the Church of England, believing in the Stuart monarchy's divine right to rule and expecting the return of the old world before the Civil War; whereas the Whigs were the party of the new aristocrats, the City merchants and religious non-conformists, known as Dissidents. I cannot say which party old Mr Richard Congreve's son – my Mr William Congreve's father, also called William – supported, perhaps neither. As a younger son he had to earn his own living as a soldier, though he later became steward to the Earl of Cork in Ireland and lived in some state in the Earl's castle at Lismore.

But if you should ask which party I support, I must remind you that it's of no consequence whatever, since nobody in our new-fledged democracy except the men of the upper classes – those with sufficient property – can vote. The women, even the greatest and richest of them, are as powerless as the plebeians, except, of course, that the duchesses and countesses and knights' and baronets' ladies and the rich merchants' wives have considerable influence over their husbands and lovers in the privacy of their bedrooms. And even we plebeians can sometimes show our feelings in riots stirred up by one party or the other, but most often by the Tories, who are apt to be the losing side. In fact, Mr Congreve himself, owning no property, usually had no vote, though he was once made temporary owner of a property in Reigate, Surrey, in order to vote for a friend of his. His high reputation as a clever and honest man, his writings and his friendships with great men gave him a certain oblique influence, but he did not, like several of the Whig and Tory poets, write political satire or propaganda for his party.

I called him an out-and-out Whig, but I'm not altogether certain that he was an inner one. He was outwardly a Whig because most of his friends were, because it was the modern thing to be, the rational thing, the urbane thing. The Tories tended to be backwoodsmen, people with muddy boots, country-made clothes and farmyard manners. Yet the man who first 'discovered' Mr Congreve, who set him on the road to fame and treated him as his poetic heir, was Mr John Dryden, a Tory. And the Reverend Dr Jonathan Swift, another friend, who had been at school and college with Mr Congreve in Ireland, was also, as I have already mentioned, a Tory. In the end my master considered that both parties – all politicians – came lower in the scheme of things than poets. I can even quote his own words to prove it, in a poem he wrote to flatter his most important political patron, Mr Charles Montagu (later Lord Halifax), who was also a poet:

> How oft, a Patriot's best laid Schemes we find
> By Party cross'd, or Faction undermin'd!
> If he succeeds he undergoes this Lot,
> The Good receiv'd, the Giver is forgot.
> But Honours which from Verse their Source derive,
> Shall both surmount Detraction, and survive:
> And Poets have unquestion'd Right, to claim
> If not the Greatest, the most Lasting Name.

Mr Congreve had no desire to be a great man of affairs himself – as his friends Mr Addison and Captain Steele and Dr Swift did – and he was content with small government posts which paid just enough for him to live on.

But the other side of this was that his only criterion for a poet, whether writing verse, prose or drama, was to attempt greatness, not to say perfection. He could not put up with anything but the very best either in his own work or in that of others. His friends considered him to be a man without vanity, but that was not entirely true. His vanity was not of the ordinary kind, visible in affectations of speech or manner, or in a parade of his learning, or in dropping the names of his many high-born or famous friends: no, it was all vested in his work. I might almost say that there were two Mr Congreves. There was the quiet, witty, convivial one who made no enemies, except those that did not know him personally, and there was the Author. I am not even sure that these two – let us call them AC (Author Congreve) and SC (Social Congreve) – were friends with each other, or took much account of each other. AC was convinced – or almost convinced – that he could and perhaps had indeed achieved greatness. I am not qualified to pronounce on this, but you can term it either justified pride or mere vanity depending on whether you judge him right or wrong.

In this context, a most interesting incident took place in 1726, a year or two before his death. He received a visit at his lodgings in London from a young and ambitious French author, Monsieur François-Marie Arouet, who had just come to England after being imprisoned in the Bastille for writing satires against the French government. He was already famous in Paris, but not then so well known here as he later became under the name of Monsieur Voltaire. The moment he and Mr Congreve sat down together, this pushy young man pitched straight in with the purpose of his visit:

'I cannot leave England, Sir, without having shaken the hand of the author of *Love for Love* and *The Way of the World*. I believe those and your other two earlier comedies to be among the finest ever written, certainly by an Englishman, and after all I am a compatriot of Monsieur Molière. Your tragedy too, *The Mourning Bride*, is excellent, but it is the comedies I most admire, for their subtle and never coarse wit, their wonderfully nuanced characters and their strict observance of the laws of drama. It is a privilege I shall never forget, Sir, to find myself at last in the company of one of the great spirits of our age.'

Mr Congreve, I should point out, had just been making his Will, was suffering severely from one of his fits of gout and had been most reluctant to receive this visitor at all, although as SC, who was always generous and helpful to other authors, especially younger ones, he had felt it his duty to do so. This ringing endorsement of AC, his other self, touched a nerve even more sensitive than those already jangling with gout.

'I thank you, Sir, for visiting a sick man,' he replied, 'but I would not have you do so on account of those trifles I was guilty of in my youth.'

'Trifles? I thought I had made it clear that I consider they raise the glory of comedy to a greater height than any English writer before or since.'

Now wasn't that exactly what AC wished to believe of himself? And here from an eager and evidently clever young foreigner, who had no axe to grind, no ulterior motive of gaining favour or employment, was pure proof that he was right. SC would have none of it:

'You should visit me,' he said, 'not as the perpetrator of some long-ago entertainments, but only as a gentleman who has led a plain and simple life.'

The young Frenchman was visibly astonished and for a moment completely at a loss what to say. He was like a man who having raised his hat in greeting receives a punch on the nose. But he recovered swiftly and said with great dignity, 'Sir, you take my breath away. I do not know what to say to you as a mere gentleman. I came to see you as a great writer.'

'Then I'm sorry to disappoint you.'

'I can only say that if you had been so unfortunate as to be a mere gentleman, I should never have come to see you at all.'

And there, after a few more cold exchanges, the interview ended but, as I showed him out of the door, Monsieur Arouet confided, 'I am quite disgusted with your master. I never would have thought that such a great man would have been so extraordinarily vain about his social standing, which is not, after all, particularly exalted.'

He misunderstood, of course. Mr Congreve (as SC) was not vain about his social standing, but on the contrary rather modest, considering that he was the much-admired friend of many of the greatest men in the kingdom as well as the lover of the young Duchess of Marlborough. The vanity lay in his standing as an author and that he could never openly admit. Any literate person with some sort of education can be an author – witness this book of mine – but a chosen few are obsessed by the craft, fancy themselves dedicated to it and called to its priesthood as if it were a sacred mystery. Mr Congreve (as AC) was one of these. He cared so deeply to be among the poets whose work was strong enough to last beyond their own time and fashions – the company of Homer, Horace, Shakespeare, Milton, Molière and Dryden – that he feared to reveal his secret, in case he should be mistaken.

1

THE TEMPLE OF BRITISH WORTHIES

When, where, did my master begin to see himself as an author – or at least to want to be one? During his boyhood, at school and university in Ireland? I should point out that although he grew up and was educated in Ireland, he was not born there, as many have assumed. No, he was born in Yorkshire and was taken to Ireland at the age of four, when his father was posted to Youghal in County Cork as a lieutenant in a regiment of foot. The boy attended Kilkenny, a school with a high reputation for scholarship, and Trinity College, Dublin, which he entered at the age of sixteen. His much-admired tutor, Dr St. George Ashe, also taught Dr Swift. Young Congreve learnt to admire the Greek and Latin authors and was able from an early age to make fine translations into English verse of Homer, Horace, Catullus and Ovid. His first published work, in a *Miscellany* put together by Mr Dryden, was a translation of the Roman satirical poet Juvenal.

The schoolboy Congreve was said to have written poems, though no one ever saw them afterwards and he told me he would be mortified if anyone had. He also discovered the pleasures of the theatre and of the company of actors and actresses at the Smock Alley Theatre in Dublin. And by the time he returned to England in 1689, or soon afterwards, he had written a novel. He was pleased enough with it at the time to dedicate it to a young woman he admired, to write a confident preface pointing out the pains he had taken with its construction, and to have it published, but he did not value it enough later to include it in the collected edition of his works.

I'll come back to that novel, but first I need to explain where we are, mnemonically speaking, in the politicised grounds of Lord Cobham's Stowe. Behold a delightful expanse of greensward sloping down to a gentle stream: these are the Elysian Fields, named after the place where the great heroes, poets and philosophers of the Ancient Greeks were supposed to go when they died. A path runs beside the stream on the eastern side and here the architect Mr William Kent built the Temple of British Worthies. It is not strictly a temple, but rather a sort of outdoor shrine, a curving wall of niches, with a pyramid at its centre. The pyramid is surmounted by a head of Mercury, the god who led the souls of the blessed to the airy and sunlit Elysian Fields instead of into the miserable dark oblivion of Hades, where everyone else ended up. There are sixteen niches containing the busts of monarchs, adventurers, philosophers, Members of Parliament, poets, an architect and a financier: an exclusive club of Whig saints. The monarchs are Alfred the Great, Elizabeth and of course William III, who headed the Glorious Revolution; the adventurers are Raleigh and Drake; the philosopher-scientists Bacon, Locke and Newton; the architect Inigo Jones, and the financier Sir Thomas Gresham, founder of the Royal Exchange. King Edward III's warrior son, the Black Prince, is there too, I forget why, probably because he used to trounce the French. I also forget who the Members of Parliament are; they are never very memorable people. The poets are Shakespeare, Milton and Pope.

Mr Pope was still alive when this shrine was built and I do not think that Mr Congreve, if he had been still alive, would have been at all pleased. He admired Mr Pope's work, but perhaps not quite as much as Mr Pope, considerably his junior, admired his. And how would he have felt to find himself omitted from the ranks of the British Worthies, this ultimate accolade, this guarantee almost of lasting fame? Social Congreve would have smiled, shrugged and remarked that he was not in the least worthy, merely a gentleman who once wrote some 'trifles', but Author Congreve would have burned inwardly with bitter bile. Perhaps Lord Cobham, in spite of his stated disbelief in his dear friend's ghost, had been haunted by it. At any rate, soon afterwards, he had Mr Kent build a separate monument to Mr Congreve further downstream.

It's a strangely crowded, somewhat ungainly object: a small brick pyramid with a stone urn in bas-relief attached to one side and adorned, again in relief, with the faces of youth, maturity and age, pan pipes, a sword, a shield, a quiver of arrows and a bunch of grapes, symbols presumably considered appropriate to my master's life, works and tastes. Certainly, he loved music and wine, and the sword and shield perhaps stand for the gentleman, but I wonder about the arrows: he was no huntsman and no soldier. Possibly they stand for his many sharp satirical hits, what the Latin memorial inscription calls his 'ingenio acri, faceto, expolito' (piercing, elegant, polished wit). This inscription also praises his 'moribus urbanis, candidis, facillimis' (civilised, candid, unaffected manners).

But the most noticeable, even grotesque part of the monument is the top of the pyramid: there sits a large stone monkey holding a mirror up to himself, while staring back at the creature from the top of the mirror is a relief of Mr Congreve's face. There is another inscription in Latin to explain it: 'Vitae imitatio, Consuetudinis speculum, Comoedia' (comedy is the imitation of life and the mirror of society).

Monkeys disturbed my master. He asked me once if I thought we were descended from them. I replied that perhaps some people reappeared as monkeys after they died.

'Oh, Jeremy,' he said, 'I'm sure you're right. We know several of them, don't we? In fact, there have been evenings when I've seemed to see a whole theatre – pit, boxes and gallery – filled with monkeys.'

In his second play, The Double-Dealer, he gave the wicked old harridan, Lady Touchwood, sitting in front of her mirror, this cruel line: 'I was surprised to see a monster in the glass, and now I find 'tis myself.' And the long verse letter entitled *Of Pleasing*, which he wrote for Lord Cobham, contained the lines:

> All Rules of Pleasing in this one unite,
> *Affect not anything in Nature's spight.*
> Baboons and Apes ridiculous we find;
> For what? For ill-resembling Human-kind.
> *None are, for being what they are, in fault,*
> *But for not being what they wou'd be thought.*

No doubt it was these lines which gave Lord Cobham and his architect the idea for the monkey and mirror on Mr Congreve's monument, but I think that the image goes much deeper into my master's character than as a mere symbol of the business of comedy – the business, I mean, of holding up a mirror to people's affectations.

I believe that after the lukewarm reception of his last play, *The Way of the World*, in 1700, when he was just thirty years old, he had become utterly sick of theatre audiences. It was not simply that tastes had changed and audiences preferred the sort of sentimental comedy and thin conventional characterisation which he disliked, though that was surely part of it. It was a real horror of crowds and their simian tendency to lose their own individualities and become a gibbering collective of half-formed ideas and desires.

This was the dark side of the Whig struggle for democracy, the inevitable outcome of those years before he and I were born when our people had cut off the king's head, been confused and divided by new forms of government and religion, lost their old certainties and not yet found fresh ones. The restoration of the Stuarts, that inept, obstinate and frankly foolish Scotch dynasty, proved merely that the old days could not be restored, and ended in King James's disastrous attempt to make the country Papist again. But even the more enlightened half-Stuarts who succeeded him, his daughters Mary and Anne and his Dutch cousin William III, were unpopular with many people, especially the Tories, who considered them illegitimate monarchs. Indeed, only about five years ago the glamorous grandson of King James II, the so-called Bonnie Prince Charlie, led an invasion force of wild Scotch Highlanders halfway down England. Fortunately they found insufficient support from the English, turned back and their army was utterly destroyed on one of their own Scotch moors. Those exiled Stuarts are perhaps no longer a real threat, yet even now in the reign of the second King George the Hanoverian dynasty is tolerated only reluctantly.

Mr Congreve hated elections because they caused so much turmoil, but in the quarter-century between the coronation of William III and the death of Queen Anne there were twelve, though the first five years were the worst, before Parliament passed a Bill keeping themselves in power for three years. Londoners loved to riot and seized any excuse to rush through the streets, overturn carriages, break shop windows, set fire to houses and of course loot any shops or houses they could get into. The little street running down to the Thames where we had our lodgings was usually well out of the rioters' way, but I remember how once after dark we heard them enter our street from the Strand. Mr Congreve was sitting in his big chair recovering from a fit of gout, with his feet up on a stool. He suddenly began to whisper in a voice almost choked with emotion, 'Snuff the candles, Jeremy, quickly, quickly! No, don't go near the windows!'

'I was going to close the shutters.'

'Don't, don't! They might see you. Did you bolt the door?'

The drunken, screaming mob came closer, seemed to be right outside our house. We heard them trying the door. I was frightened; who wouldn't be? But he was rigid. I'd never seen him in this state before, he, the cool, calm, humorous gentleman-scholar. Pain he often suffered from his gout, winced, even cried out, but then mastered it, apologised, made light of it. But he was not master of this fear and only when the mob had moved on and was out of earshot did he begin to relax and shift a little in his chair.

'Light the candles again, Jeremy!' he said in his normal voice, quiet but clear.

'Shall I bring you a glass of wine?'

'Please do! What's bad for the gout is good for the faint-hearted.'

I don't think he was a coward. His father, his uncle and cousins were military men. His grandfather, Richard Congreve, must have been a very brave man to help Prince Charles escape the Roundheads after the Battle of Worcester. Faced with any other danger, in battle, a storm at sea, or waylaid by highwaymen, I'm sure my master would have shown courage. No, it was the savage, uncontrollable nature of that crowd's hostility, its complete loss of individual human identity, its reduction to a troop of marauding monkeys that petrified him.

This may have gone back to his time in Ireland, perhaps at the time he left it, in 1689, soon after James lost his throne. Mr Congreve once spoke about that experience. We had just had a visit from Dr Swift and an actor called Mr Estcourt. Over dinner and several bottles of wine the three of them became very merry, recalling and laughing about their days together in Dublin, when Estcourt was performing in the theatre there and Dr Swift and Mr Congreve were students at Trinity College. Dr Swift confided to me when I answered the door the next time he visited that he hoped we weren't going to give him any more of that nasty white wine. He had suffered dreadful heartburn afterwards. I assured him we had something better this time. Those were the days of the long war with France and it was often difficult to get any decent wine over the counter. One had to know somebody in the government or the army in Flanders or the diplomatic service who could smuggle French wine over from Holland under another label. Mr Congreve at that time was employed in the office for Licensing Wines, so he was well placed to know what was good and what not, but on this occasion he'd been given or conned into buying some very inferior vintage from Spain or Portugal.

My master was in an expansive mood after Dr Swift and Mr Estcourt left and I remarked that they had all evidently enjoyed very happy days in Ireland.

'Yes, we did,' he said, 'until my last year or so at college, when King James made that demon Lord Tyrconnell Lord Deputy and commander of all the troops in Ireland. The actual Lord Lieutenant, Lord Clarendon, was reduced to a cipher. Tyrconnell's instruction from the king was to return Ireland to the Roman Catholics. He did that with ruthless efficiency by dismissing all the Protestant magistrates, officials, judges and army officers, including my father, and replacing them with Catholics.'

He was silent for a while, staring at the fire, which I had replenished while he was speaking and where new flames were leaping.

'Most of the population must have welcomed that,' I said. 'Aren't they all Papists?'

'Oh yes. Oh yes, a welcome was what they gave it, much like the welcome those flames are giving to your fresh lumps of coal. They burst out all over the country, invading Protestant property, driving out the owners, killing cattle and sometimes unpopular magistrates, looting, burning, destroying crops. The soldiers, under their new Catholic officers, were even worse than the peasants. They had no compunction about torturing and killing their male victims and raping the women.'

'And you?' I asked. 'Did they come after you?'

'Not immediately. The worst things were happening out in the country places. We heard rumours, but we students in Trinity College had no experience of anything much outside our studies and our pleasures. We knew nothing of politics, little of real life. King Charles was dead, King James was in his place, there were sure to be changes of policy, but what was that to us, when we had our subjects to master, our degrees to take? We were children still, innocents, little monks inside the stout walls of our alma mater.'

He sat staring at the fire again in silence.

'How I hate religion!' he said at last. 'It is nothing but politics and the worst sort of politics, the most fanatical and unforgiving.

People may punch or beat you for your politics, but they will easily kill you for your religion.'

'You don't believe in God?'

'I'm with Newton and Locke on that. If anybody can give an answer to that perennial question, it should be those great minds.'

'And what do they say?'

'You're a clever fellow, Jeremy, but there are gaps in your education. Sir Isaac Newton's words, if I remember correctly, are: "This most elegant Structure of the Sun, the Planets, and the Comets could not have come into being except by the Design and the Authority of an intelligent and powerful Being". And Mr Locke echoes him less poetically: "For the visible marks of extraordinary Wisdom and Power, appear so plainly in all the Works of Creation, that a rational Creature, who will but seriously reflect on them, cannot miss the Discovery of a Deity". So say the philosophers and so say I. But religions, dogmatic systems of belief and worship, are another matter, man-made, tyrannical and too often lethal.'

He was staring into the fire again. I felt that he was glad to have sheered off the subject of Ireland, but I wanted to hold him to it.

'You said you weren't really aware of what was going on beyond your college...'

'That winter – the winter of '88 when James ran away and left his throne to William – we thought perhaps everything would go back to normal. Tyrconnell would be sacked, the army and the state would be returned to the control of Prot- estants, the rioting peasants sent back to their hovels. We were quite wrong. James hadn't been able to defend his throne in England, but he wanted it back and he thought that, with French assistance, Ireland was the best place to start from. And William wasn't yet secure enough in England to do anything about the Irish. So Tyrconnell remained king of Ireland and all the ships to England were filled with fugitive Protestants. My parents were among them, but I still thought I could take my degree and join them later. Does all this old history really interest you, Jeremy?'

'It interests me very much, Sir. As you say, there are lamentable lacunae in my education.'

'And you know that I love filling them and showing off my own knowledge. You play me like a booby, Jeremy.'

'No, Sir. You like to tell stories and you know I like to listen to them. I am a lucky man. There are fine gentlemen all over London and in great houses in the country – and ladies too, ladies especially – who would love to hear you talk as you talk to me.'

'You are wrong there. They would prefer to be doing the talking themselves and usually are.'

I prodded him back to Ireland again. 'So you took your degree at Trinity College in spite of the Catholics?'

'No, I did not. You must remember, Jeremy, that many years later you accompanied me to Ireland to get my degree.'

'I meant that you sat your examinations for the degree.'

'No, I did not. I left Ireland in a hurry in March '89, on a boat crowded with students as well as Fellows of the College, including my tutor, Dr St. George Ashe. The degree was awarded me later on the assumption that I had sat the examinations and passed satisfactorily. I could not sit the examinations – no one could – because the college was closed and we were all, students and Fellows, driven out.'

'By angry Catholics?'

'By Tyrconnell's soldiers. They marched into the main quadrangle – marched? Better say "swarmed". They were ill-disciplined, dangerously so. They hauled us all out of our rooms, Fellows and students alike, pushed us all together into a corner, where the officer in charge addressed us, told us that we had nothing more to learn there, except that we were no longer welcome, and that anyone not out of the place by midnight would be shot. One of the Fellows protested that this was too short notice, he had a lot of books to pack up. The officer replied that he could leave the books, since they would be burning any that were not in accordance with true religion. The Fellow said that no religion could be true which practised such barbarism, whereupon the officer ordered two soldiers to drag him out to the front, slapped his face several times, kicked his legs from under him and, as he lay on the ground, kicked him again in the stomach and groin. "Does any other heretic have anything else to say?" he demanded. We were silent, horrified at this treatment of an elderly, distinguished scholar, but perhaps even more so at our own craven passivity. The soldiers now, jeering and swearing, started to move towards us, as if they too wanted to satisfy their lust for violence, hungry wolves with a tempting herd of sheep at their mercy. The officers had little control over them. The best they could do was to shout at us to get back to our rooms, pack what we needed and be sure to leave by midnight. So we all broke and ran for the cover of our various doorways and the soldiers pursued us, laughing and shouting, knocking some of us down, catching and beating others. My gown was torn from my back, but I was lucky to escape without injury.'

He gave me a strange look, almost of hostility, as if I had been guilty of violence myself in forcing him to regurgitate this sorry, humiliating experience. I said nothing.

'So ended my life in Ireland,' he concluded.

2

THE ROTONDO

The Rotondo was one of the first buildings to grace Lord Cobham's expanding garden at Stowe. It was designed by Sir John Vanbrugh, who had already built two small summer-houses, the larger of which, next to the house, was known as the Temple of Bacchus. In warm weather the guests would be served wine there before midday dinner or in the evening. None of the buildings had any political significance at this early stage of development.

It was in the year 1721 that we were enjoying a spell of fine spring sunshine at Stowe. Mr Congreve, recently recovered from his gout, was leaning on my arm as he strolled about in front of the house, when Sir John came striding out of the Temple of Bacchus and joined us.

'Cobham agrees with me,' he said, 'that we need some pretty feature over there.'

He pointed in a south-westerly direction to where the fields began to slope down to the river, later dammed to form a lake.

'What sort of feature do you envisage?' asked Mr Congreve. 'A large bubble perhaps?'

We had just been through the great financial crisis known as the South Sea Bubble. Everyone that had any money and many of those that didn't had invested in the new government-backed shares of the South Sea Company, sending their value rocketing and then, as these things will, dropping suddenly to earth when it became clear that the Company's promise of trade with South America was a phantom. The Spanish had supposedly agreed to let our ships sell African slaves and other commodities there, but in practice they had no intention of letting us interfere with their monopoly. Many people were ruined. Even King George and his mistress lost thousands of pounds and it was said that Sir Isaac Newton, poorer by £20,000, exclaimed, 'I can calculate the movement of the stars, but not the madness of men.' My master, with his usual caution, had not invested enough to cause him serious distress, but Sir John, I fancy, had only increased his permanent state of insolvency. Mr Walpole partly saved the situation and in consequence became the unassailable leader of the Whig government for the next twenty-two years.

'"Bubble" is good,' said Sir John. 'What do you say to an elegant little circular thing, a ring of pillars under a tiny dome? A classical rotondo.'

'It will need something inside,' said Mr Congreve.

'You're right. But what? A statue of some contemporary celebrity in Roman costume or a classical hero?'

'Combine the two! Mr Walpole, mender of fortunes, hero of the burst bubble.'

'Really? Whose fortunes? Not mine. Cobham admires him, but perhaps not quite enough to have him perpetually in his view. That equestrian statue of King George, Cobham's quid pro quo for his peerage, is at the back of the house.'

'Well,' said Mr Congreve, 'you've already made a temple to the god of wine and jollity – what is the next most important thing in life?'

'Money?' suggested Sir John.

'Come, come! Has marriage ended all your interest in the ladies?'

Sir John had recently married, at the age of fifty-five, a much younger lady from Yorkshire. There were some who thought that Sir John's chief interest before his marriage had been in his own sex. But my master's view was that he had been so busy building Castle Howard, Blenheim Palace, Seaton Delaval, Claremont,

Kimbolton Castle and many other grand houses, speeding all over the country in his two-wheeled calash to supervise his workmen and consult his clients, that he had no time or thought to spare for a close relationship with either sex. Mr Congreve's question was perhaps a gentle probe into this uncertain aspect of Sir John's life.

'Oh, love!' said Sir John. 'Very important of course, but you don't surely imagine that a little rotondo open to the winds and to all eyes would be a suitable bower for lovers?'

'Not a bower, no, but a tribute, an encouragement, a provocation.'

'I don't imagine Cobham would want anything too louche. No nymphs and satyrs.'

'By no means. But the goddess Venus in all her beauty?'

'You've hit it, Will! Venus straight from the sea.'

'Or her bath. Or...'

'Enough! You're making your man there blush. But Venus it shall be, as beautiful, as callipygian a rendering as we can purchase or have made to order. Gilded, I think, so that she shines out across the fields in all her golden glory from her little pillared cage.'

With which he strode back into the Temple of Bacchus to persuade Lord Cobham to open his purse.

'Callipygian, Sir?'

'From the Greek: *kállos*, beautiful, *pugé*, buttocks. Were you blushing, Jeremy, when Sir John tickled you?'

'Not from shame, sir. Heated by the sun and animated by the ardour of your conversation with Sir John.'

'I wonder what you mean by that. You are sometimes quite Delphic, Jeremy.'

'I mean that I love to see and hear you and Sir John together. He so tall and bristling with haste and activity, you so...'

'Fat and lethargic.'

'Substantial and steady.'

He laughed, we both laughed, knowing we were both right, and went with short, slow steps to join Sir John and our host in the Temple of Bacchus.

But I did not tell him the real reason for my blushing. It was partly true that I loved to see the two of them together, but also true that there suddenly came into my mind a scene between them I never witnessed but which I heard about from Mr Congreve. The pair of them had been visiting the royal palace at Hampton Court, for which Mr Vanbrugh was responsible as Comptroller of the Queen's Works, together with their mutual friend and patron, Charles Montagu, Lord Halifax, a leading Whig politician. After a long spell of bad weather, it had turned exceedingly hot, and it seems that they all decided that they had to find some way of cooling themselves. I'm sure it was Mr Vanbrugh who came up with the remedy. He led them to a fountain and they all dropped their breeches and sat in the basin. It is not an image I can forget and I wonder how many people – servants or courtiers, ladies even – glancing out of the palace windows or passing a doorway opening on the courtyard, caught sight of these three distinguished gentlemen, the government minister, the Queen's Comptroller of Works and the famous poet, seated companionably together in the cool water with bare arses.

I shall introduce more of Mr Congreve's friends under the roof of the Temple of Friendship, but Sir John's charming little Rotondo, which does indeed now enclose a golden, callipygian Venus, is a good place to recapture the memory of that extraordinary man. He first stepped into our midst as plain Mr Vanbrugh, or sometimes Captain Vanbrugh, since he served in the army for a short time, but he was not one of your military boasters, like that egregious coward Captain Bluffe in my master's first play. On the contrary, we heard of his bravery from those who had been with him, never from him. His grandfather was a Protestant immigrant from the Netherlands, his father a wealthy merchant in London and Chester and his mother the daughter of a leading diplomat, Sir Dudley Carleton, with no end of aristocratic relatives. People might have envied and ridiculed another man who seemed always to find employment and preferment from one or another influential nobleman related to his mother. But the truth was that whatever Mr Vanbrugh chose to do – whether fighting or writing plays or designing houses or as Comptroller of the Queen's Building Works or even in his most unlikely job as a member of the College of Heralds – he did as well as and usually better than anybody else.

He received his knighthood in the year 1714 when, after the death of Queen Anne, the new King George landed at Greenwich and immediately bestowed the honour on Mr Vanbrugh. It was not in recognition of his military service, nor of his architectural genius nor of those comedies he wrote in the late nineties, the only rivals for wit and popular success to my master's. Mr Vanbrugh's Whig patrons had sent him, as Clarenceux Herald, to Hanover to invest the son of Queen Anne's successor with the Order of the Garter. His knighthood was, most people assumed, like Lord Cobham's statue of King George I, the quid pro quo. His own version, however, as given to my master, was typically self-deprecating:

'I took that herald's job more in jest than earnest, and in the teeth of bitter opposition from all the other heralds, but I enjoyed my trip to Hanover and the junketings that accompanied it. When King George came ashore at Greenwich, I happened to be near the front of the reception committee. He probably thought I was more important than I was – I doubt if he had much more notion of English society than of our language. Or maybe he just recognised a friendly face and had already decided to knight somebody, anybody, as soon as he set foot on his new kingdom. Or maybe it was a German joke.'

I don't think my master envied him the title, but although they were certainly friends and seldom quarrelled, he must have envied Sir John his good health and boundless energy. Mr Congreve laboured for many months over a play, polishing, perfecting the characters and their dialogue, adjusting the scenes to achieve the exact effect he wanted from the plot. Mr Vanbrugh, as he then was, seemed to write his plays just as he spoke, with effortless fluency, without a second thought. He did not take them very seriously, whereas Mr Congreve's plays, as I've already suggested, were not the 'trifles' he pretended, but his heart's blood.

Their opposite attitudes to their plays came out in their responses to Mr Jeremy Collier's fierce attack on the theatre. Mr Collier was a maverick clergyman of the Church of England, always protesting about something. He had to go into hiding after giving his blessing to two Roman Catholic gentlemen who had plotted to assassinate King William and were strung up at Tyburn. But his attack on the theatre was considered by many people to be reasonable enough, since after the Restoration of King Charles II the theatre seemed to have been growing more and more scandalous in its depiction of lascivious ladies and gentlemen, seduction and adultery. Mr Collier also strongly objected to the way plays sometimes showed clergyman to be hypocrites and made witticisms out of Christian teaching. For instance, he singled out this exchange from Mr Congreve's first play, *The Old Bachelor*:

VAINLOVE: Could you be content to go to heaven?'
BELLMOUR: Hum, not immediately, in my conscience not heartily. I'd do a little more good in my generation first, in order to merit it.

With the implication, I'm afraid, that he would like to get more children on loose ladies. Nor could Mr Collier approve of this exchange from Mr Vanbrugh's *The Provok'd Wife*:

BELINDA: Ay, but you know we must return good for evil.
LADY BRUTE: That may be a mistake in the translation.

But what Mr Collier really wanted was to go back to the days of Oliver's Commonwealth and close down the theatre altogether.

The playwrights named and shamed by Mr Collier included Mr Vanbrugh, Mr Congreve and Mr Dryden. Mr Dryden responded by admitting his guilt. Mr Congreve wrote a long and detailed dissection of Mr Collier's arguments, intelligence and character, which was generally considered to be undermined by its barely concealed anger. My master *was* angry, very angry.

He brooded for several weeks before deciding to publish his response, but he did not wait long enough to cool his head.

'This man pretends to be a scholar,' he said to me, 'but he is an ignoramus. He pretends to be defending sacred texts, but he and his like draw dubious lessons from them every day in their sermons. He thinks clergymen are so special that no one has the right to criticise them. He is a religious fanatic who believes that his narrow view of religion is divine revelation. He is a public pest and I shall tell the world as much.'

I tried to calm him. 'He is all the things you say, but it will do no good to tell him so. Mr Vanbrugh's response was simply not to take him seriously.'

'Van takes nothing seriously, but somebody must counter these dangerous ideas of Collier's or we shall have our theatres closed again.'

He would not be advised and spent many days writing and rewriting his invective, making himself angrier and angrier. When I tried again to argue for moderation, he even lost his temper with me – a very rare occurrence.

'Go away, Jeremy! Do what you're paid to do and leave me to do what I do! This Collier creature has to be trodden into the ground.'

When Mr Vanbrugh called to see whether my master was going to respond to Collier's attack, I asked him on the doorstep to try to bring my master round to a cooler way of thinking. I heard them arguing a little, but Mr Vanbrugh really could not understand my master's passion. He didn't believe, as Mr Congreve did, that there was nothing more important in the world than literature and the special quality of drama. He said in a low voice, as I let him out of the door at the end of their interview, 'No use, Jeremy, no use at all, I'm afraid. Birds of a feather, you see, Collier and Congreve, both fanatics, birds with red wattles and their crests up. It's a cockfight.'

Mr Congreve's reputation was temporarily damaged by this altercation with Collier. The theatres were not closed down, but a law was passed making the plays subject to censorship by the Lord Chamberlain and the playwrights had to be careful in future to license themselves. Even Mr Congreve himself made a few alterations to his texts when he published his collected works some years later. But in the long run he was rewarded with the admiration of all his peers, whereas Mr Vanbrugh's plays were never considered to be great literature so much as delightful entertainments. Nevertheless they were popular and remain so, and what price a play if it is not?

And then Mr Vanbrugh was such a character in himself. Tall and imposing, with a face dominated by the long, straight nose, soft brown eyes, a small mouth, a slightly cleft chin and a quizzical expression, he was six years older than my master. As a very young man, during the war with France, he was captured by the French in Calais and spent several years in French prisons, thought to be a spy. He always denied it, but debonair and courageous as he was, he would surely have made a first-rate spy. After his release from the Bastille in Paris in exchange for a real French spy imprisoned in London, he evidently felt the French deserved some requital, for he joined the British battle fleet as a volunteer when it sailed out to engage a French invasion fleet off the Normandy coast. The French, who had been hoping to set ex-King James back on his throne, were completely routed and many of their ships destroyed in the great English victory of La Hogue. The bells of London rang for three days and the streets were filled with happy festive people who lit bonfires at every corner.

Two years later Captain Vanbrugh took part as a marine – a kind of seagoing soldier – in a very dangerous and nearly disastrous attack on the French port of Brest and was particularly commended by his commander, the Marquis of Carmarthen – another noble relative – for his courage in rescuing men under heavy fire. After that he turned dramatist and then architect and seemed to discover new ideas and designs for buildings as easily as he tossed off comedies.

My admiration for Sir John did not make me wish to exchange masters. Far from it. Mr Congreve's sedentary style of life suited me perfectly. Mr Vanbrugh's manservants came and went, worn out, their nerves strained beyond bearing, scattered behind him like clods from the wheels of his galloping calash. But I must say for Mr Vanbrugh that however short of money he was or in hock to creditors, he always somehow found enough to pay his servants and his workmen.

To judge from his comedies, Mr Vanbrugh surely loved women not men, though he had no illusions about their faults and affectations, any more than he did about those of men – witness his malicious Lady Fancyful in *The Provok'd Wife* and his preening beau Lord Foppington in *The Relapse*. But he did not think much of marriage, and his friends – not least my master, a bachelor to his dying day – were all amazed when he finally succumbed in his late fifties to a colonel's daughter, young Mrs Henrietta Yarburgh of Scarborough, and even had children with her. By then I suppose he was growing tired and dispirited by his long battle with the Marlboroughs over Blenheim Palace. The Christmas before he married he was staying with his cousin Lord Carlisle at Castle Howard and making the arrangements for the wedding in the city of York. When he returned to London he excused himself to my master for betraying the club of bachelors: 'It was so bloody cold in that house that I had a mind to marry to keep myself warm.'

But he went on to say, 'You know I've always envied you, Will, your quietness of mind, your way of keeping out of the world's way except when it suits you to engage with it. You have the excuse of your gout, of course, which I don't, but I fancy it's your philosophy that rules you more than your illness. Ever since I was twenty years old I've understood that it's quietness of mind that brings happiness. Every other delight is like drinking too much – three days' pain for three days' pleasure.'

'You astonish me,' said Mr Congreve. 'You have lived the lives and accomplished the work of at least three highly active men. Where did all that come from if your mind was set on being quiet?'

'I've no idea. Chance, I suppose. Life threw these things at me and I wasn't strong enough to resist picking them up.'

'Not strong enough to resist!' said my master to me afterwards. 'Arrant poppycock! He went after them. Life couldn't resist *him* is more like the truth.'

There was a brief period, about a year, when Mr Vanbrugh and my master collaborated on the creation of a new theatre. They had both had successes with Mr Betterton's breakaway company at the former tennis-court theatre in Lincoln's Inn Fields and Mr Vanbrugh thought the company deserved better premises. Mr Congreve, displeased with the reception of his latest play, *The Way of the World*, had determined to write no more plays but felt he owed it to the company, in which he held a share, to do anything he could on their behalf. So Mr Vanbrugh bought a plot of land beside the Haymarket and rapidly produced designs for the new theatre, while Mr Congreve undertook to raise subscriptions for it, at £100 a share. Most if not all of the subscribers were, of course, Whigs, and belonged to the Kit-Cat Club. The foundation stone was laid by the Duke of Somerset, with an inscription dedicating it to 'the little Whig, Toast and Pride of the Party'; the Duke of Marlborough's second daughter, Lady Anne, married to the Duke of Sunderland. This was less than a year after that visit by Lord Halifax, Mr Vanbrugh and Mr Congreve to Hampton Court and the three of them had been discussing the plans for the new theatre over dinner there and afterwards, bare-arsed, in the fountain.

The new Queen's Theatre, named in honour of Queen Anne, was built in record time and opened within a year of the laying of the foundation stone. It was a fine, impressive building – Mr Vanbrugh liked grandeur – with room for at least two hundred more spectators than the rival Theatre Royal in Drury Lane, but unfortunately turned out to have the wrong acoustics for actors. Their voices echoed in the lofty space of the ceiling and their words could not be easily deciphered. The building was much more suitable for music and in fact opened with an Italian opera. But it was never a success and after a year or so Mr Congreve had had enough of its problems and resigned his place as co-manager. Mr Vanbrugh was naturally put out.

'You are an unreliable fellow, Will, and I wish I'd never brought you into this.'

'I know, and you shouldn't have, and I'm very sorry.'

'You did well to get all those subscriptions, but really what have you contributed compared to my labour in actually getting the damned thing built?'

'I have been of little worth, Van, and the sap is not in me. You will do much better without me.'

But he did not. Italian singers were expensive and the audience wanted only the most celebrated sopranos and *castrati*. Mr Vanbrugh's debts mounted and my master was well out of the affair.

Mr Vanbrugh's problems with the theatre, however, were as nothing compared with his commission, at about the same time as he finished the theatre, to build the palace of Blenheim. After the Duke of Marlborough's great victory of Blenheim over the French in the year 1704, the queen rewarded him with the royal estate of Woodstock and the duke determined to build himself a mansion there. But who was to pay for it was not entirely clear. Mr Vanbrugh was sure that the duke had asked him to build the house and intended to pay for it and that the queen had appointed him as Surveyor under a warrant from the Treasury, which he presumed meant there would be some input of funds from the government. But there seems to have been no proper contract and when the money ran short – anything designed by Mr Vanbrugh, especially on such a vast scale, did tend to come out expensive – the duke, who was rich enough, but a skinflint, egged on by his duchess, who was a termagant, was unwilling to make up the difference. Besides, the duchess disagreed with many aspects of Mr Vanbrugh's designs, gave instructions for the whole garden front to be demolished and rebuilt, and ousted him altogether after the duke's death. Then she took him to the courts to try to deprive him of his fees and settle most of the extra expense on him. The case went up to the House of Lords.

'That B.B.B.B. old B. of a duchess would like to beggar me,' said Sir John, 'but I have influential friends as well as she and besides the evidence is on my side. I believe I shall smite that wicked old witch of Marlborough hip and thigh.'

Which he did. Her case was dismissed and when she sued him and all the workmen in the Court of Chancery she lost again. Many years later Sir John visited Woodstock with his new wife and his cousin and patron, Lord Carlisle, for whom he had built Castle Howard. He wanted to show them this still mightier masterpiece. But neither he nor his wife was allowed even to pass the gate into the grounds of Blenheim Palace.

Although Lord Cobham admired and employed Sir John, he did not include him in the Temple of British Worthies, where the only architect's bust was that of Inigo Jones. However, after Sir John's sudden death early in the year 1726, Lord Cobham assuaged that no doubt restless spirit, like Mr Congreve's a little later, by dedicating the sixty-foot obelisk which Sir John had built in the middle of the Octagon Lake to his memory. Mr Congreve, I'm sure, loved Sir John as a lively friend and valued him as a man of outstanding versatility and achievement, yet on the shelves of my master's extensive library, stocked with so many plays by English, French, Greek, Latin and even Spanish authors, there was not a single one by Vanbrugh. Wanting to read *The Relapse* when we heard of Sir John's death and not finding it, I asked my master whether someone had borrowed it.

'No. I don't think I ever had a copy.'

'That's surprising.'

'Why should it be?'

'You have so many plays by other people and he was a close friend.'

'Friend, but not teacher. The plays in my library are those of my predecessors and masters. I had nothing to learn from Van. He came along after I'd found my own voice.'

'Then he probably learnt something from you.'

'Very likely. He was a quick learner. When he first started designing buildings he had no training and couldn't do proper drawings. He made rough sketches, but his assistant, young Hawksmoor, did the detailed drawings. Just so, he was no poet, but he could run up a play any time you asked him. I daresay, if anyone had asked him, he could have led an army or captained a battleship or governed the country.'

I was not entirely satisfied with this explanation and Mr Congreve must have read my thoughts on my face.

'You think I was envious.'

'No, sir. Not exactly.'

'What exactly?'

'You don't particularly like the plays.'

'No, I don't. There are fine, witty passages, certainly, but the characters have no depth, no development in them. Lord Foppington in *The Relapse* and Sir John Brute in *The Provok'd Wife* will live for ever, I dare say, but they are caricatures, not real men. His ladies are quite standard types. He never gave himself time to disclose character through the design of the whole play or work out a proper structure through character. The endings, therefore, are very unsatisfactory, very scrambled. And those two plays are his only originals, you know. All the others are adaptations of plays by other authors.'

'You are a severe critic, sir. I would not care to submit my work to you, if I were an author.'

'Never resort to that, Jeremy! It's an unforgiving trade, with more backbiters than there are nits in a cheap wig, and less reward for your labour in turning life into words than the wig-maker gets for turning somebody else's curls into my peruke.'

3

THE TEMPLE OF FAME

Mr Joseph Addison, poet, journalist, Member of Parliament and, towards the end of his life, the government's senior Secretary of State, is held partly responsible for the new sort of meaningful English gardens created by Lord Cobham, Mr Pope and others. Mr Addison had a dream, which he described in *Tatler*, the journal founded by Captain Richard Steele. Finding himself in a wood filled with people following many different paths, Mr Addison joined a group of middle-aged men marching along a broad straight path behind a standard bearing the word 'Ambition'. They came to a Temple of Virtue and beyond it a Temple of Honour and saw many statues and monuments to the heroes, gods and great men of ages past. Were there any to great women? I think not, although there were goddesses inside the temples. Lord Cobham's garden, however, boasts a statue of Queen Caroline, raised on a lofty pillar. At the time when the statue was made, she was still Princess of Wales, married to George I's son, now King George II, for whom Lord Cobham, grateful to the Hanoverians for making him a viscount, also commissioned a statue.

Mr Addison in his dream left the Temple of Honour to explore other narrower and more winding paths through the wood and came to a crumbling Temple of Vanity, crowded with pedants, hypocrites, politicians, people with titles but no other claim to honour, and a huge press of women. Elsewhere he discovered a fortified Temple of Avarice, in which the filthy god of Avarice sat between Rapine and Parsimony and there were stalls devoted to Corruption, Bribery, Extortion and Fraud. This very busy temple was intermittently haunted by the terrifying spectre of Poverty.

The moral of the vision was obvious, especially since it was dreamed by Mr Addison, whose ambition for office and influence was almost as limitless as it was successful. He even wrote a very successful tragedy, *Cato*, about the last days of the great Roman Republican who committed suicide rather than surrender to the tyrant Caesar. Mr Congreve had ceased to have much to do with the theatre by then, but he attended the first performance and told me how it was received with frenzied applause. Such a subject, of course, treated by a Whig at a time when the Tories were in power, was bound to be seen as highly political. Queen Anne was ailing in that last year of her reign and the Tory leaders were known to be trying to persuade her – she was herself inclined to be Tory – to break the Act of Settlement which passed the throne to her Hanoverian cousins and leave it instead to her half-brother James Stuart, the Catholic Pretender. The fear of a return to absolute monarchy and a renewed Papist tyranny was widespread, especially among Whigs. Mr Addison, careful to avoid taking sides too obviously, got the Tory Mr Pope to write his prologue, and Dr Samuel Garth, a Whig, the epilogue. In the event both parties in the audience competed to applaud, trying to make out that the play's appeal to Stoic virtue and liberty spoke for them. The Whigs interpreted the tyrant Caesar as James II, the Tories as the Duke of Marlborough, by then in exile. At the curtain call both party-leaders from their boxes either side of the stage summoned the actor who played Cato, Mr Barton Booth, and presented him with fifty guineas. I hope he did not take Mr Addison's path to the Temple of Avarice, but was as virtuous as his role and shared some of the gold pieces with his fellow actors.

Mr Congreve agreed privately with his friend, John Dennis, a notoriously severe critic, that the play was hollow, pretentious and clumsily constructed, but naturally did not say so to Mr Addison, who was also a friend. It was my master, in fact, who first set Mr Addison on his triumphant path behind the banner Ambition. He was then a brilliant graduate of Oxford University and fledgling poet, whom Mr Congreve had met through Mr Dryden and their mutual publisher Mr Jacob Tonson. Mr Addison's masters at Oxford wanted him to enter the Church in the wake of his father, the Dean of Lichfield, but Mr Congreve told his friend and patron, Mr Charles Montagu, that Mr Addison would be wasted on the Church and should be given diplomatic training. Mr Montagu, later ennobled as Lord Halifax, was already a powerful figure in the government, the so-called Whig Junto, and known as the Maecenas of the age.

Maecenas, I should say for the benefit of any reader whose memory is not as reliable as mine, was the friend and minister of the Roman Emperor Augustus, and championed Virgil and Horace among other great poets of his time. We are all these days, at least those of us with a little learning, living half in that ancient classical world and half in the modern world of Mr Locke and Sir Isaac Newton and the Bank of England. That too, by the way, was created by the ingenious Mr Montagu. He took my master's advice and sent Mr Addison to Paris and other places on the Continent; laying the ground for his subsequent rise, once the Whigs were back in power, to the top ranks of administration and wealth.

Mr Addison eventually bought a country estate of his own, at Bilton near Rugby, which he seldom had the time to visit but which was being extended, planted and stocked with game by a relative. I never heard, however, that he got round to furnishing it with temples and statuary in the manner of his dream. By then, as Secretary of State for the South, he was running half the country, as well as the colonies and relations with the rest of Europe, and was living near London in a mansion called Holland House, where he had once been tutor to the young Earl of Warwick and was now married to the earl's rich mother, the widowed Countess Dowager.

Inspired by Mr Addison's vision, Lord Cobham started to transform the grounds of his house at Stowe into a similar allegory of liberty and virtue. What a wonderful progression that was! From a dream to words to physical reality. As a poor, low-class person myself, born from an obscure, illicit liaison, you might expect me, like so many poor, low-class people, to hate the rich and condemn their extravagance, but if we were all equally poor there would be no such places as Stowe. You will say that not many people of my kind have the entry to such places, but I wonder whether we could even imagine them, or dream them, if the rich had not spent their riches making them.

The first buildings at Stowe, designed by Sir John Vanbrugh, might not have appealed to Mr Addison and might in his dream have been located only in the wilder parts of his wood, down crooked paths. Much as Mr Addison liked his drink, he did not approve of drinking and would surely have considered that a Temple of Bacchus set a bad example. Nor would he have been better pleased, I suspect, with that naked callipygian Venus in the Rotondo. However, after Sir John's death Lord Cobham brought in another leading architect, Mr James Gibbs, who soon raised the moral tone with his Temple of Fame. This is a modest, octagonal structure with arched entrances on the four broader sides and a tiled dome; and to each corner on the outside is attached a column surmounted by the head and shoulders of a youth. I'm not sure what or whom these youths represent – perhaps poets, perhaps young men destined for fame in journalism or government like Mr Addison himself, perhaps simply the acolytes or servants of fame. I like to think it is the latter and that one of them may be representing me, Jeremy Fetch, the useful servant of a poet. Certainly if anyone deserves to be celebrated in such a temple it should be Mr Congreve, whose fame was already assured by the time he was thirty years old.

Alas, he never entered this building. The construction of the Temple of Fame coincided with the end of his life. Too ill to visit Stowe again he turned to his favourite Latin poet, Horace, for inspiration, and wrote a last letter in verse to his friend and generous host:

> Sincerest Critick of my Prose, or Rhime,
> Tell how thy pleasing STOWE employs thy Time.
> Say COBHAM, what amuses thy Retreat?
> Or Stratagems of War, or Schemes of State?

He wonders whether Lord Cobham, who fought under the Duke of Marlborough to subdue the ambitions of Louis XIV, is now grieved to see the French, sixteen years later, disputing the terms of the original peace treaty achieved by Marlborough's victories:

> As if BRITANNIA now were sunk so low,
> To beg that Peace she wonted to bestow.
> Be far that Guilt! be never known that Shame!
> That ENGLAND shou'd retract her rightful Claim,
> Or ceasing to be dreaded and ador'd,
> Stain with her Pen the Lustre of her Sword.

But perhaps Lord Cobham is busy making more lakes and fountains?

> Or dost Thou, weary grown, these Works neglect,
> No Temples, Statues, Obelisques erect,
> But catch the morning Breeze from fragrant Meads,
> Or shun the noontide Ray in Wholsome Shades,
> Or slowly walk along the mazy Wood,
> To meditate on all that's wise and good?

Then he turns to praising Lord Cobham in person:

> At Home in Peace, Abroad in Arms Renown'd,
> Graceful in Form, and winning in Address,
> While well you think, what aptly you express,

With Health, with Honour, with a fair Estate,
A Table free, and eloquently neat.
What can be added more to mortal Bliss?
What can he want who stands possest of this?

Yet there is one ingredient of happiness missing, and here Mr
Congreve, taking advantage of his six-year seniority to Lord
Cobham, hints at the former general's very short temper with
his servants and workmen, if not with his guests:

Whatever Passions may thy Mind infest,
(Where is that Mind which Passions ne'er molest?)
Amidst the Pangs of such intestine Strife,
Still think the present Day, the last of Life;
Defer not till to Morrow to be wise,
To Morrow's Sun to thee may never rise.

Indeed, for the poet himself, this tomorrow had become all too
contingent. But he insists:

Come, see thy Friend, retir'd without Regret.
Forgetting Care, or striving to forget;
In easy Contemplation soothing Time
With Morals much, and now and then with Rhime,
Not so robust in Body, as in Mind,
And always undejected, tho' declined;

He was a little wide of the mark there, I'm afraid, though he
certainly tried to keep his spirits up and conceal any fears he had of
not seeing the next day's sun. And he ends with a subtle reminder
of the title of his last play, *The Way of the World*, conjuring up the
supposedly golden Elizabethan age a century earlier and even the
legendary past imagined by the Roman poet Ovid:

Not wond'ring at the World's new wicked Ways,
Compar'd with those of our Fore-fathers Days,

For Virtue now is neither more or less,
And Vice is only varied in the Dress;
Believe it, Men have ever been the same,
And OVID's Golden Age, is but a Dream.

Mr Congreve's own golden age was the 1690s when he was in his twenties. Picked out by Mr Dryden as his poetic heir, he wrote his four comedies, his single tragedy and much verse: songs, lyrics, odes and English versions of Homer, Juvenal, Horace and Ovid. I shall come to the plays in another place, but I think it a pity that although you may sometimes find verses by Mr Pope inscribed on stone in English gardens you will never, to my knowledge, find my master's. Why not these lines, for instance, adapting an ode by Horace? They were among his earliest writings, composed at the age of twenty-two, but expressed, significantly enough if one may read a person's character from his philosophy, the very same sentiment as in those last verses to Lord Cobham, thirty-six years later:

Seek not to know to Morrow's Doom;
That is not ours, which is to come.
The present Moment's all our store:
The next, should Heav'n allow,
Then this will be no more:
So all our Life is but one Instant *Now*.

Or these sardonic reflections, from his earlier Epistle to Sir Richard Temple, not then ennobled as Lord Cobham:

The Foolish, Ugly, Dull, Impertinent
Are with their Persons and their Parts content.
Nor is that all: so odd a thing is Man.
He most would be what least he should or can.
[...]
Cowards extol true Courage to the Skies,

And Fools are still most forward to advise;
Th' untrusted Wretch, to Secresie pretends,
Whisp'ring his *Nothing* round to *All* as Friends.
Dull Rogues affect the Politician's part;
And learn to nod, and smile, and shrug with Art;
Who nothing has to lose, the War bewails;
And he who nothing pays, at Taxes rails.
Thus, Man, perverse, against plain Nature strives,
And to be artfully absurd, contrives.

But the best of his poems are perhaps too personal to be set in stone around garden-walks, more concerned with the character of the individual addressed than with descriptions of nature or moral precepts.

My own favourites are those he wrote for his first and perhaps only great love during the Nineties. Mr Congreve's affairs of the heart will be better treated when we reach the Temple of Venus, but the lovely face of Mrs Anne Bracegirdle, who played leading roles in all his plays, must inevitably peep from many a corner of this memorial tapestry I am weaving. Mrs Bracegirdle, or Bracey as she was universally known, was famous for bewitching every man that set eyes on her in the theatre – and many a woman – yet, unlike most actresses, never giving in to their amorous advances. When she died, twenty years after my master, she was still a spinster. This was how Mr Congreve, when he first fell in love with her – he was twenty-three years old and she younger by a year – expressed his frustration:

Pious Selinda goes to Pray'rs,
Whene'er I ask the Favour;
Yet the tender Fool's in Tears,
When she believes I'll leave her.
Wou'd I were free from this Restraint,
Or else had Hopes to win her;
Wou'd she could make of me a Saint,
Or I of her a Sinner.

I will quote his beautiful 'Elegy to Cynthia', written a year or so later, when we visit the Temple of Venus, since it is there that we must enter more fully into Mr Congreve's frustration and discover whether it was ever surmounted.

The Temple of Friendship, which we shall also visit later, was not built until a decade after my master's death, but I mention it here because its impressive classical pediment of stone concealed brickwork behind. Just so, behind my master's bright facade of calm ironical humour and cheerful enjoyment of the *Now*, which endeared him to so many people and made him friends who remained friends for life, there was a deep shade of melancholy. Few people ever saw it, though he occasionally allowed a glimpse of it in his comments on the English weather: 'Our sickly Clime, which has for ten Years past,/With one continu'd Winter been o'er cast...' So began the prologue he wrote for Bracey to speak at a special performance in Whitehall of his play *Love for Love,* commanded by King William for Princess Anne's birthday early in the year 1697. Then a year later his reply to Mr Collier's attack on the theatre ended with this paragraph:

Is there in the world a climate more uncertain than our own? And which is a natural consequence, is there anywhere a people more unsteady, more apt to discontent, more saturnine, dark, and melancholic than ourselves? Are we not of all people the most unfit to be alone, and most unsafe to be trusted with ourselves? Are there not more self-murderers, and melancholic lunatics in England, heard of in one year, than a great part of Europe besides? From whence are all our sects, schisms, and innumerable sub-divisions in religion? Whence our plots and conspiracies, and seditions? Who are the authors and contrivers of these things? Not they who frequent the theatre and concerts of music. No, if they had, it may be Mr Collier's invective had not been levelled that way; his gun-powder-treason plot upon music and plays (for he says music is as dangerous as gun-powder) had broke out in another place, and all his false-witnesses had been summoned elsewhere.

Mr Congreve loved music perhaps even more than the theatre, attended concerts, was the friend of musicians such as the Purcell brothers and Mr John Eccles, who set to music the songs he wrote for his plays. After he ceased writing plays he wrote the text of a masque, *The Judgment of Paris*, set to music by four different composers in competition, and the libretto for an opera, *Semele*, with music by Mr Eccles. Bracey, whose singing, said Mr Dryden, outdid professional singers, took the part of Venus in the masque, and Mr Congreve meant her to sing Semele's role in the opera, but that is a story I will return to.

My master's secret melancholia was sometimes alleviated by music, but he could hardly conceal it from his servant. His more immediate remedy was to take down a book from his shelves, but his eyesight was deteriorating and although to the end of his life he was still able to read with a magnifying glass, that was a slow and irritating business. So he often asked me to read to him and I could always tell by the tone of his voice whether he simply wished to be informed or diverted or whether he urgently needed to be rescued from the gloom of his thoughts. Once – it was soon after he and Mr Vanbrugh had decided they could not after all open their new theatre in the Haymarket with Mr Congreve's opera *Semele* – he admitted as much to me:

'I am very low, Jeremy, very short of any reason for my existence. Yes, it is wise to live only for the day, not to expect anything from the future, since expectations are usually chimeras. But the truth is that for those of us not constantly immersed in some activity, however dreary and humble – I do not mean your relatively easy services to me, but labouring in the fields or a bakery or a government office – there must always be a purpose in view, something awaiting our attention. I have none left. I am an empty flask, drained of my spirits, my *eau de vie.*'

'Will you not write another play for the new theatre?'

'No, I will not. Not for any theatre. All successful playwrights have a time, a short time, when their ideas chime with those of the public. My time is past, my chime is cracked, my day is done.'

'*Love for Love* is always popular. You could put that on again in the new theatre.'

'Oh, please! Reviving their stale trifles is the last resort of played-out poets.'

'But that play is no trifle and need not be stale.'

'It is.'

'Not if it tickled the public's fancy in some new way.'

'How could it? Performed backwards, do you mean, or by acrobats on high wires, or by a troop of monkeys?'

'No. But suppose by a troupe of ladies...'

'What? All the parts played by actresses?'

His voice sounded so fierce that I only mumbled in reply, 'Yes, sir.'

A pause. Mr Congreve got up from his chair and came towards the window where I was standing. I tensed myself. I could not read his expression and thought he might be going to hit me, though he had never done so before and never did in all our time together. He raised his arm and laid it round my shoulders.

'Jeremy, dear man, I am infinitely obliged to you. Your idea is ridiculous, demeaning, cheap, but Van will love it and no doubt the greedy, gaping audience will too.'

So my master's gloom was temporarily dispelled and the season ended with an all-female revival of *Love for Love*. It was only mildly successful and many serious people thought like its author that it was a cheap trick, but it briefly filled the seats.

Mr Congreve's known love of music led to his being commissioned to compose a hymn for St Cecilia's Day in the year 1701. This day was celebrated every year on 22 November in the Stationers' Hall with a great feast for the noblemen, merchants and citizens of London, accompanied by the music of hautboys and trumpets. Mr Congreve's text was set for soloist and chorus by Mr Eccles and addressed not to the saint – his opinion of religion made saints as little to be admired, let alone worshipped, as parsons – but to Harmony:

> O *Harmony*, to thee we sing,
> To thee the grateful Tribute bring
> Of Sacred Verse, and sweet resounding Lays,
> Thy Aid invoking while thy Pow'r we praise.
> All Hail to thee
> All-pow'rful *Harmony*
> Wise Nature owns thy undisputed Sway,
> Her wond'rous Works resigning to thy Care;
> The Planetary Orbs thy Rule obey,
> And tuneful roll, unerring in their way,
> Thy Voice informing each melodious Sphere.

Not one of his best efforts. Compare the true feeling in his 'Ode on Mrs Arabella Hunt Singing', written ten years earlier. Mrs Hunt played the lute and sang in a very high voice, 'like the pipe of a bullfinch' as somebody said. Mr Congreve greatly admired her and I remember him working on this poem soon after I joined him, when we were both very young.

> Let all be husht, each softest Motion cease,
> Be ev'ry loud tumultuous Thought at Peace,
> And ev'ry ruder Gasp of *Breath*
> Be calm, as in the *Arms* of Death.
> And thou most fickle, most uneasie Part,
> Thou restless Wanderer, my Heart,
> Be still, gently, ah gently, leave
> Thou busie, idle thing, to heave.
> Stir not a Pulse, and let my *Blood*,
> That turbulent, unruly Flood,
> Be softly staid:
> Let me be all, but my Attention, dead.
> Go, rest, unnecessary Springs of Life,
> Leave your officious Toil and Strife;

For I would hear her Voice, and try
If it be possible to die.

Doesn't that catch the very essence of a music-lover? Perhaps even of a lover too, for this was before he met Bracey and that last line often has a double meaning in love poems. When Mrs Hunt died prematurely in the year 1705, my master wrote a brief epitaph for her to be engraved below Sir Godfrey Kneller's portrait of her playing the lute.

I made the comparison above in order to demonstrate the difference between Mr Congreve's public and private verse. He wrote many public odes: on the death of Queen Mary, for which King William sent him 100 guineas; to King William after he captured the town of Namur from the French, probably hoping for another contribution, but receiving none; on the Duke of Marlborough's great victories over the French; and on the death of the Duke's only son, Lord Blandford, aged sixteen; and so on. But in my opinion and I believe that of many of his friends, his public verse did him little credit. It was too laboured, too dependent on classical models and references, too far from his own experience in its description of warfare or grief, too self-consciously public. No doubt it was pleasing or consoling enough to the grandees for whom it was written and who seldom read any verse at all, but although he reprinted most of it in his *Collected Works*, I wonder whether it really pleased its author. I could never, of course, ask him that question, for fear of losing my job, nor did I ever hear any of his friends mention the matter except with a few conventional compliments, which I judged to be insincere.

There was a scholarly, almost pedantic side to Mr Congreve, part of his perpetual quest for perfection. It never mars his plays, for he knew by his assiduous study of Greek, Roman, French and Spanish playwrights and his many youthful visits to the Smock Alley Theatre in Dublin, that actors must be given dialogue they can quickly memorise and easily speak. In his public verse, however, he was led astray by bouts of solemnity, an infectious need to conform to ancient classical models and rules. I think he caught that from his mentor, Mr Dryden. For instance, he took it upon himself to reform the so-called Pindaric Ode, which the poet Cowley had naturalised into English verse. These poems made for singers and dancers were originally composed by the ancient Greek poet Pindar in honour of victors in the athletic games held in Olympia and various cities around Greece. But Cowley had misunderstood their strict form and made it a vehicle for informal irregularity. Mr Congreve not only wrote an essay correcting Cowley's error and the still more erroneous compositions of his imitators, but exemplified his teaching with his own true Pindaric Odes in English. One such was his ode to the queen celebrating the Duke of Marlborough's victories; another his ode to the duke's close associate, the Earl of Godolphin, Lord Treasurer and the queen's chief minister.

Lord Godolphin was a most suitable recipient for this form of verse, which originally celebrated sporting prowess, since he, like the queen herself, was especially keen on horse racing and often visited Newmarket to watch and make bets on it. It was at about this time that the first Arabian horse was imported from Aleppo to inaugurate the breeding of English thoroughbreds, which was continued and much improved nearly thirty years later by the importation of that famous stallion, the Godolphin Arabian, owned by Lord Godolphin's son Francis. Mr Congreve's Pindaric Ode to Lord Godolphin begins:

Whether, Affairs of most important Weight
Require thy aiding Hand,
And ANNA's Cause and *Europe's* Fate
Thy serious Thoughts demand;
Whether, thy Days and Nights are spent
In Cares, on Publick Good intent;
Or, whether, leisure Hours invite
To manly Sports, or to refin'd Delight;
In Courts residing, or to Plains retir'd,
Where gen'rous Steeds contest, with Emulation fir'd

But for all 'the Air-born Racers [...] impatient of the Rein [...] in matchless Speed' etcetera, the verses are too heavy with classical references, formal discipline and blatant flattery to fly very far or win any races themselves.

No, Mr Congreve's entitlement as a poet to enter the Temple of Fame must rest on his quieter, more melancholic, more heart-felt verses. Let me end this chapter with one of the most elegant, an elegy entitled 'The Candle':

> Thou watchful Taper, by whose silent Light,
> I lonely pass the melancholy Night;
> Thou faithful Witness of my secret Pain,
> To whom alone I venture to complain;
> O learn with me, my hopeless Love to moan;
> Commiserate a Life so like thy own.
> Like thine, my Flames to my Destruction turn,
> Wasting that Heart, by which supply'd they burn.
> Like thine, my Joy and Suffering they display,
> At once, are Signs of Life, and Symptoms of Decay,
> And as thy fearful Flames the Day decline,
> And only during Night presume to shine;
> Their humble Rays not daring to aspire
> Before the Sun, the Fountain of their Fire:
> So mine, with conscious Shame, and equal Awe,
> To Shades obscure and Solitude withdraw;
> Nor dare their Light before her Eyes disclose,
> From whose bright Beams their Being first arose.

Was that also addressed to Bracey? Very likely, since there was no other woman in his life whom he loved to quite that degree, not even Henrietta, the young Duchess of Marlborough, who loved him with such devotion.

4

THE QUEEN'S THEATRE

The Queen's Theatre at Stowe is named after Sir John Vanbrugh's theatre in London. The comparison is absurd and no doubt deliberately so, given Sir John's sense of humour. The latter is a huge enclosed edifice with pit, gallery and boxes, capable of seating at least nine hundred people. The former is a small open air amphitheatre sited between the Rotondo and the statue of the Princess of Wales (now Queen Caroline). I am not sure whether it has ever actually been used as a theatre. At the time it was planned, at more or less the same time as the Rotondo, I remember a terse exchange between Sir John and Mr Congreve:

'Will you write something for it, Will?'

'No. Will you?'

'Hardly. One's jewelled wit would be blown away on the wind.'

'Even if it didn't rain.'

'The sun might shine, of course.'

'In the actors' eyes.'

'Perhaps an evening performance?'

'Too chill.'

'And the candles would blow out.'

'Where would the actors change their costumes?'

'We shall plant hedges.'

'Actresses undressing behind hedges, Van?'

'Yes, it does have possibilities, doesn't it?'

It was constructed more, I think, as a classical reference, a nod to those great stone amphitheatres where the ancient Greek tragedies were performed, than with any idea that a company of actors from London or Lord Cobham's guests be asked to brave the English weather. It will serve very well now, however, as the trigger for my master's brilliant and explosive career in the theatre, when, like Mr Halley's comet, he appeared from nowhere, blazed briefly across the sky and passed suddenly out of sight, though never out of memory.

After he was driven out of Ireland by Tyrconnell's soldiers in such haste and distress, he took refuge in his grandfather's home, Stretton Hall in Staffordshire, built earlier that century by the great architect Inigo Jones. The Congreve family took their name from a hamlet in that county, where they had lived for centuries. Young Mr William Congreve was then nineteen years of age and had brought with him the nearly finished manuscript of his novel, *Incognita,* or in English, *The Unknown Woman.* In those peaceful surroundings, a modest estate more or less restored to prosperity after the depredations of the Roundheads in the Civil War, he settled down to complete and polish his novel. He had some advice from the daughter of a neighbouring landowner, Mrs Katharine Leveson, to whom he dedicated the book when it was finished. She was ten years older than him and I could never discover how deep their relationship went – I was not, of course, in his service at the time. But he certainly admired her wit and judgement and in the dedication calls himself her 'Friend, a Title which I am proud you have thought me worthy of'. She was evidently unmarried, since she still bore the same name as her father who, together with Mr Congreve's grandfather, was a local magistrate, and must have been a lady of some learning and address, for her brother was a Member of Parliament and a Groom of the King's Bedchamber and she had been to London several times. Mr Congreve told me this long afterwards when I expressed curiosity about the novel and its dedicatee, and asked him why he was not including it in his *Collected Works*.

'Juvenilia,' he said.

'But it's not the sort of clumsy, over-written thing one expects of someone so young.'

'True. I took a lot of trouble over it and thought highly of it at the time and was keen to have it published. But I moved on.'

'You were always moving on. Every one of your plays moves on from the last. Why should this not stand as your starting-point?'

'It was in the wrong form. It was trying to be a drama and I soon understood that it was a play I wanted not a novel.'

'But wouldn't the readers of your *Collected Works* like to share that understanding?'

'I don't wish to include something I quickly outgrew.'

'You think the novel an inferior form to drama?'

'Undoubtedly. Spoken dialogue delivered with appropriate gestures and facial expressions by real people in character is far more telling and lifelike than mere words on a page.'

'But you have Mr Defoe's novel *Robinson Crusoe* on your shelves. Is that so inferior?'

'A remarkable book, I concede, but I think most people read it as a true story of travel and adventure rather than a novel. There is also that much earlier Spanish novel, *Don Quixote*, which if you haven't yet read, you should, since you'll be glad to find that the Don's manservant, though not as clever as you, is a lot more sensible than his deluded master. It's a masterpiece, but unique. The form is too loose, too untidy, too lengthy to have any future. Who could spare the time or take the trouble to read such inventions if they didn't believe them true?'

Well, he didn't think of the legions of leisured ladies, and died too soon to hear of the huge success of that untidy form in the hands of Mr Samuel Richardson and Mr Henry Fielding.

Mr Congreve's *Incognita* was a very different kind of novel from theirs, neither loose nor untidy, and extremely short, much more akin to drama. It was set in Florence and observed to some degree the classical unities of time, place and action laid down by Aristotle. The plot, as tightly wound up as the mechanism of a clock and with as many cogs turning and engaging one another in rapid sequence, traced the tangled love affairs of two young men and two young women. It seemed to me to resemble the similarly Italianate disguises, intrigues and misapprehensions of Shakespeare's minor comedies.

But to return to Stretton Hall in the year 1689, where this young, ambitious Mr Congreve, still healthy and energetic, a hearty eater and drinker, his mind full of classical learning, was the guest of his grandfather, that old Cavalier hero, Mr Richard Congreve. It was possibly then that my master composed those early lines about living in the *Now* and, suiting the action to the thought, turned immediately from the novel that aspired to be drama to writing a play. Inside the house he felt oppressed by the atmosphere of gloom as his grandfather, eighty years old and weak with fever and gout, sank towards death. But the English weather, which later depressed my master so much, must have smiled on him then, for he began this play partly out of doors, under an old oak tree near the lake, and I believe he modelled one of his characters, the witty, sophisticated Araminta on his kind friend Mrs Leveson.

Four years later, when it was performed at the Theatre Royal, Drury Lane, she attended a performance and afterwards spoke to Mr Congreve, as I was shepherding him through a crowd of admirers to his hackney carriage.

'I did enjoy myself, Will, a great deal. What a lot of lively characters you've invented!'

'Perhaps less invented than observed, but thank you.'

'You've certainly observed the ladies with a sharp eye. Those in your novel were pure angels. But you treat us less gently in this play.'

'Not unjustly, I hope.'

'Oh, I don't complain. We're humans, not angels. I think my favourite is Araminta, who is clever without showing off and adventurous without losing control. But perhaps I was influenced by that spirited young actress who plays her. Mrs Bracegirdle? A name to remember, an actress to watch.'

'You are right. Her Araminta was perfection, the character to the life, far beyond what my poor lines had laid out for her.'

I smiled to myself as they kissed politely and parted, his original Araminta all unknowing that it was she herself who had been transformed by the magic of the stage into Bracey.

His grandfather died that August, leaving the manor of Stretton by entail to his grandson John, since his eldest son was already dead. My master attended the funeral in the family chapel and was joined by his father, who as the second son received a much-needed bequest of £100. After his expulsion from his regiment in Ireland, he and his wife had been living in London on their small savings, while Mr William Congreve Senior looked for another commission. Now his son accompanied him to London, where the bequest went some way to keeping them all three in reasonable comfort. Mr William Congreve Junior continued to work on his play, though he was somewhat distracted, he told me, by his first encounter with this teeming, roaring city, glamorous, enticing, dangerous and filthy. But he did not lack friends or indeed relatives here. His cousins Ralph and William Congreve were about his own age and just starting successful military careers, and his mother's rich female cousins from Yorkshire had both married noblemen, the Earls of Huntingdon and Scarsdale, with substantial town residences. He also knew one or two actors whom he had met at the Smock Alley Theatre in Dublin and it was naturally towards them rather than his noble or military cousins that he gravitated.

The leading playwrights of the period were Sir George Etherege, Mr William Wycherley, Mr Thomas Shadwell, Mrs Aphra Behn and, of course, Mr John Dryden. All were of the previous generation and for better or worse – certainly worse in Mr Collier's eyes – had used the re-opening of the theatres after the Restoration to reflect the scurrility and immorality of the pleasure-seeking Cavaliers, triumphant and rampant after their return from exile with King Charles. But by the time

Mr Congreve reached London, Sir George Etherege and Mr Wycherley had ceased to write plays, Mrs Behn had died, Mr Shadwell was writing his last play, performed posthumously with little success, and Mr Dryden had virtually abandoned the theatre for poetry. The theatre was looking for a new master.

So was I. After the death of my demanding, irascible, but fundamentally fond master in Oxford, I used the small bequest he left me to move to London. Here I began to frequent a tavern near Drury Lane, where I could observe some of the actors from the Theatre Royal out of their roles and sometimes in their cups. They seemed very ordinary people off the stage, preoccupied with their domestic difficulties, lack of money, grasping landlords, sexual frustrations and professional jealousies. They cheered themselves up with streams of comic anecdotes about the misadventures and eccentricities of their absent colleagues. One of them, Mr William Mountfort, noticed that I was always listening to their conversation and asked me if I wanted to be an actor myself. I told him no, I lacked the confidence.

'Why is that? You're handsome enough and you speak well.'

'I couldn't pretend to be someone else.'

'But you're evidently interested in other people.'

'I do like to watch them, but I don't think I would care to be watched myself.'

'What do you do for a living?'

'Nothing at present. I was manservant to a scholar in Oxford, but he died and I must find another place before the money he left me runs out.'

'I suppose you can read?'

'Oh, yes, English. And Latin too. A little French, but not Greek.'

'You are a rather superior sort of servant.'

'I like to believe so.'

'Too much so for many masters, I should think. But if I hear of anyone who deserves to employ you, I will let you know. Mention my name at the door of the theatre if you would like a free seat any night this season!'

What a kind, good man! He was a brave one too, as I shall explain later, but, alas, that cost him his life.

Meanwhile, we were all suddenly alarmed by the threat of a French invasion. Our warships defending the Channel coast were defeated by a fleet from France in a battle off Beachy Head in Sussex, while the exiled King James, determined to recover his throne, landed with a large French army in Ireland. The Protestants in the north of Ireland were driven back into the city of Derry. Closely besieged for months, they refused to surrender, but starving and battered by artillery, could not hold out much longer. King William led an army to Ireland, leaving England, after the failure of our navy, almost defenceless. Mr Congreve Senior was commissioned captain in an emergency regiment of dragoons. But what use would a hastily recruited regiment of volunteers be against a fully trained invasion force? Those were grim days.

No true Englishman or Irish Protestant, I'm sure, needs to be reminded, even sixty years later, of the glorious turn of fortune that followed. King William's troops utterly routed the French in the Battle of the River Boyne, Derry was relieved and ex-King James fled back to France. The English army under the then Earl of Marlborough gradually subdued the whole island and finished their victorious campaign with the capture of the Catholics' last redoubt, the city of Limerick. King James's evil Governor, Lord Tyrconnell, died of an apoplexy. Now indeed we had reason to ring all the church bells of London and light bonfires in every street.

Captain Congreve, never called upon, after all, to confront invaders, was once more unemployed, though not for long. As an officer stationed in Cork he had been acquainted with the Earl of Cork and Burlington. This great Protestant nobleman, now again in possession of his sequestered and ravaged estates, invited Captain Congreve to take charge of them. So in October of that memorable year 1690 my master's father, now become Colonel Congreve, and his lady returned to Ireland. They remained there for the next twelve years, living in the earl's chief seat beside the

River Blackwater, Lismore Castle, overseeing its restoration from the ruin inflicted by Tyrconnell's savages.

My master – not yet my master – remained in London, where his father, ignorant of his son's genius, entered him as a law student in the Middle Temple and paid him a small allowance. Mr Congreve told me that, although the law bored him and he soon abandoned any idea of becoming a practising barrister, he gratefully accepted his father's generosity since it gave him time to find his feet in London and complete his play. Indeed he was following what had almost become a tradition, since the Inns of Court had been the school, or at least the shelter, for three of his Restoration predecessors – Messrs. Etherege, Wycherley and Shadwell – as well as a still active playwright, Captain Thomas Southerne.

This Irishman, ten years older than my master and also an alumnus of Trinity College, Dublin, had served as a soldier before the Glorious Revolution, so it may have been Mr Congreve's military cousins rather than any theatrical friends who first brought them together. However it was to Captain Southerne, by courtesy of Mr Mountfort, that I owed my introduction to Mr Congreve. I had taken up Mr Mountfort's kind offer of a free seat in the theatre and afterwards went to the stage door to thank him and congratulate him on his performance of Sir Courtly Nice in a revival of Mr Crowne's play of that name. He emerged in conversation with Captain Southerne and introduced me to him, saying that I was looking for employment as a manservant but that he thought I would be wasted on most masters.

'Are you such a catch, then, young man?' asked the Captain.

'I would not say so myself,' I replied. 'But if Mr Mountfort is good enough to think so…'

'He reads Latin as well as English,' said Mr Mountfort.

'Then I know where you should apply,' said the Captain. 'There is a very young gentleman come to town – about your age – and enrolled at the Middle Temple, though I think he's more poet than lawyer, who is looking for a servant. He's a serious scholar, from my own alma mater, but I should guess as poor as the rest of us and you might find the wages too meagre.'

'I would rather have a good master than excessive wages,' I said, though thinking that I would prefer to have both.

'Well, I cannot say whether he's a good master, but I'm sure he's a good man.'

He gave me the name and address – in Arundel Street off the Strand – of Mr Congreve.

'Would you be wanting me to write that down for you?' he said.

'No, sir. I have an excellent memory.'

'That too? You are a paragon, I see. One piece of advice, however, young fellow: do not be tempted to turn author yourself! The profession is less lucrative than that of a footpad and as full of anxiety, and even if you don't die prematurely of strangulation or a broken neck you most likely would of starvation.'

'I will remember what you say, sir.'

So I made my way to Arundel Street, quite near the theatre, and knocked on the door of the house next to the Blue Ball tavern. After some minutes, when I was about to knock again, Mr Congreve opened the door. He looked confused and said abruptly, 'Yes?'

'I believe you are looking for a manservant, sir?'

'Am I? Yes, I believe I am.' He looked me up and down. 'Are you him?'

'Captain Southerne gave me your name and address, sir, and said I might suit.'

He looked me up and down again. 'Excellent! How soon can you start?'

'Any time that is convenient to you, sir.'

'Good! Come in!'

I said that if he wanted me to start at once, I needed to fetch my few belongings from where I had been lodging in the East End, some distance off.

'Of course you do. Fetch away, then! Fetch away!'

I daresay it was the memory of that first doorstep interview, when his mind was less on me than the translation of Juvenal he was making for Mr Dryden, which suggested the surname he gave the manservant in his famous comedy *Love for Love:* Jeremy Fetch.

My new master had met Mr Dryden at Will's Coffee House near Covent Garden. There the great man held court, sitting by the fire in winter and in the window in summer, while all the aspiring poets, wits and critics of the day vied to sit near him and gain his attention. He was by then an old man of sixty and, since the death of Milton, recognised as the chief of English poets. During the Commonwealth period he was a Roundhead and worked for Mr Thurloe, the Secretary of State, but changed sides after the Restoration and was created our first ever Poet Laureate by King Charles. He lost that honour, however, after the Revolution which removed King James, when he declined to change sides again and swear allegiance to King William and Queen Mary.

It may have been Captain Southerne or else a fellow law student called Mr Arthur Maynwaring who guided Mr Congreve through the crowd of Mr Dryden's disciples in Will's Coffee House to a place beside the great man's chair. He made a favourable impression and Mr Dryden, who was about to publish the Roman poet Juvenal's sixteen satires in English verse translations by several hands, including his own, asked my master to take on the eleventh. My first task on entering his service was to compare his version with the original and give my opinion. Knowing him so little at this point I was uncertain whether to be honest or merely to praise, and chose the latter. He was not pleased.

'Jeremy,' he said, 'this will never do. I must have your true opinion or we must part. You were recommended as a Latinist and I care less about my shirts and stockings than I do about my verses. This will be the first thing of mine to appear under my own name and in the company of Mr Dryden's, no less. I cannot afford to fail and you will be on the street again if I do.'

'I will try to mend my ways, sir.'

'Yes, sir, and tell me how to mend my verses!'

Which I did, as judiciously as possible, and flatter myself that the result, which almost immediately promoted Mr Congreve to a prime place among Mr Dryden's disciples and was the first rung on his ladder to fame, contained several nice touches of my own. Just as important from my point of view was that we ceased to be strangers and that Mr Congreve, who was renowned for his ability to make and keep friends, made me his friend and kept me as such until his dying day. I shall never forget one little passage from that Juvenal translation. We laughed over it together as we tinkered with its wording and he was apt to quote from it mockingly long afterwards, whenever he thought I was becoming too pleased with myself and intruding too much on his friends:

> On me attends a raw unskilful Lad,
> On Fragments fed, in homely Garments clad,
> At once my *Carver*, and my *Ganymede*;
> With diligence he'll serve us while we Dine,
> And in plain Beechen Vessels, fill our Wine.

I believe it was I who suggested improving his 'simple' to 'homely' and 'wooden' to 'Beechen'.

I should make it clear that I was Mr Congreve's Ganymede only in that I poured the wine for him and his guests. Neither he nor I was inclined to prefer our own sex to the ladies. I have no objection to those that do, nor I'm sure did he, except in so far as they were liable to affectation, always a target for his satire whether in man or woman. My previous master's occasional clumsy attempts on my virtue had left me with little liking for the practice of man on man, but every servant of either sex must be prepared to comply with such advances or seek another employer – it is a hazard of our trade. I was relieved to find that Mr Congreve had no such designs on me.

That translation of Juvenal proved, as he hoped, to be my master's passport to success. He had already published his little novel, *Incognita: or, Love and Duty Reconcil'd*, under the pseudonym Cleophil, but it received little notice. Mr Dryden next asked him to translate two passages from Homer. Lacking any knowledge of Greek, I was unable to help him with these, but Mr Dryden was mightily pleased with them and said so in the dedication to his publication *Examen Poeticum*, in which they appeared the following year. 'I cannot mention Mr Congreve,' wrote Mr Dryden, 'without the honour which is due to his excellent parts, and that entire affection which I bear him. I wish Mr Congreve had the leisure to translate the whole of Homer and the world the good nature and justice to encourage him in that noble design, of which he is more capable than any man I know.' Such unequivocal praise from that quarter he was more than pleased to accept.

Before that, however, Mr Congreve had picked up his play again. The previous summer we had left London on the public coach to stay with friends called Port in a country house at Ilam in Staffordshire. They may have been relatives of our landlord Mr Edward Porter or else connections of the Congreve family in the same county. It is so long ago that even my memory fails here. Mr Congreve carried his unfinished manuscript in his portmanteau – or rather, I did – and the weather smiling again as it had three years earlier at Stretton Hall, he sought solitude and inspiration out of doors, beside the River Manifold. Carrying a folding stool and the hamper of cold meats, cheeses, fruit and ale provided for his dinner by his kind hosts, I accompanied him down a narrow, precipitous path round the crag on which the house was built to a niche among the rocks. Shaded by an overhanging boulder and a yew tree whose exposed roots spread out across this natural awning, he sat down facing a steep black mountainside across the river bed, while directly below, the river, emerging from underground, bubbled up in a loud cascade. I left him there and returned to fetch him and the empty hamper – he was very fond of his food – before darkness fell. The weather held for nearly a week, and he returned to the same spot with a well-stocked hamper each day, until a spell of rain forced him to continue his work in his hosts' parlour. He was frequently disturbed there, either by hushed enquiries after his comfort or the summons to meals and I could understand why he preferred to work out of doors. What I could never understand, when I read the finished manuscript, was how he fixed his imagination on such wholly urban scenes in the midst of wild nature, or preserved the rhythms of his witty exchanges against the noise of that cascade.

By the time we returned to London the play was almost finished and the last scenes were written in our lodgings. When we were both satisfied with it, for Mr Congreve insisted I should criticise it 'with honest malice', he went to Will's and laid the manuscript on the table beside Mr Dryden's cup of coffee.

'What's this, Will?' asked the old man. 'Have you translated more Latin verses or composed some of your own?'

'I have been rash enough to write a modern comedy.'

Mr Dryden looked at the title page.

'*The Old Bachelor?* I often wish I were such myself.'

Mr Dryden was well known to have married an aristocratic wife who lived mostly in the country and treated him with none of the adulation he received from his friends and admirers in London.

'It's somewhat after Etherege's *Plain Dealer*, especially his character Manly, but I hope sufficiently fresh in the working out.'

Mr Dryden took it away with him and my master could put his mind to nothing but what might be the verdict. He kept away from Will's, not wishing to seem importunate, and he even tried to distract himself by reading his law books.

After two or three days a boy delivered a note at the door. It was from Mr Dryden: *We never see you at Will's. Are you unwell?*

It was late in the day. The crowd of critics would soon be out from the theatre, eager as crows at carrion to tear chunks off the latest play. Mr Congreve decided to wait till morning to go to Will's, but it cost him his night's rest and I did not sleep well myself.

Next morning I could hardly tie his stock and, brushing his coat, dropped the brush on the floor. We were both trembling with nerves. At Will's he found Mr Dryden seated in his usual warm-weather place by the window and was given a seat beside him. There was no sign of his manuscript. His conversation with Mr Dryden went like this – he remembered it word for word and I wrote it down immediately after he told me:

'Your play needs a little improvement,' began Mr Dryden, putting his hand on Mr Congreve's arm as if to comfort him.

Mr Congreve said nothing. He assumed that all was lost.

'I will make some suggestions myself and Captain Southerne, who has also read it, will add some of his own.'

'I am most grateful to you and Captain Southerne for taking the trouble…' began Mr Congreve in a low, humble tone.

'No trouble. None at all. I never saw such a first play in my life and Captain Southerne has already passed it to Mr Davenant at the Theatre Royal with his recommendation to produce it. All it needs are a few tweaks of a technical kind to give it the fashionable cut of the town and those, with your agreement, we can supply.'

Mr Congreve was again silent. He was not sure, he told me, that he was not still tossing on his mattress and had briefly dropped off to dream what he wanted to hear.

'Will you allow us to give it a professional polish, dear boy?' Mr Dryden said. 'Both Captain Southerne and I are very experienced play-doctors.'

'Polish' – 'doctors' – the words echoed in Mr Congreve's brain, he said, and he had difficulty associating 'polish' with 'doctors', or finding an appropriate response. He could only think that he was blushing like a girl and that all the people seated around him and watching keenly for his reaction must be secretly despising his ineptitude.

But slowly his brain cleared a little and he managed to say, 'I am lost for words, Sir. I shall never in all my life hear anything to match your words. Please do polish my play and doctor its faults – and thank you, and thank Captain Southerne.'

Then he got up, pushed his way out of Will's and weaved his way home, narrowly avoiding collisions on the crowded streets, as if he was drunk. Indeed, he soon was, we both were, in the Blue Ball next door, and I fetched his friend and landlord Mr Porter, and Mr Porter sent his servant to fetch other friends from the Temple and we all drank bottle after bottle of wine to *The Old Bachelor* and the young genius we suddenly found in our midst. And so at last to bed and slept much better than the night before.

Mr Dryden changed the order of one or two scenes, Captain Southerne cut a few lines and reworded others, and Mr Davenant scheduled the play for the Christmas season. He also gave Mr Congreve free entrance to the Theatre Royal, so that he could gain more experience of the actors' capacities and what Mr Dryden called 'the fashionable cut of the town'. I believe this was the first time that anyone, let alone a new young playwright, had been granted such a privilege. Mr Congreve and his manservant walked about the town and the parks with shining faces and noses in the air. At Will's, Mr Congreve found himself almost as much the centre of attention as Mr Dryden, but he knew better than to flaunt himself and dominate the conversation, as many young men would have done in his shoes. Talking of shoes, however, he did order new clothes and wigs and called on me to dress him with more care and elegance. My frowsty former master had not given me any experience of fashionable valeting, but I was as happy to learn by observation and advice about town as he was in the theatre.

It came at last, as winter drew in, to his first meeting with his cast, when he was to read the play to them. There they sat around him, this assembly of the best actors in the land, led by the greatest of them all, Mr Betterton. He could play comedy or tragedy, heroes or villains or sometimes even minor roles with equal brilliance and now was to be Heartwell, the old bachelor of the title. There was Mr Mountfort in the young hero's role as Bellmour, with his wife as the flirtatious heroine, Belinda. Young Mr Doggett, who had just joined the company but whom my master already knew from Dublin, was the foolish old banker

Fondlewife, while Laetitia, his light-minded wife, was to be played by the celebrated and much older Mrs Barry. (Mrs Barry was equally celebrated for her remarkable love life: she would take a man to her bed for the night and next day behave as if she hardly knew him.) Mr Williams was to be Vainlove, the character who goes off a lady as soon as she begins to show her feelings for him, and the lady who finally nails him, Araminta, was, as I've already mentioned, none other than bewitching Mrs Bracegirdle. Imagine Mr Congreve's feelings as he faced this glittering ring of stars with his play in his lap! Imagine his sense of wonder and triumph that this could be happening to him! But imagine also his strung nerves, his sudden fear that his lines would fall flat, his wit lose its savour, his plot plummet into a void!

He began to read, he told me, in a daze, mouthing the speeches but understanding nothing of their meaning, mumbling and stumbling over words. The actors shifted on their chairs, coughed, sniffed, sneezed and rubbed their hands and knees against the cold. At last, in a break between scenes, kind Mr Mountfort rose from his chair.

'You are not doing your fine work justice, Mr Congreve. Will you permit me to read it for you?'

'With all my heart, Sir.'

So he did and at the end they all came round my poor shivering master, patted him and kissed him (the ladies too) and promised they would make his play shake the town. Actors are often said to be shallow creatures displaying false emotion, but I don't think this fair. They are trained and accustomed to project emotion onstage and therefore when they feel real emotion offstage they show it fully and openly, not trying partly to conceal it like the rest of us.

The Old Bachelor was intended to open soon after Christmas, but had to be postponed. The reason was an incident that took place at the stage door early in December. It was at night, after a performance. Mrs Bracegirdle came out of the stage door and was suddenly surrounded by a gang of drunken gentlemen, if

one can call them so, for they were more like cut-throats, led by
the notorious rake Lord Mohun and a Captain Hill. This captain
grabbed her arm and they were about to make off with her,
when Mr Mountfort came out, saw what was happening, rushed
forward, dealt Captain Hill a blow in the face that made him
let go of Bracey and pushed her to safety inside the stage door,
shouting to the door-keeper to close and lock it. But now the
whole gang turned on Mr Mountfort, who ran to his lodgings
in a street nearby. They caught up with him before he could get
through the door and Lord Mohun seized him by his coat-tail,
wrapped his arms round him and shouting drunkenly, 'Oh, my
hero!', kissed him on the lips. But Captain Hill, in revenge, I
suppose, for the blow to his face, drew his sword and ran him
through the belly. The whole gang then ran away, as the watch,
alerted by people on the street, approached. They carried Mr
Mountfort into his lodging and fetched a surgeon, but nothing
could be done for him and he died the next day. The murderer,
I believe, fled the country before he could be taken, but Lord
Mohun was caught, imprisoned and tried by his peers in the
House of Lords. They let him off. He had not after all done this
murder or probably intended it, though he had killed men before
in duels and was to die himself some years later duelling with the
Duke of Hamilton, after which the duke also died of his wounds.

Brave Mr Mountfort was buried at St Clement's and more
than a thousand people attended the funeral, as Mr Congreve
and I did in great sorrow. He was truly as much a hero in real life
as he so often appeared on the stage. But now the hero's part in
The Old Bachelor was vacant, and as if there was suddenly an evil
spell cast on the play, two other members of the cast, Mr Nokes
and Mr Leigh, died soon afterwards of natural causes. The play
was therefore postponed until March, when Mr Mountfort's part
as Bellmour, which he should have played opposite his wife as
Belinda, was taken by Mr Powell. He was a promising young
actor and had also written a comedy, *A Very Good Wife*, which was
performed the same year as Mr Congreve's, but unfortunately he
spoiled his career by drinking too much, forgetting his lines and

quarrelling with the other actors. None of these faults, however, had yet appeared when he played Bellmour in *The Old Bachelor*.

Mr Congreve attended all the rehearsals, though, inexperienced as he was, he left most of the direction to Mr Betterton. He would usually return to our lodgings in a trance of pleasure, though whether more from seeing his characters take life and his lines flight as the actors grew into their roles or from being constantly in the company of Bracey, I could not be quite sure. His eyes shone, he spoke little, he was infatuated.

My master sat in a box and I in the gallery for the first performance. Among many noblemen in the boxes were Mr Dryden and Captain Southerne, and among the ladies our landlord Mr Porter's wife, Mrs Elizabeth, who, we had recently been surprised to learn, was Bracey's sister. Mr Shadwell and, I think, Mr Wycherley, with other playwrights and poets were in the pit with the beaux and critics, as were many of my master's friends from the Temple. After the opening music from the orchestra of lutes, viols and theorbos, Bracey came to the front of the apron stage and spoke the prologue:

> But for your comfort, it falls out today,
> We've a young author and his first-born play;
> So, standing only on his good behaviour,
> He's very civil, and entreats your favour.
> Not but the man has malice, would he show it,
> But on my conscience he's a bashful poet;
> You think that strange – no matter, he'll outgrow it.

And then, pretending to forget her lines, ran off. From that moment, Mr Congreve's wit, rapid as musketry fire, and the obvious delight and confidence with which the actors revelled in their roles, first astonished and soon ravished the packed house. And if you doubt my partiality, here is what Lord Cork wrote to his agent, my master's father, across the Irish sea in Lismore Castle, after that first performance:

Your Sons play was Acted on Thursday last & was by all the hearers applauded to bee the best that has been Acted for many yeares, Monday is to bee his day which will bring him in a better sum of money than the writers of late have had, for the house will bee so full that very many persons of Quality cannot have a Seate all the places having been bespoken many days since.

When, at the end of the play the four beautiful actresses, Mrs Barry, Mrs Bracegirdle, Mrs Mountfort and Mrs Bowman appeared together, the applause shook the theatre and, as the actors had promised, the town, in the sense, I mean, of its best-dressed, most critical citizens. *The Old Bachelor* continued to be played for an unprecedented thirteen days more and three printed editions of the text were sold out within the month. Brave Mr Mountfort and kind Captain Southerne had made me the most fashionable manservant in the land.

But now I think I have already attached too many memories to that puny amphitheatre at Stowe, so I will pin my account of Mr Congreve's further theatrical adventures to another building.

5

THE LAKE PAVILIONS – WESTERN

These two identical buildings, designed by Sir John Vanbrugh, were completed in my master's lifetime. They stand facing the south front of the house on the far side of the Octagon Lake, at the bottom of the garden laid out by Mr Charles Bridgman. They are not exactly pavilions, if that implies something temporary and tent-like, but small sturdy Greekish temples with open interiors, raised above broad flights of steps, while a row of columns with Ionic capitals supports their triangular pediments. I remember that we walked down and sat in the western one – in those last years I was usually Mr Congreve's necessary prop – in company with Lord Cobham. He had been re-reading my master's second play, *The Double-Dealer*.

'It's a very dark story,' he said, 'and that cunning villain Maskwell, like Shakespeare's Iago, has no redeeming feature.'

'Except his cunning,' said Mr Congreve.

'You think that redeeming?'

'Perhaps not. But it raises him above brutes.'

I note, by the way, that Mr Congreve was quite willing to talk about his work with an old and valued friend like Lord Cobham, though he would not do so with a young whippersnapper like Monsieur Voltaire.

'But his utter disloyalty to the hero, Mellefont, his supposed friend – that seems to me,' said Lord Cobham, 'to put him beyond any hope of redemption.'

'There are such people.'

'Were you thinking of anyone in particular?'

'I don't recall it. I was still very young then. My knowledge of people was limited and came mostly from literature. Iago, as you say. I was probably trying to see what might be the result of such a ruthlessly selfish person operating in civilised society.'

'Lord Mohun?' I murmured in his ear, not presuming to take part in the conversation.

'Mohun, of course. But he was simply a brute – no brains at all. Some years later, I suppose, I might have been influenced by the extraordinary treachery of a very clever man – Matt Prior.'

'Oh dear, yes!' said Lord Cobham.

They both shook their heads and sat in silence for a while.

Mr Matthew Prior had been partly educated at Westminster School until his father died. His uncle, who kept a fashionable tavern, withdrew him from the school and put him behind the bar. Mr Prior, a particularly good-looking boy with dark hair and bright blue eyes, was serving the customers one day when the Earl of Dorset came in and noticed that this young bartender was holding a copy of Horace. Lord Dorset asked him if he knew enough Latin to read it. 'Oh, yes,' he said. Lord Dorset, not believing him, took the book, opened it at one of Horace's *Odes* and asked him to translate it. Young Prior went into a back room and returned soon afterwards with his own translation in verse. Lord Dorset, after testing him again on several more visits to the tavern, paid for him to be re-admitted to Westminster School. There he became a close friend of Mr Charles Montagu, a grandson of the Earl of Manchester, but the younger son of a younger son. Both these very clever young men went on to Cambridge University, after which, again with the help of Lord Dorset, now Lord Chamberlain to the new King William, Mr Montagu soon became a leading Whig politician, while Mr Prior was posted as a diplomat to the Hague. There, as Mr Montagu's representative, he was involved in the intermittent feelers towards peace which punctuated the war in Flanders between King William and the French King Louis XIV.

One of the main issues between these kings and other European leaders, especially the Emperor of Austria, was the future of Spain and its huge possessions after the death of its weak-minded and sickly King Carlos II, who had no direct heir. This was finally settled – or apparently so – in the year 1701 by secret negotiations leading to the Treaty of Ryswick, in which the Spanish dominions were divided between the various claimants to the throne after the King of Spain's death.

The Whigs were still in power at the time, but they lost that year's election to the Tories, who proceeded to attack the treaty and its secrecy and impeach the Whig ministers who had made it. Mr Prior, who was up to then a Whig and a member of the Kit-Cat Club, had just been elected a Member of Parliament. He astonished everyone by voting for the impeachment of the Whig ministers, including his school friend and patron, Mr Montagu, now ennobled as Lord Halifax. Mr Prior was never forgiven by his former friends, was eventually ejected from the Club and, when the Whigs returned to power, was thrown into prison. No one ever quite understood why he behaved as he did, though he wrote a verse which perhaps explained it, at least from his own point of view:

For conscience, like a fiery horse,
Will stumble, if you check his course;
But ride him with an easy rein,
And rub him down with worldly gain,
He'll carry you through thick and thin,
Safe, although dirty, to your inn.

Was it truly a matter of conscience, that he believed the treaties misguided and their secrecy dangerous? Or the worldly gain of siding with the party in power? The verse seems to suggest a combination of both. But he certainly got dirty in the process.

Mr Congreve began to write his second play, *The Double-Dealer*, on the springtide of his success with the first. But he was already starting to suffer from the gout which was to afflict him for the rest of his life, with hot sharp pains in his feet and hands. Most people thought it was due to his overindulgence in food and wine, but, while admitting the charge, he remarked that the disease also attacked other people, such as his father, who lived much more austerely. His friend Dr Samuel Garth said he thought it *was* hereditary. At any rate there was no lasting cure, though the doctors sent him to spas such as Tunbridge Wells, Epsom and later Bath to drink and bathe in the sulphurous waters, which did seem to help a little, if only by suggestion. Mr Congreve also spent some time that summer at a friend's house in Surrey, again making use of the peace and quiet of the countryside, as he had with his first play, to inspire him with the quick-fire exchanges of city sophisticates. Here, though, the scene is not set in London parks, streets and lodgings, but confined to the gallery and adjoining rooms of his character Lord Touchwood's country house.

I return now to the conversation, nearly thirty years later, between Mr Congreve and his host in the Lake Pavilion at Stowe.

'*The Double-Dealer* is almost a tragedy,' said Lord Cobham, 'ending happily only at the last moment through some lucky eavesdropping. Perhaps that was why the first audience took against it? They were expecting to laugh at affectation, not to be horrified by sheer evil.'

'There's surely no shortage of affectation? Lord and Lady Froth, Sir Paul and Lady Plyant, Lady Touchwood…'

'But Lady Touchwood is almost as wicked as Maskwell. That line she has, "I was surprised to see a monster in the glass, and now I find 'tis myself". You run in and out of laughter and the most sinister emotions.'

'Set against the clear and ultimately triumphant love of the hero and heroine.'

'It is a very complex mixture to be swallowed all at one sitting.'

'More like life. But you are right, Dick. I should not have been so surprised and angry at its poor reception.'

He was indeed very angry after those first performances of *The Double-Dealer* in the winter of 1694, following his phenomenal spring success with *The Old Bachelor*; and he showed his anger in the dedication to Mr Montagu of the first printed version of *The Double-Dealer*:

> Give me leave, without any flattery to you, or vanity in myself, to tell my illiterate critics, as an answer to their impotent objections, that they have found fault with that which has been pleasing to you [...] They were not long since so kind to a very imperfect comedy of mine that I thought myself justly indebted to them [...] But I find they are to be treated cheaply, and I have been at an unnecessary expense.

He toned that down in subsequent editions after I ventured to hint that he had cheapened himself.

'Do you say so, Jeremy? You are a damned interfering jackass and if ever I want the mud cleaned from my prose as casually as you brush it off my boots, I will let you know.'

But he took my advice. My master's sensitivity to criticism indicates clearly enough his real feelings about those 'trifles' he affected to dismiss to Monsieur Voltaire.

This second play, which he claimed was entirely his own, without his borrowing 'one hint of it anywhere', in my opinion owed something to Monsieur Molière's *Tartuffe* as well as to Shakespeare's *Othello*. It was performed by most of the same actors as the first. Mr Betterton took the part of the villain Maskwell, Mr Doggett was Sir Paul Plyant and Mrs Leigh his lady. Mrs Barry played Lady Touchwood and Mrs Mountfort Lady Froth to Mr Bowman's Lord Froth. Mrs Bracegirdle was, of course, the heroine Cynthia and her lover Mellefont was Mr Williams, acting, as they were all aware, a part the author wished to play in real life: 'Love, love, downright, very villainous love', as his alter ego puts it. Mellefont even tells the musicians to sing a song to his beloved which sounds like an echo of his author's early poem to Bracey, 'Pious Selinda':

Cynthia frowns whene'er I woo her,
Yet she's vexed if I give over;
Much she fears I should undo her,
But much more to lose her lover;
Thus in doubting she refuses:
And not winning, thus she loses.

Mr Dryden and other friends stood by the play's quality and it gradually gained the town's acceptance, especially after Queen Mary commanded a special performance early the next year. On that occasion the celebrated Mr Edward Kynaston, who took the role of Lord Touchwood, was ill. He was now about fifty years old and noted for playing kings and nobles, but he was once a boy actor who played women's parts. Mr Congreve gave his role to a young unknown actor, Mr Colley Cibber, who got up the lines overnight, modelled his performance on Mr Kynaston's and did so well that Mr Congreve recommended him for a higher salary. In effect he launched Mr Cibber's subsequent career as actor, manager, playwright and author of a popular autobiography, *Apology for the Life of Mr Colley Cibber, Comedian.* Mr Cibber says that when Mr Kynaston was still acting female parts, but growing a little too old for it, King Charles II had to be kept waiting for the performance to start while the boy was shaved. Snippets like this are what actors amuse each other with when they're not onstage.

My master died before Mr Cibber's book was published and, although he had set him on the way to success, never much liked him personally – he became very tactless and arrogant – and thought he was largely to blame for the sort of shallow, sentimental stuff with which the theatre was soon infested and which, in my time at least, it still is. But was it really Mr Cibber who brought that about or was it the low taste of the public? Mr Cibber simply gave them what they wanted.

Queen Mary, having enjoyed *The Double-Dealer,* commanded a special performance of *The Old Bachelor,* but at the very end of that year, three days after Christmas in such cold weather that the Thames froze over, she died of smallpox. My master, grateful for her encouragement, wrote an elegy for her, a classical pastoral called 'The Mourning Muse of Alexis'. I thought it embarrassingly florid, though I did not say so to Mr Congreve and fortunately he did not ask for my opinion. The poem proved popular, however, and King William, deeply saddened by his wife's death, rewarded him with a hundred guineas.

Meanwhile he had another play ready for the Theatre Royal and the same actors as before. But the theatres were closed during the public mourning for the queen's death and besides the actors were in rebellion against their new manager. This was Mr Christopher Rich, a niggardly lawyer, who had obtained complete control of the theatre from the Davenant family. Noting that the public was beginning to tire of comedy and preferred singing and dancing, he cut the actors' salaries, pared back expenses, gave their parts to younger actors costing less, and used the savings to raise the salaries and spend more on the costumes of his singers and dancers. Mr Betterton, backed by Mrs Barry and Bracey, who as one of the youngsters had been offered Mrs Barry's parts but loyally refused them, led the rebellion and formed an association of the other actors to negotiate with the management. They got nowhere. But the public, always capricious, now began to sympathise with the rebels and the theatre lost their favour and their money.

Mr Congreve, about to sign the contract for his new play with Mr Rich, held back while Mr Betterton, Mrs Barry and Bracey made their case to the royal official responsible for theatres, the Lord Chamberlain, still that admirable Lord Dorset who had been such a help to Mr Prior and Mr Montagu. He passed their complaints on to King William, who asked to hear them himself. The upshot was that the rebel actors were given a licence to set up a new company in the old tennis courts in Lincoln's Inn Fields, which had been used as a theatre after the Restoration by Sir William Davenant. The young Mr Betterton and his future wife as well as Mr Kynaston had in those days been part of Sir William's company, but after his death, the company merged with Mr Killigrew's company at the Theatre Royal in Drury Lane and the theatre in Lincoln's Inn Fields reverted to being a tennis court. Thus, since well before my master or I came to London, there had been only one theatre and one company in town. Now there were to be two again and my master sided with the rebels. How could he do otherwise considering what they had done for him, that they were now his friends and that above all Bracey was among them? He had not yet signed the contract with Mr Rich, so he gave his new play to the new company. Everything hung on their opening production and they agreed it should be this very play, *Love for Love*.

But there were problems. Mr Williams, for whom the part of the hero, Valentine, was intended, chose the seemingly safer part of staying with the Theatre Royal, as did Mrs Mountfort. Mr Congreve referred to this in his prologue:

But since in Paradise frail flesh gave way,
And when but two were made, both went astray;
Forbear your wonder and the fault forgive,
If in our larger family we grieve
One falling Adam, and one tempted Eve.

Mr Collier no doubt ground his teeth at this impudent use of a sacred text, and I should guess that Mr Williams and Mrs Mountfort came to regret their choice. But Mr Congreve himself was not at all happy when he learnt that Mr Betterton would take Mr Williams's role as Valentine.

'How can he do it?' Mr Congreve said to me as soon as he got back to our lodgings with this news. 'He may be the greatest actor in the land, but he's short and heavily built and at least sixty years old, much the same age as my father. How can he play the handsome young Valentine to Bracey's Angelica? Or the tearaway son to that mean old booby Sir Sampson? Cave Underhill will play Sir Sampson, but he's if anything younger

than Betterton. The whole machinery of my play will be
disordered and disrupted. It will be a disaster.'

It was not, of course, just the damage to his machinery that
upset him, but the damage to this latest embodiment of his
passion for Bracey in the love of Valentine for Angelica and hers
for him.

'Does Mr Betterton know your views?' I asked.

'If you mean, did I tell him that he was far too old and stout
and not handsome enough? No, I did not. I said that I had
written the part of Sir Sampson specially for him and I didn't
think Underhill would manage it quite so well.'

'And...?'

'He knew perfectly well what I meant, but he looked me
straight in the eye and said, "You are a very young man, Will, and
still learning your trade. I have grown old in mine and have never
been content to be bound by my physical limitations. Offstage
I am as you see me – not very shapely. Onstage I am another
person, an actor. An actor, moreover, of very long experience
and some talent, and I can play any role I choose to, young or
old, rough or smooth, minor or major, comic or tragic, good or
evil. My greatest role is Hamlet. If I can play Hamlet, I can play
Valentine." What could I say?'

'What does Mrs Bracegirdle think?'

'I've no idea. She keeps her thoughts to herself. But she is
Betterton's protégé, she joined his household as a girl and he
taught her to act. She is like a daughter to him.'

'Father and daughter is hardly how you envisaged Valentine
and Angelica.'

'Jeremy, would you like to go and repeat that to Mr Betterton?'

'No, sir.'

'Then keep your mouth shut and do not go mentioning a
word of this to your friends about town!'

Mr Betterton did play Valentine. He managed it adroitly, but
could not, in my opinion, quite overcome his unsuitability. He
had all the mannerisms of youth and even his voice had the
careless energy of a man in his twenties, but he was still an

old man playing a young man. It was the tour de force of a consummate actor rather than the living portrait of a young lover, whose feigned madness in the fourth act is only a step beyond his real state of mind. As my own character in the play, Valentine's witty manservant Jeremy Fetch, remarks, 'he that was so near turning poet yesterday morning, can't be much to seek in playing the madman today'. Yet Mr Betterton himself must have relished the role and been pleased with his handling of it, for fourteen years later when he retired he chose to play Valentine again for his benefit performance. He was then well over seventy years old, a martyr like my master to gout, and died a year later.

Mr Bowen played my part, Jeremy, sharply enough, but if there is rivalry between actors for the audience's favour – and there always is – it was young Mr Doggett as the salty sailor Ben who got the prize. My master had visited taverns near the docks to get the sailors' jargon and Mr Doggett, who was a member of the Fishmongers' Company, was very familiar with the Thames watermen. He even inaugurated their annual race, The Doggett's Coat and Badge. He had performed well in both Mr Congreve's earlier plays, as the ridiculous merchant Fondlewife in *The Old Bachelor* and the equally ludicrous Sir Paul Plyant in *The Double-Dealer*, but his career put on full sails from that first performance of sailor Ben in *Love for Love* on 30 April, 1695.

So did Mr Congreve's. *The Old Bachelor* had made him the most promising comedian since the glory days of Mr Wycherley and Sir George Etherege, but *Love for Love* stamped and sealed that promise. It was a particularly sympathetic audience, of course, so keen to support this company of rebels in their new theatre that they applauded every actor as he or she appeared onstage. Mr Congreve had many admirers among the titled as well as the literary nobility and they were all there in the boxes or the pit, expecting from the word that had got round an unusual success.

Mr Congreve himself sat in a box by the stage with his hat pulled over his sensitive eyes, perhaps against too much dazzle from the lights, though more, I think, to hide his expression and perhaps his tears – he wept easily when his emotions were stirred – from the crowd. Once, before the play began, he pushed his hat back and looked up, searching the gallery, and when he saw me in a front seat, lifted his hat to me. Was that the proudest day of my life, as the people sitting around and behind me and even many of the ladies and gentlemen in the boxes and pits craned and peered to see who, up there in the cheap seats, could be receiving this special mark of recognition?

It was surely among the proudest days my master ever knew, for that play took the town by storm. All acknowledged that they had never in their lives seen a new comedy to match it, and that Mr Congreve now joined the select company of master playwrights, Shakespeare, Jonson and Monsieur Molière, though he even excelled the latter two in the depth of his individual characterisation. The actors – especially Mr Doggett in his tarpaulin part, Mrs Ayliff as Miss Prue, the innocent country girl voracious for love, and Mr Trefusis as the foolish old astrologer Foresight – had frequently to pause while the audience spluttered and rolled about, dug each other in the ribs and howled with laughter. What a celebration we had, after the applause had finally died away and the excited audience began to leave, many of them red in the face and laughing again as they and their companions recalled particular lines and scenes! The play was performed throughout that season and the rebel company in their new theatre were vindicated and established for the rest of that decade.

Mr Congreve's ambition now, having reached the summit of comedy, was to claim a still loftier peak: tragedy. The actors gave him a share in their new company and he promised to write them a play a year, *if his health permitted*. That escape clause was fortunate, for although his first three plays had all been performed within the past two years, it took him the next five years to write his next two, and after that there were none. He was reasonably well off now and even raised my wages, since, in addition to his takings from the plays, his Whig patrons –

Mr Montagu or Lord Dorset or both – had found him part-time government employment as one of five commissioners for licensing hackney carriages. The commissioners' office was in Surrey Street, quite close to our lodgings, but the licensing was mostly done by a full-time secretary and did not require much work on the commissioners' part. The post only became available because the government had just cut the salary by half and the previous commissioners all resigned. Nonetheless, as my master said, it was money for crossing the road.

Various diversions conspired to prevent him writing his tragedy, some of them created by himself. To begin with, there was the first printing of *Love for Love*, for which Mr Congreve wrote a dedication to Lord Dorset, the kind nobleman who had helped the rebel company into their new theatre and whom my master, among other flattering remarks, praised as the monarch of poetry. That was somewhat of an exaggeration and a little hard on his other friend and patron, Mr Dryden. Lord Dorset had, however, written a well-known ballad, 'To all you ladies now at hand', and was descended from a famous Elizabethan poet, the first Earl of Dorset, Thomas Sackville, who had some hand in a miscellany of poetic biographies called *The Mirror for Magistrates*. Mr Congreve was intrigued by that book, though he said that most of the poems, except Lord Dorset's ancestor's, were poor stuff.

'What is your interest in it, then?' I asked him.

'The general idea,' he said. 'It describes the lives and deaths of famous historical people, bad and good, Roman Emperors, English kings and nobles, even mythical characters, as moral lessons for the leaders of society in the time of Queen Elizabeth.'

'You think we need something similar nowadays?'

'Don't all societies need to study the mistakes and successes of the past? No, it's not really the moral side of it that appeals to me. I leave that to the politicians and the clergy – good luck to them! What intrigues me is the way many of the poems tackle the subject.'

'Which is?'

'They imagine the ghosts of the various subjects – King Alfred, Richard the Third, Julius Caesar and so on – examining themselves and their actions in front of a mirror.'

'Like Lady Touchwood in your play – "the monster in the glass"?'

'It's a gruesome thought, isn't it, that after death we might have to haunt a mirror to be reminded of our failings?'

'Only famous people like you, sir. Nobodies like me would be excused, I'm sure.'

'Jeremy, you're as bad as a clergyman, always pretending humility. If I am famous, so are you, the most celebrated manservant in town. But I think we're both safe enough. The lives of poets or their manservants, however famous, would not make much of a mirror for magistrates.'

'But for other poets perhaps?'

'No, rather a mirror for those monkeys, the critics and the public, to gibber and gob at.'

It was at this time that Mr Congreve was sitting to the painter Mr Godfrey Kneller for his portrait. He did not much enjoy the experience of being observed so closely and it perhaps made him think of becoming the ghost in the mirror. But his portrait, when it was finished, showed him as no sort of ghost, but a very pink, well-fleshed and healthy young man in an elegant grey velvet coat.

Not that he was so healthy. His gout was gripping him again and causing him much trouble with his stomach, so we travelled to Tunbridge Wells to relieve it with that disgusting 'steel-water' they boast of. It seemed to work better this time than it had the year before and my master recovered his temper and his appetite. He remarked that the steel-water seemed to be less like the streams of Helicon, which were sacred to the Muses and supposed to inspire poetry, than the water of Lethe, inducing stupor and empty-headedness, but I think he actually enjoyed the temporary relaxation of having nothing in his head. However he never stopped observing his fellow water-drinkers, a few of whom he made friends with, but most of whom, he said, were only used to conversing with their own relations at home and quite unable to extend their circle of acquaintances.

He did emerge for a day or two from his pleasant idleness to write a long letter to his friend Mr John Dennis, the critic, on the subject of Humour. Mr Dennis was much feared and even hated for his savage criticism, but he admired Mr Congreve's work and they always remained friends. The letter was published the following year as 'An Essay Concerning Humour in Comedy', in a book edited by Mr Dennis. I make no attempt to summarise its content, any more than I do with the plots of the plays – why make a tedious abbreviation of what anyone may read in full and fully savour? – but will just quote two short passages:

Humour is neither wit, nor Folly, nor personal Defect, nor Affectation, nor Habit. I take it to be a singular and unavoidable manner of doing, or saying, anything, peculiar and natural to one man only, by which his Speech and Actions are distinguished from other Men.

In other words, humour derives from individuality. It is that unique quirkiness that he seeks to give to each of his characters, where other comedians are content with types and caricature. But he does not look for humour in women:

For if any thing does appear comical or ridiculous in a Woman, I think it is little more than an acquired Folly, or an Affectation. We may call them the weaker Sex, but I think the true reason is, because our Follies are stronger, and our Faults are more prevailing.

That I take to be simply another escape clause, his attempt to avoid offending the ladies. He was not afraid of offending them in his plays – witness the wicked Lady Touchwood, Lady Wishfort and Mrs Marwood and several fluttering softheads – but he was very wary of them in real life. Towards the end of his life I asked him why.

'They have no outward power,' he said. 'They cannot hurt us as government officials, taxmen, lawyers, judges, doctors, surgeons, creditors, robbers, rioters can. But their power to hurt our more inward selves – our feelings, self-respect, confidence, peace of mind – is formidable. Not all women exercise that power, of course, but just as only experience will teach you the difference between insects that sting and those that don't, so it is with women. You must treat them all with care until you know whether they are stingers or not. I don't blame them, any more than I blame wasps for defending themselves. If women had any outward power, they would likely exercise it just as we do, kindly or cruelly, generously or meanly, cleverly or incompetently. We have examples of that in the difference between Queen Mary I's reign and her sister Elizabeth's, and again between Queen Mary II's and her sister Anne's. As it is, lacking outward power, they are forced to manipulate their own lives and those of the men that presume to rule them by more subtle, more foxy means. But if those fail, they can become vengeful, pitiless, hateful – to other more successful women as well as to men – and will sting if they can. Consider that old Duchess of Marlborough and how, ever since Queen Anne tired of her domineering ways and turned her out of her service, she has become an almost legendary stinger.'

'Even of her own daughters.'

'Quite so.'

This put an end to our conversation, for, as I shall relate in another place, Mr Congreve's intimacy with the Duchess Sarah's eldest daughter, Henrietta, was not a subject for discussion.

I return now to the year 1695 and the distractions which prevented Mr Congreve from making progress with his tragedy. Before leaving London for Tunbridge, he was enlisted by Mr Dryden to read his translation of Virgil's *Aeneid* and check it against the original, for which Mr Dryden thanked him effusively in his Preface, never aware, of course, that a certain fellow Latinist on the premises had contributed several improvements.

At about the same time we had to move all our possessions to Chancery Lane, where we were to share lodgings at the Judges

Head tavern with Mr Dryden's and my master's publisher, Mr Jacob Tonson. But on our return to London we received a visit from Mr Congreve's mother. His father was too busy to leave Ireland, where, in addition to administering the Earl of Cork's estate, he had recently been appointed a Commissioner of Supply for the county of Waterford. Mrs Congreve had travelled to England with the Marquis of Carmarthen and the sister of Lord Cork and stayed with them at Plymouth and Bath before coming to London as the guest of her cousins Lord and Lady Scarsdale in Duke Street, where her son went to call on her. I met her for the first time when she came to see our new lodgings in Chancery Lane.

She was a small rather round person, with a certain resemblance to her son, very much the lady in manner – she was used to entertaining many distinguished visitors at Lismore Castle whenever the Earl of Cork was away on his English estates, which was most of the time. But she had a warm, direct way of speaking which did away with any difference of birth or status and put one immediately on friendly terms with her. That too was a trait she had passed to her son.

'I suppose you are the famous Jeremy,' she said as I helped her out of the Earl of Scarsdale's carriage in Chancery Lane.

'I have been told so, madam,' I said, 'but my real name is—'

'Jeremy suits you,' she said. 'I will call you that, if I may, since my memory for names is very poor these days and I have got that fixed.'

'I daresay I shall soon forget my real name myself,' I said, 'since Mr Congreve took the liberty of turning me into one of his characters.'

'Did you dislike that? I will call you by your real name if you prefer.'

'Not at all, madam. I was proud to be characterised. Mr Congreve has lifted me out of myself.'

'How well you put it! Of course, he's done the same to us in Ireland. We are no longer Colonel and Mrs Congreve, but Mr Congreve's parents.'

At this point my master came to the front door himself.

'What is detaining you, mother? Oh, it's that garrulous popinjay of a servant of mine.'

'You are quite wrong, Will. *I* was detaining *him*.'

She was a lovely lady, that mother of his, and I'm sure it was she who from the outset gave him his easy way with the world.

It was during this summer that the allied army, still fighting the French in Flanders, as they had been ever since King William became king in the year 1688, had a great victory. King William himself, still grieving for the loss of his queen, was leading the English and Dutch troops and the Bavarians were commanded by their Elector. They were intent on recapturing the city of Namur, which had been previously taken by the French and was now occupied by a large French army under their Marshal Boufflers. Another large French army led by Marshal Villeroi approached to lift the siege, but King William outmanoeuvred them and pressed the siege, breaking into the city itself after a month's fierce fighting, and shutting up the French in the citadel. Finally, after another month, Marshal Boufflers surrendered and was allowed to march out with the remains of his army, while Marshal Villeroi and his troops retreated. London celebrated with its usual bells and bonfires and Mr Congreve, jubilant with the rest, wrote an ode, 'To the King On the Taking of Namur', which began:

Of Arms and War my Muse aspires to Sing,
And strike the Lyre upon an untry'd String:
New Fire informs my Soul, unfelt before;
And, on new Wings, to Heights unknown I soar.

Alas, I cannot say that he did. Although he had so many military relatives, he knew nothing of war himself and his Muse was anything but military in sympathy. I kept mum, however, and Mr Congreve, aglow with patriotism, delivered his ode to Lord Dorset to give to the king. He may have hoped to be rewarded with another hundred guineas, but his main motive was pure enthusiasm for a king who had now decisively trounced the best French generals both in Ireland and Flanders, and curbed the expansive ambitions of the so-called Sun King. At any rate, no reward followed. King William also kept mum.

6

THE LAKE PAVILIONS – EASTERN

On our final visit to Stowe we were fellow guests with the famous poet Mr Alexander Pope. It surprised me that Lord Cobham should be friends with somebody who was not only a Roman Catholic but a Tory. Mr Pope was also a friend of Lord Bolingbroke, who had led the Tory government up to the death of Queen Anne and then fled the country. He had been plotting to give her throne to the Old Pretender, son of James II. However, Lord Bolingbroke later fell out with the Jacobites in exile and returned to live in England, where he contrived to lead the Tory opposition to Mr Walpole's Whig government without doing so openly. Lord Cobham, who at that time was still a supporter of Mr Walpole, though he later quarrelled with him, must have considered that Mr Pope's brilliance as a poet cancelled his unfortunate political connections. Indeed, as I've already mentioned, he thought so highly of Mr Pope that he included him in the Temple of Worthies with Shakespeare and Milton while he was still alive. The Reverend Dr Swift, who was also a Tory and friend of Lord Bolingbroke, was likewise an occasional guest at Stowe. Dr Swift, however, had used his influence during the time of Tory power under Queen Anne to save his Whig friends, especially Mr Congreve, from losing their government jobs. He boasted that in those days he never visited the Tory ministers 'without a Whig in my sleeve'.

Mr Pope, like Dr Swift, was a great admirer of Mr Congreve and dedicated the first volume of his translation of Homer's *Iliad* to him in the warmest terms: 'Let me leave behind me a memorial of my friendship, with one of the most valuable men and finest writers, of my age and country.' By 'age' he meant era, since he was half a generation younger than Mr Congreve and in spite of his own poor health lived another half generation after him.

During that visit to Stowe, Mr Pope joined us on a stroll round the Octagon Lake. I say 'stroll', but any onlooker would have seen it less as a confabulation of poets at their leisure than an outing for cripples. I pushed Mr Congreve in a wheeled chair, while Mr Pope, small and hunched, scrambled along beside us with his strange twisted way of walking, talking all the way. As a boy he had caught some dire disease and nearly died. His growth was stunted, his legs were damaged and his health continued to deteriorate as he got older. He had a sharp, thin face, suffered bad headaches and often looked as if he were in pain. He was kind and polite to me as Mr Congreve's prop-and-stay, but I'm afraid I was sometimes reminded of a very ill-natured jibe of Mr Dennis's – he and Mr Pope heartily hated one other – describing him as 'in shape a Monkey… and he is so in his every Action, in his senseless Chattering, and his merry Grimaces'. It's only fair to say that Mr Pope had attacked Mr Dennis first, in his biting *An Essay on Criticism*.

By the time we reached the Eastern Pavilion – it was warm weather – these two pain-wracked poets were glad to rest on the bench inside. I helped Mr Congreve up the steps and Mr Pope went up them crabwise. By then he was telling my master of his acquaintance with Mr Betterton, after the great actor had retired from the stage and gone to live in the country. Mr Pope was then about twenty years old and living with his parents in a house not very far from Mr Betterton's near Reading.

'One of our neighbours introduced me to old Betterton,' said Mr Pope, 'who was keeping himself busy by modernising Chaucer and suggested I do the same.'

'Which you did, I think,' said Mr Congreve.

'A couple of the *Canterbury Tales*, yes. But you know that Betterton had started his career with Sir William Davenant's company, and Davenant was Shakespeare's godson – perhaps even his natural son. So he told his actors stories about Shakespeare's private life and Betterton passed them on to me. Probably not true, but with a person as extraordinary and extraordinarily private as Shakespeare, one is glad to gobble up any tidbits. Betterton also told me, by the way, about his days acting in your plays. He said that you weren't at all happy about him taking the part of Valentine in *Love for Love*. You thought he couldn't do it.'

'He was far too old. And having carried it off to his own satisfaction he insisted on taking the young lead's part in my next play too.'

'Your tragedy? Yes, but he said they made an even greater success with that than they had with *Love for Love*. He laughed about your opposition and said you were very young still, obsessed with Mrs Bracegirdle, and really wanted to play the part of Osmyn yourself.'

'I am not an actor. But I wanted Jack Verbruggen to do it. He came over to us from the Theatre Royal company, although his wife, Mountfort's widow, stayed with them. Verbruggen was a very lively and talented performer. As it was, he had to play King Manuel, which was the part I intended for Betterton. So we had a young man playing an old man and an old man playing a young one. It was irritating.'

'The penalty of writing plays. You get the applause, which mere printed poets never get unless they read their work in public, but you have to suffer the inadequacies or waywardness of the actors. I suppose you had no trouble from the ladies?'

'None at all. Bracey was a ravishing Almeria, and Mrs Barry gave one of her greatest performances as the fiery African queen, Zara.'

Mr Congreve had no reason to complain, even of Mr Betterton's obstinacy. *The Mourning Bride* proved his most popular play, often revived, and brought in a good income.

But he found it hard to write. It was still barely begun when we travelled to Ireland early in the year 1696. Mr Congreve and Captain Southerne, among others, attended a ceremony in Trinity College, Dublin, where they were given their Master of Arts degrees, which the troubles in Ireland at the beginning of King William's reign had prevented them receiving at the time. I thought my master well suited by his cap and gown and asked him if he didn't think now of taking a doctorate.

'I'm far too lazy to go back to studying.'

'But you spend much of your time studying. What have you been doing recently with all those Spanish books, the history of ancient Granada?'

'Pilfering, Jeremy. I pilfer what I need and invent the rest.'

'I'm sure you are quite as learned as most doctors of philosophy or letters.'

'That may be, but not in the formal, dogged way required by universities. You would make a much better doctor than me, with your prodigious memory.'

'You really think so, sir?'

'What have I said? Am I to lose my useful manservant because he wants to go off and become a doctor of philosophy?'

'Dr Jeremy Fetch. It has a ring to it.'

I was teasing him now.

'Please, Jeremy, put this out of your head! If my tragedy takes as well as *Love for Love*, I will raise your wages.'

'I will bear that in mind.'

But I could not help smiling at his anxious expression and he noticed.

'You are a devil, Jeremy. You're making fun of me.'

'Dr Jeremy Fetch!' I said, and burst out laughing, when he too began laughing. After that he sometimes called out, 'Fetch me my pipe, Dr Fetch!' or 'Fetch me my boots, Dr Fetch!' But he never did so in company, he was always careful to respect my dignity, as he was with everyone else's, high or low. When he told Monsieur Voltaire that he should be treated as just a gentleman, he meant it in both senses: his birth and his manners.

After our stay in Dublin we travelled to Lismore Castle to stay with Mr Congreve's parents, who had a whole wing to themselves. Mrs Congreve greeted me almost as warmly as her son, first kissing him, then taking both my hands and saying, 'Dear Jeremy, we have no end of servants here, so you are to have a holiday.'

'Mother!' said my master, 'the fellow is an inveterate idler. You should not encourage him. I shall need him close by to sharpen my quill and keep my inkwell full.'

'Are you going to work here, then?' she asked.

'Who knows? But in case I do, I cannot have Jeremy mooning about the fields looking for milkmaids.'

'I'm sure they are more likely to come looking for him, such a handsome young man.'

'If there's too much of that we shall have to go straight back to London.'

Colonel Congreve appeared at this moment.

'What nonsense is this?' he said. 'You're here at least till the end of summer. There is hardly a person in Ireland who is not determined to meet you and we have already arranged a whole series of visits both to and from our neighbours. And you must know that in Ireland we count as neighbours anyone within a radius of fifty or sixty miles.'

'Very well, father,' said Mr Congreve, 'I am at your disposal.'

'Certainly you are, and must now redeem the burden you have put upon us as father and mother of the new Shakespeare.'

He smiled and hugged his son. Mr Congreve smiled back, but I thought equivocally, as if he both liked and disliked the compliment. Later, when I was unpacking his trunk, he muttered, 'Shakespeare! *Absit omen!*'

He meant, I think, that he couldn't help being flattered, but at the same time, still not having written his tragedy, was superstitious about invoking the greatest name of all in that line.

He would not like me to reveal this, but he was very superstitious. Nobody could make some promise for the future without his touching wood, and he had certain little rituals about the house which he did not like to omit. Perhaps they were just the signs of an orderly mind and a cautious disposition, but I noticed once that as he was about to go out to a rehearsal, he suddenly rushed back into his study and saluted a bust of Aristotle which Bracey had given him. Whether he felt the need to acknowledge the philosopher's wisdom or the donor's love or that he thought it brought him luck, I cannot say. He saw that I had noticed his gesture and pretended to scratch his head. I would not have dared to enquire further. But I suspect that few of us, though we may lose our belief in church religion, are quite immune to a respect for some invisible power, chance or fate or providence, whatever we like to call it. Mr Congreve made us laugh at his character Foresight, the ridiculous astrologer in *Love for Love*, whose elaborate prognostications are always wrong and who fails to observe that Scandal is making love to his wife, but I do believe that his characters, however exaggerated and absurd, take their life from his own sympathy with their feelings, from touching some aspect of himself.

I'm sure that his carefully concealed sense of unseen forces was the mill-stream that turned the wheel of his historical tragedy, *The Mourning Bride*. Our visit to Lismore Castle supplied the setting he had not been able to envisage in the relentlessly up-to-date world of London, and thus the opening to hitherto unexplored feelings of dread and disaster. Not that they were entirely unexplored. He had brushed against them in a night scene in his novel *Incognita*, when one of the two heroes rescues his beloved from abduction and rape, while his character Maskwell in *The Double-Dealer* creeps out from some dark alley of the spirit unknown to the other characters in his comedies.

Lismore Castle in County Waterford was built in the twelfth century by King John on the site of an even more ancient abbey, and belonged later to the great Earls of Desmond who were virtually the kings of Ireland, until their power was broken by the English in the reign of Queen Elizabeth. The next owner was the queen's favourite Sir Walter Raleigh, but when he was imprisoned by King James I he sold it to Richard Boyle, who was an adventurer like himself but proved more prosperous and became the first Earl of Cork. His son, the second earl, was now the owner and Colonel Congreve's employer. The Congreves had enjoyed the friendship of Lord Cork ever since Colonel Congreve had been posted as a young lieutenant to Ireland; and the printed edition of my master's first play, *The Old Bachelor*, was dedicated to Lord Cork's grandson, Charles, soon to succeed to the title and estates, since his father had died a few years earlier and his grandfather, aged eighty-five, died the year after our visit to Ireland. The second earl's younger brother was the famous Robert Boyle, philosopher, physicist, chemist, inventor of 'Boyle's law' – something to do with the volume and pressure of gases which I cannot attempt to explain – and author of *The Sceptical Chymist*. He was born at Lismore.

The castle stands high above the River Blackwater and was partly rebuilt and modernised by Lord Cork after the damage done by Lord Tyrconnell's soldiers. He surrounded it with a castellated wall and built a grand new gatehouse into the central courtyard. There was a delightful walled garden and sloping lawns, and a huge estate beyond of farms and woods, all of which Colonel Congreve managed. It was a beautiful and peaceful place, the servants were friendly (especially a pretty housemaid called Siobhan), and as Colonel Congreve had warned, relays of visitors came to meet 'the heir to Mr Dryden and Shakespeare'. My master was civil enough to them all, though I don't think they were as impressed with his witty conversation as they hoped. It takes at least two people to make a witty conversation and few of them supplied the second person. Besides, he was preoccupied with his play and the ideas the castle was giving him.

It was not the beauty or the peace of the place, not the swift river below nor the garden nor the countryside beyond that caught his imagination. It was the ancient dungeon-like vaults below the castle which no doubt dated back to its time as a monastery and where monks in another period of Irish troubles had hidden the so-called *Book of Lismore*, tales of the deeds of Celtic heroes. I went down into these dark cellars several times with him and cannot say I enjoyed the experience. They were deathly chill and deathly depressing to my usually cheerful temperament, but they had almost the opposite effect on him. He would rub his cold hands, wipe his red and runny nose on his sleeve and say, 'Good, very good! Isn't it wonderful, Jeremy? Don't you feel clammy hands at your throat and see the ghost of a monk flit past that doorway there?'

'If you say so, sir.'

'Your teeth are chattering, Jeremy. You're not frightened?'

'No, sir, just very cold.'

'Icy fingers laid on your hand.'

'The icy fingers are my own.'

'That dark heap in the corner! Not a corpse, I hope? Hold the lantern over it!'

'An empty sack, I fancy.'

'You fancy! Can you fancy nothing, Jeremy?'

'I fancy a blazing fire.'

'You are quite hopeless.'

'No, sir. I am full of hope that we shall soon see the blessed sun again.'

'These cellars are very extensive. We still have a lot to see here.'

'We haven't seen much so far.'

'Deeper in, I daresay there may be tombs or even a charnel house.'

'That would indeed be a real frisson.'

'Footsteps! Do you hear footsteps?'

'Rats.'

'What's that? Some passing phantom?'

'Your own shadow, sir, as I changed the lantern from my frozen right hand to my gelid left hand.'

'I wonder if we shall ever find our way out again.'

'Trust me to do that, sir! I can think of little else.'

But I have to admit that when I read the passages in his play inspired by these vaults under Lismore Castle, I felt that my discomfort had been almost justified. And when, early next year, I saw his actors transform what he had imagined into an atmosphere of fear and cruelty that gripped the whole audience, I repented of my unhelpfulness at Lismore.

LEONORA (Mrs Bowman): Hark!
ALMERIA (Bracey): No, all is hushed, and still as death. –
'Tis dreadful!
How reverend is the face of this tall pile,
Whose ancient pillars rear their marble heads,
To bear aloft its arched and ponderous roof,
By its own weight made steadfast and immoveable,
Looking tranquillity! It strikes an awe
And terror on my aching sight; the tombs
And monumental caves of death look cold,
And shoot a chillness to my trembling heart.
Give me thy hand, and let me hear thy voice!
Nay, quickly speak to me, and let me hear
Thy voice – my own affrights me with its echoes!
LEONORA: Let us return; the horrors of this place,
And silence, will increase your melancholy.
ALMERIA: It may my fears, but cannot add to that.
No, I will on; show me Anselmo's tomb,
Lead me o'er bones and skulls and mouldering earth
Of human bodies; for I'll mix with them...

Well, perhaps I did give him some help. After all, I held the lantern and drew attention to the cold, and I'm sure if there had been bones or bodies or tombs, I would have been less surly. All I can say is that I was better suited to be the servant of a comedian than a tragedian. But against all expectations he did, that once, climb the highest mountain, where Shakespeare, Otway and Dryden had stood before him. The play was a mighty success, not least because it had a political dimension in its story of the tyrannical King Manuel of Granada and his eventual overthrow by Osmyn, the disguised prince of Valentia, with the collusion of the tyrant's own daughter Almeria. It seemed to the Whigs a reflection of their victory nine years earlier, when the tyrannical

King James was overthrown by his daughter Mary and her husband, Prince William of Orange. The published version was even dedicated to the tyrant's younger daughter, Princess Anne, pointing out that 'this poem' – so he called it – was 'constituted on a moral whose end is to recommend and to encourage virtue'. Mr Congreve himself clearly considered it a kind of 'mirror for magistrates' – Whig magistrates, of course.

Where is the tragedy, though, you might ask, if the tyrant is defeated and the noble lovers, Osmyn and Almeria, succeed to his throne? A good question, for I wonder if you can really have a tragedy with a happy ending. King Lear recovers his throne and Cordelia lives to succeed him? Othello at last thinks of asking his wife Desdemona if she slept with Cassio and, convinced that she didn't, forbears smothering her? Ophelia recovers from her madness and decides not to drown herself, her brother is reconciled with Hamlet, who kills the wicked king, marries Ophelia and they become king and queen of Denmark? No, Mr Congreve's *The Mourning Bride* is not, in my opinion, a proper tragedy. He could not bring himself to make it so. Neither he nor his audience could stomach real tragedy and that is why, no doubt, tragedy seldom flourished in our softer times. Perhaps we are too conscious of the reverse, that the comedies of our lives, unlike those in the theatre, generally have sad endings, to which this one I am writing is, I'm afraid, no exception.

But tragedy or not, *The Mourning Bride* filled the theatre for thirteen successive nights and certain lines from it became so well known that, like lines from Shakespeare, people would quote them without even knowing where they came from: 'Music has charms to soothe the savage breast' and 'Heaven has no rage, like love to hatred turned,/ Nor hell a fury, like a woman scorned'.

Later the same year, after nine years of war, King William and his European allies at last made peace with the French and signed the Treaty of Ryswick. The guns in the Tower of London boomed, bells rang and bonfires appeared all over the town. My master shared the general rejoicing and wrote another public poem, *The Birth of the Muse*. It's an odd mixture of classical myth and British history leading up to King William's great achievement in making peace, and contains that patriotic passage beginning 'Britannia, rise; awake, O Fairest Isle' which I quoted in my Prologue. But to show how my master's own sense of achievement and further ambition had soared with the success of his tragedy, I will quote his remarkable, almost Miltonic image of the creation of the world by 'the Father', a classical rather than a Biblical deity:

> Not yet the loosen'd Earth aloft was slung,
> Or pois'd amid the Skies in Ballance hung.
> Nor yet, had *Time* Commission to begin,
> Of Fate the many-twisted Web to spin;
> When all the Heav'nly Host assembled came
> To view the World yet resting on its Frame;
> Eager they press, to see the Sire dismiss
> And rowl the Globe along the vast Abyss.
> [...]
> The Father now, within his spacious Hands,
> Encompass'd all the mingled Mass of Seas and Lands;
> And having heav'd aloft the pond'rous Sphere,
> He launch'd the World to float in ambient Air.

But what kept it floating? Sir Isaac Newton's newly discovered Force of Gravity, I suppose, unless it was Mr Boyle's Law of Gases – such extraordinary times of new knowledge we live in!

The poem was finished less than a month after peace was declared and a few days before King William returned to England. Mr Congreve was pleased with it, gave it to me to read and asked my opinion. I thought it patchy, but did not care to say so.

'I am not qualified...' I said.

'It's not meant just for the "qualified" and in any case you are certainly as well qualified as anybody, Dr Fetch.'

'Well, then,' I said, 'it does make me feel a little giddy.'

'Giddy?'

'Dizzy. That great ball rolling off into the air and as yet no Time.'

'But that's when Time begins, as the earth begins to spin on its axis round the sun.'

'Incredible.'

'But true.'

'It still makes my head spin.'

'Cagey b—'

He was about to say 'bastard', broke off as he remembered that I really was one and did not press me further. The poem was published a week later and dedicated to his loyal patron, Mr Charles Montagu, who responded by finding him another small post as the manager of a state lottery, though this post was very poorly paid and had little success with the public. Mr Montagu, at my master's suggestion, also persuaded Mr Vanbrugh, whose first play *The Relapse* had been successful at the Theatre Royal the year before, to give his second comedy *The Provok'd Wife* to the new company at Lincoln's Inn Fields.

Mr Congreve was now, after Mr Betterton, the leading voice in the management of the new theatre, and he brought in new plays by three playwrights, Mr Charles Hopkins, Mrs Catharine Trotter and Mrs Mary Pix. Their first plays had all been performed at the Theatre Royal and its manager, Mr Rich, was naturally enraged by their departure, so that I feared he might send a couple of lowlifes to waylay my master and give him a beating. But Mr Rich was a sly lawyer and responded more craftily by getting hold of the manuscript of Mrs Pix's new comedy before it was performed and having Mr George Powell – another actor who had stayed behind when the rebels left the Theatre Royal – steal its plot for a play of his own. Mrs Pix was furious in her turn and took her grievance to Mr Congreve. Then he, she and Mrs Trotter, with actors from Lincoln's Inn Fields and other friends, all attended Mr Powell's opening night in order to hiss it down. An anonymous pamphlet written by a friend of Mr Powell claimed that when they failed to get the audience on their side, 'this very generous, obliging Mr Congreve' – sarcastic reference to my master's universal reputation – 'was heard to say, "We'll find out a new way for this Spark, take my word there is a way of clapping of a Play down".' I was not there and cannot confirm the story, but he may well have said it and even followed up with bursts of derisive clapping. His loyalty to friends and protégés was absolute and he was certainly incensed by Mr Powell's blatant theft.

The other lady poet he championed, Mrs Catharine Trotter, a relative of two Scotch noblemen, was only eighteen years old and wrote a poem to Mr Congreve comparing him to Alexander the Great:

> Alike in youth you both sought early fame,
> Both sure to vanquish too where'er you came;
> But he by others' aid his conquests gain'd,
> By others too the fame of them remain'd;
> Thou sov'reign o'er the vast poetic land,
> Unaided, as unrival'd, do'st command,
> And not oblig'd for fame, which records give,
> In thy own works thou shalt for ever live.

Mr Congreve replied, not entirely truthfully, that 'it is the first thing, that ever happened to me, upon which I should make it my choice to be vain'. However, he was not so pleased when Mr Charles Hopkins, son of the Bishop of Derry and graduate of Trinity College, Dublin, dedicated his tragedy *Boadicea* to him in almost equally flattering terms:

> O! *Congreve*, could I write in Verse like thine,
> Then in each Page, in every Charming Line,
> Should Gratitude, and Sacred Friendship shine.
> [...]
> Nor does your Verse alone our Passions move,
> Beyond the Poet, we the Person love.
> In you, and almost only you; we find
> Sublimity of Wit, and Candour of the Mind.

Why should that have displeased him? He said it was because Mr Hopkins had not first asked him if he could dedicate the play to him, but I believe it was because of his secret superstition, his fear that all this brilliant success and the excessive praise it engendered must tempt Providence to turn the tables.

It soon did, in the shape of Mr Jeremy Collier and his *A Short View of the Immorality and Profaneness of the English Stage.* I have already indicated how much this angered Mr Congreve, but have perhaps not sufficiently shown how much it hurt him. Here is Mr Collier's mocking comment on a scene in *The Mourning Bride*:

> When Zara in the fifth act finds the dead body, she falls
> into a most terrible fit of fustian:
> "Ha, prostrate, bloody, headless, O – start eyes,
> Split ear, burst every vein, at this dire object;
> At once dissolve and flow; meet blood with blood;
> Dash your encountering streams, with mutual violence,
> Till surges roll, and foaming billows rise,
> And curl, their crimson heads, to kiss the clouds."
> One would think by this rant that Zara had blood enough
> in her veins to fill the Bay of Biscay or the Gulf of Lyons –
> at this rate a man may let the Thames out of his little finger.

In the play's second printed edition Mr Congreve took care to omit all those lines except the first.

But angry as he was with Mr Collier, scornful of most of his arguments, contemptuous of his narrow outlook, and determined to prevent him and others like him from closing the theatres again, he thought he recognised the workings of the ancient Greek belief that hubris is inevitably followed by nemesis. And he was quite sure of it when Mr Collier's diatribe led to his prosecution, with Mr Vanbrugh and Mr Durfey and their booksellers, before the Middlesex Grand Jury for immoral and irreligious expressions in their printed plays. They were found guilty and had to trim their plays accordingly, but the worst of it was that the public and even King William approved in general of Mr Collier's strictures. Ever since the Restoration of King Charles II, playwrights and actors had been permitted great freedom of expression and suggestion. They had, of course, merely reflected and satirised the same freedom in upper-class society. No longer. Mr Collier did not succeed in closing the theatres, but he floated in on a rising tide of disapproval for the Cavalier licentiousness of the past forty years and brought much comfort to the puritans.

Perhaps we should have expected it. Our society has a history of alternating puritanism and moral latitude. In Shakespeare's play *Twelfth Night*, performed in the last years of Queen Elizabeth's reign at the beginning of the last century, the drunken knights Sir Toby Belch and Sir Andrew Aguecheek make a monkey out of the puritan steward Malvolio. By the middle of that same century, after the Civil War, the puritans had closed the theatres and were in complete control of our country. In the last part of the century, after the Restoration of King Charles, the theatres reopened and the roistering Belches and Aguecheeks – Lords Rochester and Dorset, Colonel Tidcomb and all – again rode high. Mr Collier and his renewed moral corsetry were almost inevitable.

My master was chastened or, I should rather say, brought back to himself. Would any of us, promoted to the company of Shakespeare and Alexander the Great at the still tender age of twenty-seven, not have become somewhat self-conceited? As his indispensable staff of one, I have to admit that I too became a little high and mighty in my dealings with people of my own class. But at least, I think, we both knew it and were relieved to descend from our clouds and become ordinary mortals again. It took nearly a year and a half after the Collier commotion for my master to complete his next and last play, in which he again gave an important role to the hero's manservant. This intelligent and polished character, named Waitwell, is recruited by his master, Mirabell, into an elaborate plot to disarm his enemy, Lady Wishfort, the disagreeable old aunt of Mirabell's beloved, Millamant. Waitwell is required to marry Lady Wishfort's maidservant, Foible, which he is very happy to do, and to masquerade as Sir Rowland, a knight seeking to marry

Lady Wishfort. This is the exchange Mr Congreve wrote for his master and servant:

MIRABELL: Come, sir, will you endeavour to forget yourself, and transform into Sir Rowland?
WAITWELL: Why, sir, it will be impossible I should remember myself. Married, knighted, and attended all in one day! 'Tis enough to make any man forget himself. The difficulty will be how to recover my acquaintance and familiarity with my former self, and fall from my transformation to a reformation into Waitwell.

There in a nutshell you have my real situation, and Mr Congreve's too, as we returned to our former selves. Never believe that a poet's inventions are not abstracted, however obliquely, from his own circumstances! But Mr Congreve actually spelt out his disillusioned return to earth in the Prologue to his new play:

Poets are bubbles, by the town drawn in,
Suffered at first some trifling stakes to win;
But what unequal hazards do they run!
Each time they write they venture all they've won:
The squire that's buttered still, is sure to be undone.
This author heretofore has found your favour;
But pleads no merit from his past behaviour.
[...]
Satire, he thinks, you ought not to expect;
For so reformed a town who dares correct?
To please, this time, has been his sole pretence,
He'll not instruct, lest it should give offence.
Should he by chance a knave or fool expose,
That hurts none here, sure here are none of those...

By quoting from his new play I have got ahead of myself and him. In the spring of the year following the Collier affair, the new company revived *The Double-Dealer*, which had been the particular play of his arraigned by the Middlesex Grand Jury. This was not an act of defiance so much as a trade on the publicity given to the play by the court case, for the offending expressions were omitted and Mr Congreve's name appeared on the playbill, which was unusual if not unprecedented for a living author. What the company really wanted was Mr Congreve's new play, but that was not ready yet, far from it. He had begun to work towards it by reading the comedies he admired, Shakespeare's, Ben Jonson's and the Roman playwright Terence's, and thought he saw his way to a plot. But there was nothing on paper when he accepted a last-minute invitation from the Earl of Montagu to spend part of August at his great country house, Boughton, in Northamptonshire.

These Montagus are a very confusing tribe and I will try to sort them out. They are all descended from Sir Edward Montagu, Chief Justice in the time of King Henry VIII and King Edward VI. Then, in the days of King James I and King Charles I, three brothers – Henry, Sydney and Edward – sired separate lines of successful Montagus. (Forgive me if I make it sound like the breeding of thoroughbred horses or pedigree dogs.) *Henry* Montagu was the ancestor of the Dukes of Manchester and of that Maecenas of the arts, my master's patron Mr Charles Montagu, the youngest member of the Whig Junto, who later became Earl of Halifax. *Sydney* was the father of Edward Montagu, who was joint High-Admiral under King Charles II, became Earl of Sandwich, and went down with his flagship in a great sea-battle with the Dutch off the little Suffolk fishing-port of Southwold. *Edward* was the grandfather of this Earl of Montagu, owner of Boughton House. There are times when I am inclined to bless my obscure birth for saddling me with no need to breed leaders of men and nobody to live up to.

Ralph, Lord Montagu had married as his second wife a very rich woman, daughter of the second Duke of Newcastle and widow of the Duke of Albemarle. Now this is a strange story, but I'm assured it is true. Her previous husband had been appointed by King James as Governor of Jamaica, but had died there and she had experienced a most hair-raising voyage back to England in the company of her husband's embalmed body and a large treasure recovered from a sunken Spanish galleon. It was the year 1688, when King James lost his throne, and the sailors on the naval frigate accompanying the duchess's vessel deserted in favour of King James. There were various exotic creatures on board her own ship – a crocodile, an iguana and a seven-foot snake. They cannot have been well looked after. The crocodile died and the others escaped from their cages. The iguana leapt overboard, but the snake slithered away through the ship causing general terror until it was finally shot dead. Whether all this had turned her head or she had always been somewhat unhinged, the duchess when she reached England made a vow to marry nobody again unless he were of royal birth. Lord Montagu therefore wooed and won her in the guise of the Emperor of China. He did not look very Chinese, so I think that by then she must have been quite mad.

At any rate, her wealth was what he needed to improve his property and by 'improving' I mean something far beyond modernisation. He had formerly been our ambassador to the court of King Louis XIV, whom he much admired and who seemed to like him – at any rate the king would have the fountains at Versailles turned on specially for Lord Montagu's visits. It became Lord Montagu's ambition to transform Boughton, the grounds as well as the house, into an English Versailles. Most of the workmen he employed for that purpose were also courtesy of the Sun King, for that tyrannical Catholic monarch had recently revoked the Edict of Nantes (which had given freedom of worship to Protestants) and caused large numbers of his most intelligent, skilled and hard-working, but Protestant citizens to flee from his dominions and settle in England, to our lasting advantage.

Lord Montagu was a collector of fine furniture and paintings and a highly educated man, so he did not invite guests who were likely to bore him or each other, and Mr Congreve was delighted to be one of them. The visit proved to be all he had hoped and a kind of correlative to the visit to Lismore Castle which had given him the clue to his tragedy. Now he wanted the clue to another comedy and he found it at Boughton, not in the great house or even the fountains and canals it overlooked, but, so he said in his dedication of the play to Lord Montagu, in the conversation and friendship of many of the finest minds in the land. Three of them he knew already from the Kit-Cat Club, but as he said to me when we were returning to London in His Lordship's coach, 'To know people one meets occasionally for an hour or two in a coffee-house or at a dinner party is not the same as to know them from daily companionship in the pleasantest circumstances, walking, talking, looking at pictures, eating and drinking with them.'

It so happened, that summer of the year 1699, when we still had an uneasy peace treaty with France, that the king's ministers were in disarray. King William's preferred minister was Lord Sunderland, but neither the Whigs nor the Tories liked or trusted him – he had previously served King James, had converted to Catholicism and was now a Protestant again – and he had resigned at the end of the previous year. The king, displeased with his ministers' squabbling, left for the Low Countries to continue negotiations with France, leaving political confusion behind him. Lord Montagu, not himself a minister, but always active in politics, offered his house at Boughton as a place where a deal might be done, since it was conveniently close to other country retreats where some of the grandees were spending the summer. Several came: the Duke of Shrewsbury; the Earl of Godolphin and the Earl of Marlborough (as he then was); Lord Montagu's cousin, Mr Charles Montagu, Chancellor of the Exchequer; Mr Henry Boyle, younger grandson of the second Earl of Cork; and his friend Mr Robert Harley, both Members of Parliament. The two latter were moderate Tories, willing to work with Whigs. But other important people did not come and apparently nothing could be decided without them. Baulked of their political purposes, the guests had to be content with enjoying their host's lavish hospitality, his magnificent, newly recreated house – the old Tudor building enclosed within a mighty modern mansion in the French style with a long colonnade on the ground floor and a suite of State Rooms above – and the Versailles-inspired canals and waterworks in the grounds.

Mr Congreve, who by this date was inclined to avoid coffee-house company and preferred to mix only with his own particular friends, was at first a little intimidated, I think, to find himself, much the youngest guest, in this den of political lions. He was relieved to be joined by another poet, the physician Dr Samuel Garth, author of the mock-heroic poem *The Dispensary*, published that same year, as well as by Mr John Locke, the famous scientist and philosopher who had once been Lord Montagu's physician. Mr Charles Montagu, of course, was already my master's friend and patron, while Mr Boyle belonged to the family which employed Colonel Congreve in Ireland and was the younger brother of Charles Boyle, the third Earl of Cork, to whom my master had dedicated his first play. Lords Marlborough and Godolphin were civil enough, but, linked now by the marriage of Lord Marlborough's daughter Henrietta to Lord Godolphin's son Francis, as well as by some inkling perhaps of how they would become the twin military and political leaders of another great war with France in the years ahead, kept themselves somewhat apart. The debonair Duke of Shrewsbury, however, who wore a piratical patch over one eye and was well known for his charm, won my master's admiration immediately. Bracey excepted, I do not remember him ever being so impressed before by a new acquaintance.

'A most remarkable man,' he said as I dressed him on the second or third morning of our visit. 'And a Talbot. Does that mean anything to you, Jeremy? His ancestor, the first Earl of Shrewsbury, was that famous general who fought with King Henry V in our old wars in France and died fighting for Henry VI: Shakespeare made much of him: "stout Lord Talbot, the great Alcides of the field".'

'Alcides?'

'Another name for Hercules, fits the line better.'

'But the Duke of Shrewsbury is not a military man himself?'

'No longer, but he fought for King James during Monmouth's rebellion.'

My master, although he made fun in his first play of the cowardly Captain Bluffe, always had a soft spot for military men. His family, after all, were almost all soldiers. He was the odd one out.

'It's unfortunate,' he continued, 'that his health is poor, or there would be no question who should run the country.'

'His eyes give him trouble, I suppose.'

'No doubt, but that proverb might have been invented for him: "in the country of the blind the one-eyed man is king". No, he sees better than most with his one eye, but he suffers from asthma. That can knock a person down and must often exhaust him. Yet consider his record! He was one of the "Immortal Seven" who signed the invitation to the Prince of Orange to take the throne away from James. He actually sailed with Admiral Russell to fetch the prince from Holland and mortgaged his estate so as to contribute to the prince's expenses. Since then he has been a pillar of King William's government, as Secretary of State both for the South and the North. Yet he was quite frank with me: he does not want power, he takes these jobs because the king and his fellow ministers insist, and when he tries to resign, they refuse to let him go.'

I must have looked doubtful.

'You think he is not sincere? On the contrary. A man of unusual integrity. Mr Montagu says that he's difficult to understand, that he seems sometimes to vacillate, that his loyalties are uncertain and that he may have sympathy with the Tories or even the Jacobites. That may be true. He is not a Whig. He was born a Catholic, but converted to the Church of England, then served King James as a colonel of horse, then played a leading part in the removal of King James. But I disagree with Mr Montagu. I don't think that was vacillation or uncertainty, or even time-serving. That's how a man behaves who thinks deeply before he acts, who puts principle before party, and the good of the country before his own ambition, or even safety.'

This gathering was unusual for a summer house party in being all male, probably because it had been intended as a political cabal.

Mr Congreve, Dr Garth, Mr Boyle, Mr Locke and the Duke of Shrewsbury were in any case unmarried, and Mr Montagu's wife had recently died. Lords Marlborough and Godolphin and Mr Harley, expecting business rather than pleasure, had left their wives at home. Lord Montagu's wife, the lady he had wooed in the guise of the Emperor of China, was present in the house, but never seen. She kept or was kept to her own secluded rooms, where she was served by a separate group of servants, who also had their own rooms separate from ours and, so I was told, were always dressed as Chinese and, entering her presence on their knees, treated her as if she was truly the Empress of China. I was disturbed by the thought of this mad lady somewhere in the vicinity and that Lord Montagu, who had married her for her great wealth and used it to make and furnish this great house, was able to behave, at least in front of his guests, as if she did not exist, as if he had not made these elaborate and hidden arrangements to humour her insanity. I could not help asking Mr Congreve if he had seen his hostess.

'You know as well as I do that she is not to be seen by anyone.'

'Isn't that strange?'

'Not in the circumstances. It is inevitable.'

'Poor lady!'

'On the contrary. She is, I imagine, happy to suppose herself an empress and lives luxuriously in her delusion. Any other husband might have snatched it all away from her and ceased to indulge her once he had secured her hand and her fortune in marriage.'

'It would make a play.'

'Not of the kind I write.'

'You had Valentine feign madness in *Love for Love*.'

'Feign! That's the difference. Real madness is something I could not compass. Ophelia? Lear? I'm not sure that even Shakespeare could depict it to the life, or actors carry it off convincingly.'

He thought for a moment.

'But there is another possibility.'

'That she is not...'

'That she indulges him, yes. That she loves playing the empress and loves her husband's play-acting as the Emperor of China too much to disillusion him.'

We both fell silent, considering this unlikely but really dreadful scenario: two people trapped in a double illusion. I believe that when my master came to write his next play, the thought of his invisible hostess contributed something to the plot – the manservant Waitwell disguised as a knight proposing marriage – as well as to the lady being deceived, his frightening character Lady Wishfort. But of course he made no mention of that in his dedication of the play to Lord Montagu, referring instead to 'the honour of Your Lordship's admitting me into your conversation, and that of a society where everybody else was so worthy of you'.

I was not myself admitted into any of these great men's conversation, though I did once exchange a few words with Mr Harley. And on one occasion Lord Montagu's butler sent me to pass on a message from His Lordship to my master, asking him if he wished to be included in a party riding out into the countryside the next morning. I found Mr Congreve in the grounds contemplating an immense spout of water rising out of a rectangular sheet of water, so still on a windless day that it looked like glass. He was in the company of the Duke of Shrewsbury, Mr Montagu and Dr Garth and, while I waited to pass on my message, heard Mr Montagu say that he feared Mr Collier had somewhat 'narrowed the scope for wit in the theatre'.

'Not entirely,' said Mr Congreve. 'He is such a narrow-minded fellow that he puts us on our mettle to be both bolder and more subtle. The problem is not so much Collier himself as the shallow public he appeals to.'

'Hasn't the public always been shallow?' suggested Dr Garth.

'No doubt, but they follow fashion. The fashion used to be to appear worldly-wise and witty and to admire wit. Now it is to seem sententious and sentimental.'

'I wonder,' said the Duke of Shrewsbury, 'that a man of your learning and wit writes for the theatre at all, considering how little grateful the public is.'

'But Your Grace works for the public in public office. Are you rewarded with much gratitude?'

'None. You are right. Why then do we do it?'

'There is some satisfaction, I think,' said Mr Montagu, 'in the sense that one may direct things better than they might be directed by others.'

'You are leaving out ambition,' said Dr Garth. 'Aren't you all ambitious of success and perhaps lasting fame, in spite of the risk of being misunderstood and disparaged?'

'Ah, Dr Garth,' said the duke, 'you observe the symptoms and diagnose the disease. I'm afraid there is something in what you say. But for my own part I would be glad enough to put such ambition as I ever had to rest and retire to some more humble homestead than this one.'

'The doctor leaves himself out of his diagnosis,' said Mr Congreve. 'But I think he too has some ambition to be remembered. If not as an admired physician, then as a poet.'

'To be remembered, no,' said Dr Garth. 'Only to amuse myself and my friends. To enjoy life while I have it, that's all I ask.'

'Which of us will be remembered, after all?' said Mr Montagu.

All looked thoughtfully at the ground and said nothing, so I took the opportunity to intervene:

'Mr Congreve!' I said.

They turned and stared at me with surprise.

'Who are you?' asked the Duke.

'I have a message from Lord Montagu for my master,' I said.

'Your master being Mr Congreve?' said the Duke.

'Quite so, Your Grace.'

'We thought for a moment that you were claiming an undying future for him,' said Dr Garth.

'No, sir. I am sure his work will be long remembered, but I was not meaning anything but to catch his present attention.'

'But you spoke truth,' said Mr Montagu. 'Of all four of us here, I would lay a bet that Will Congreve is the one who will be best remembered. Poets, as he himself has written, have a better chance of that than politicians.'

'You are too kind, Charles,' said my master in a low voice, pink with embarrassment. 'What is your message, Jeremy?'

I think he added 'Damn you!', but in such a whisper that I may have imagined it from the angry movement of his lips.

'His Lordship asks whether you care to ride tomorrow morning, sir.'

He gave me his answer in one sharp word and as I bowed and turned to go I heard the duke say, 'You are well served, Congreve, when even your valet comes in on cue.'

I left them laughing merrily at my innocently prophetic intervention and Mr Congreve's confusion. I might remark, by the way, that his high opinion of the Duke of Shrewsbury was confirmed many years later when, in her last moments of life, Queen Anne gave him the Lord Treasurer's wand. Thus Lord Bolingbroke's secret scheming to pass the throne to the Pretender was defeated and the Protestant succession made sure. And so for the second time this modest duke, neither Whig nor Tory, saved us from the Catholic Stuarts and perhaps another Civil War.

My encounter with Mr Harley took place on a back staircase usually used only by servants. He was a shortish, quite slender man of about forty years old then, though he put on weight later when he became Lord Treasurer in the Tory government at the end of Queen Anne's reign and was created Earl of Oxford. It was he, at that crucial moment in the year 1714, who had to give up the Lord Treasurer's wand to the Duke of Shrewsbury as the queen lay dying.

'I am quite lost,' he said. 'Looking for the Archive.'

'It is a very confusing place, sir – one house inside another – so many stairs and corridors – and I am myself only a visitor.'

'Whom do you serve?'

'Mr Congreve, sir. The poet.'

'And a very fine one too. I am an admirer of his work.'

'Thank you, sir. I will pass that on to him.'

'Oh, I have already told him so myself. The pity is that he's a Whig.'

'Should I mention that to him?'

'No, no. I'm not against Whigs in general, only those that are deaf to anything but party. We need moderate men, men that can hear both sides of an argument. I'm sure you are one such yourself.'

'I hope so, sir. *Quot homines, tot sententiae* [as many opinions as there are men].'

'My dear fellow! Does Mr Congreve teach you Latin?'

'That phrase, sir, if I recall correctly. Its author, the poet Terence, is a great favourite of my master. But it was my previous master at Oxford who first taught me Latin and it was partly that facility that brought me into Mr Congreve's service.'

'Well, your master is a lucky man. But if you ever think of leaving him, don't fail to come knocking on my door! Now how can I find the Archive? I believe it contains some interesting manuscripts and private papers and I have a curious passion for such things.'

'I must find somebody to direct you, sir, or it will be the blind leading the blind.'

Fortunately at that moment one of Lord Montagu's footmen was passing at the foot of the stairs and took charge of Mr Harley's quest for the Archive.

It was at Boughton that Mr Congreve first met and talked to Mr John Locke whose *An Essay Concerning Human Understanding* he greatly admired. Mr Locke, who, like the Duke of Shrewsbury, suffered from asthma, was in poor health and never, I think, an easy person to converse with, but no doubt my master's evident esteem for his work won him over. He had probably not imagined that a young celebrity renowned for his wit and fanciful inventions in the make-believe world of the theatre might be a man of Reason too. Indeed, as Mr Congreve showed me, after our return, in his copy of Mr Locke's book, he specifically distinguishes wit from reason:

Men who have a great deal of Wit, and prompt Memories
[…]

'That's you, Dr Fetch.'

[…] have not always the clearest Judgment, or deepest
Reason. For *Wit* lying mostly in the assemblage of *Ideas*, and
putting those together with quickness and variety, wherein
can be found any resemblance or congruity, thereby to
make up pleasant Pictures, and agreeable Visions in the
fancy: *Judgment*, on the contrary, lies quite on the other side,
in separating carefully, one from another, *Ideas*, wherein can
be found the least difference, thereby to avoid being misled
by Similitude, and by affinity to take one thing for another.

'Well,' said Mr Congreve, 'we are both hung out to dry there,
Jeremy, but I explained to Mr Locke that there is a difference
between the use of a character in a play as part of the author's
whole construction, which might be considered a matter of
reason and judgement, and what the character himself may say
or do, witty and fanciful as that may be.'

'Was he convinced?'

'He did not deny it and said he was continually revising his
work for fresh editions, so would consider my argument at more
leisure. But I don't think he will, now that I look at his book
again. Consider this passage: "Would it not be an insufferable
thing for a learned Professor, and that which his Scarlet would
blush at, to have his Authority of forty years standing wrought
out of hard Rock Greek and Latin, with no small expense of
Time and Candle, and confirmed by general Tradition, and a
reverend Beard, in an instant overturned by an upstart Novelist?"'

'Yes,' I said, 'but he is surely ridiculing other people with fixed
opinions there, not describing himself? He doesn't have a beard,
does he?'

'True, but we are all human, Jeremy, and, as the Bible says, apt
to see the small mote in another's eyes when we have a large

beam in our own. Notwithstanding my liking for him, I think he has somewhat fixed opinions and a virtual beard.'

However, the value Mr Congreve derived from his stay at Boughton was not any particular conversation, let alone the witticisms or characteristics of his fellow-guests. It was the sense that in spite of Jeremy Collier and the increasingly alien public taste, there remained a small section of society worth the trouble of writing for. He began at once that autumn to compose a comedy which should satisfy both his own desire to perfect the form and appeal to the exacting taste of Lord Montagu and his friends, noting in his dedication to Lord Montagu that 'if I am not mistaken, poetry is almost the only art which has not yet laid claim to Your Lordship's patronage'.

The Way of the World is the height of my master's art and the peak of a tradition of satirical comedy with a serious underlay, which ended there. It was not generally recognised as such when it was first performed in the early spring of the new century and did not much help the new company's fortunes, which had begun to languish. Mr Betterton did not this time insist on playing the hero, Mirabell, a part everyone saw as a self-portrait of Mr Congreve. That part was given to the more suitable Mr Verbruggen. Mr Betterton was content with the villain's part, the greedy, seedy Fainall. Mrs Barry was the self-deceiving old Lady Wishfort, and Bracey, of course, played the heroine Millamant, perhaps the most perfectly feminine, most elusively attractive woman ever created by my master or any other playwright. Bracey's performance reminded me of a highly bred horse that shies and rears in the paddock, yet effortlessly wins the race. Everyone knows the scene in the Third Act when Millamant states her conditions for marrying Mirabell and he retorts with his. I asked Mr Congreve how he could depict so clearly what usually brings a marriage to grief, yet still have his lovers marry.

'"The world must be peopled",' he replied, quoting one of Shakespeare's fastidious bachelors on the verge of marriage.

'But you believe that marriage almost always leads to unhappiness.'

'I do and it does. But you see if two people fall desperately in love – something nobody can help – they have little alternative. Nature has taken them in its grip and nature is only concerned in the outcome, more people. True, the man only ruins his life if he marries, but the woman ruins her life whether she marries or not; and so the man ruins *her* life either way and, if he truly loves her, has at least the hope that theirs may be the rare marriage that turns out well.'

The Way of the World was Mr Congreve's last word on the many varieties of women and their volatile moods, young, old, married, jealous, vengeful, forgiving; and on their attendant males, the husbands, lovers, fools, gold-diggers who stalk them for their money or their beauty or both. But my favourite characters, of course, are the servants Waitwell and his sweet new wife Foible, played by Mr Bright and Mrs Willis; for amongst all the butterfly fluttering of the society ladies and the peacockery of the gentlemen, these two are unconditional lovers, reliable confidants, bright, brisk and sensible people working for adequate wages and the promise of a farm. I regret that I never found my real-life Foible or owned a farm, but at least this once I saw myself briefly enlarged into a married man and even a respectable knight in the mirror of my master's reflected world.

Seated in the Eastern Lake Pavilion at Stowe so many years later, Mr Pope and Mr Congreve came on to the subject of this play and Mr Pope asked the question which so many have asked and answered to their own satisfaction:

'Why did you never write another play?'

'I had no more to write.'

'Your bucket was empty?'

'No, my bucket was full.'

'It was not because the audience wanted lighter, more sentimental stuff?'

'No, although they did.'

'Nor that Mr Jeremy Collier's attack on the theatre – and you especially – made you unwilling to make yourself a target for any further criticism?'

'No. *The Way of the World* was in part a dismissal of Collier and all his tribe.'

'I recall that you gave your character Lady Wishfort a copy of Collier's *Short View* in her closet.'

'Precisely. Lady Wishfort, with her cracked cream face, her unseemly vanity and her jealous malice was just the person to admire Collier.'

'It wasn't that you preferred the quiet life of a gentleman to the ups and downs of the theatre?'

'I did prefer it, certainly. But, as I said, I had filled my bucket.'

'At the age of thirty?'

'Perhaps I had learnt from Betterton that young men's roles should be taken by young men.'

'Writing plays is only for young men?'

'Not always, not necessarily. But it was for me. I might have been the age I am now, over fifty, but I happened to be thirty. I had filled my bucket.'

But even a quarter of a century after he had done so, at about the time of this conversation with Mr Pope at Stowe, his early retirement from writing plays still rankled with those who valued quality. Mr Edward Young the poet wrote:

Congreve, who crown'd with Lawrels fairly won,
Sits smiling at the Goal while Others run,
He will not Write; and (more provoking still!)
Ye Gods! He will not write, and *Maevius* will.

7

THE TEMPLE OF FRIENDSHIP

Mr Congreve never saw this temple, which was built some ten years after his death. By that time the Whig party had split. Mr Walpole's Excise Bill in the year 1733 proposed to extend the tax on imported tea, coffee and chocolate to tobacco and wine, but would also, in the view of its opponents, Whig as well as Tory, give yet more power and patronage to government officials and further erode the liberty of citizens. Lord Cobham sided with the Mayor and Corporation of London and the populace in general in opposing the Bill. When it failed, Mr Walpole punished his Whig opponents by depriving them of their public offices, and Lord Cobham, this illustrious general under King William and the great Duke of Marlborough, was dismissed from his regiment. He retaliated by turning his grounds at Stowe into a manifesto for liberty and virtue and a protest against the Prime Minister's corrupt and autocratic government. But since Mr Walpole and Lord Cobham had been for many years close allies, he could equally well have called this edifice the Temple of *Broken* Friendship,

It is a substantial two-storey building with one-storey porches on either side, and fronted by a pillared and pedimented Tuscan portico. Inside, there is a basement kitchen beneath the banqueting hall, whose ceiling is decorated with an allegorical picture of Britannia saluting the reigns of King Edward III and Queen

Elizabeth, while decently veiling with her cloak 'The Reign of...', presumably that of our present monarch, King George II, hand-in-glove with Mr Walpole. Along the walls are ten busts of Lord Cobham's friends and relations, the so-called 'Patriots', chief among them Frederick, Prince of Wales. This prince was as much at odds with his father, King George II, as *he* had been when Prince of Wales with *his* father, George I. But for our purposes we can leave aside the Hanoverian dynasty's perennial family problems, Lord Cobham's anger with Mr Walpole, and the temple's political significance, since all this happened after Mr Congreve's time. Its name at least can cover an important part of my master's life: his diverse and ever *un*broken friendships.

His personal friends were mostly Irishmen he had known as fellow pupils at Kilkenny School or Trinity College, Dublin, or as fellow students of the law at the Middle Temple. They were heavy drinkers and hearty eaters like himself and several grew very fat as they got older. He would no doubt have done so too if he had not suffered from severe fits of the gout, which forced him to be more abstemious and drink mineral water as often as wine. They were jovial people and in their company he joked and laughed and teased them in a way that would have surprised his other groups of friends, the poets and noblemen, with whom he behaved more circumspectly. Those who didn't know him well even thought him cold and stand-offish, but that was a protective mask he wore when he became a celebrity and wished to avoid being treated as such. Celebrities divide roughly into two types: those that bask in the bright light and adoration, which is all they sought in the first place; and those that hate the social flattery inseparable from a successful career. My master belonged among the latter and so could only relax fully in the company of those who had known him before he became famous.

His closest personal friend was Mr Joseph Keally. They had known each other as boys at Kilkenny, though Mr Keally was three years younger and still at school when Lord Tyrconnell began driving out Protestants, including the headmaster of

Kilkenny College, Dr Hinton. Young Keally escaped to England and entered Pembroke College, Oxford, at about the time my master left Trinity College, Dublin, under the same compulsion. They met again as fellow students at the Middle Temple.

When I first joined Mr Congreve in his lodgings in Arundel Street, Mr Keally had lodgings in the same house and they saw each other almost daily, whether in each other's rooms, in the Blue Ball tavern next door, or in the Middle Temple. Mr Keally, however, unlike my master, was a serious student of law, which he later practised very successfully back in Ireland, becoming a member of the Irish Parliament, Recorder of Kilkenny, Attorney-General of the Palatinate of Tipperary and eventually Commissioner of Appeals. By that time he was married, with two children. I once overheard my master ask Mr Keally about his name:

'It seems both Irish and not Irish.'

'My great-great-grandfather,' said Mr Keally, 'was called O'Kelly. He fled to Kilkenny in the time of Queen Elizabeth's Irish massacres and changed his name to Keally.'

'Changed his religion too perhaps?

'Very likely. His grandson John Keally, my father, was certainly a Protestant. He married the daughter of a Captain Joseph Cuffe, who commanded a troop of horse under Cromwell and was rewarded with substantial grants of land.'

'Captain Cuffe? That's a good name for a soldier.'

'Yes, and I remember my grandfather, Captain Cuffe, as a very bluff soldier indeed.'

Mr Congreve was still working on *The Old Bachelor* then and I have little doubt that he borrowed Mr Keally's military grandfather's name and changed it to Captain Bluffe, the braggart soldier in that play.

'And your father? What sort of man was he?'

'I hardly know. I was only five years old when he died. But he must have been a serious and ambitious man. At the time of his death he had just been made High Sheriff of county Kilkenny and was building our family seat, Kellymount House.'

Alas, Mr Keally himself also died early, at the age of forty, in the year 1713, a great sadness to my master and to Mr Keally's many other friends, who included Captain Steele and Mr Addison. Like them, Mr Keally was not only an active man of the world but also a sensitive and learned person who read books, enjoyed plays and music, and once translated a ballad of Mr Congreve's into Latin. Mr Congreve corresponded with him frequently after his return to Ireland in the autumn of the year 1697, by which time he had seen his friend, my master, changed from a young stage-struck student of law into the famous author of three comedies and a tragedy. After that, Mr Keally visited London occasionally, but Mr Congreve never went to Ireland again after his visit in 1696, though he sometimes thought he might.

On that score I knew him better than he knew himself. He had little desire to go far beyond London, partly because of his gout, partly because of what he called 'my natural laziness', and partly because nobody much – except perhaps Sir John Vanbrugh in his calash – enjoyed travelling on muddy roads with dangerous cavities and the constant risk of highwaymen, or across seas which might be either storm-tossed or becalmed. Stowe and Boughton to the north, Bath to the west and Tunbridge Wells, Richmond and Epsom to the south were about the limits of his excursions.

We did, however, take advantage of the peace with France in the summer of the year 1700, to travel to the Low Countries in the company of Mr Tonson, the publisher, and Mr Charles Mein. Mr Mein worked for the Custom House in London and was another fat and jolly Irishman, with a very loud laugh. Indeed he was always laughing. It seemed to be his natural reaction to anything that surprised or pleased him, not just in conversation, but when looking at pictures or even listening to music, which was disconcerting to the musicians. Our Channel crossing, however, stifled even Mr Mein's laughter. We left Dover at four in the morning and lacking any wind were still only halfway over nine hours later. Fortunately then we were met by a French rowing boat, which took us in tow and finally brought us to Calais by six o'clock in the evening. There we found excellent champagne and burgundy wines at very moderate prices and you can be sure that we drank sufficient quantities of both to put us all to sleep before travelling on by coach with heavy heads the next day.

Mr Mein had only short leave of absence from his Custom House duties, and Mr Tonson had some book business to transact in Rotterdam, so they both went on to that city directly. Mr Congreve and I, however, made a tour through French Flanders, by way of Brussels, Namur (which he was particularly anxious to visit because of his poem on its capture) and Antwerp, and then into Dutch Gelderland. My master was very angry with me for forgetting to post a letter he had written to our friends and landlords, Mr and Mrs Porter, and accused me of being habitually drunk. It's true that I did drink more than usual on that trip, but so did he and I should say that I was the soberer of the two, at least when it came to catching coaches or finding a lift on open wagons, which in those rustic places were often the most convenient mode of conveyance.

Neither of us spoke the Dutch language, which sounds from a distance like English, but close-to like monkey-jabber, so it was me rather than him, with an extensive repertoire of gesture and grimace, who contrived to make our needs known to the natives. Perhaps after all I could have been an actor, as Mr Mountfort once suggested. Easiest of all, of course, is to lift one's elbow and command a tankard and, the natives being even greater drunkards than the English, it is not surprising we spent many of our days in a pleasant haze or occasionally a bleary fog. We did sometimes meet a person who spoke some English or French, usually a soldier or gentleman who had fought in King William's war with the French, but my master's most intense conversations were conducted in Latin on the open wagons with itinerant monks and friars or Calvinist preachers, all of whom seemed intent on converting him to their own beliefs and whom he listened to with extraordinary patience.

'Are you intending to write a treatise on comparative religion?' I asked him, 'or a play satirising religious fanatics so as to infuriate Mr Collier afresh?'

'Neither. I am stocking up on these various beliefs, in order to converse intelligently with Bracey's mother when we get home. You know she thinks of little but religion and she regards me as hardly better than an atheist.'

'But aren't you?'

'No, no. Not an atheist. I am trying to discover which belief is the least absurd or unsavoury so as to expound its finer points to Mrs Bracegirdle.'

'You think that if the mother approves of your new interest in religion, she may smooth your way to the daughter?'

'Oh come, Jeremy! Do you take me for a hypocrite?'

'You sound as if you might be.'

'There is no smooth way to Bracey through her mother or anybody else. All roads to Bracey are rough, circuitous and perilous. The shattered, still groaning bodies of unsuccessful suitors lie on every side. Brambles, false turnings and pitfalls await the infatuated pursuer. No, the problem is purely practical. Whenever I visit their lodgings I must perforce converse with the mother as well as the daughter and, since the mother's chief interest lies where it does, I require a little more religious powder in my musket or grist to my mill.'

All this I thought somewhat nonsensical. He was fond of Bracey's mother and had no difficulty in talking to her on any subject, while his colourful version of his pursuit of Bracey was equally inventive, but I will come to that in another place.

We arrived eventually at Rotterdam to catch a vessel home, only to find Mr Mein still there for lack of an easterly wind. With our arrival it soon blew and we were back in London just in time to hear of a new war with France, which broke out again in Flanders that winter. The sickly king of Spain, Carlos II, had finally died and, instead of adhering to the partition of the Spanish dominions laid down in two secret treaties after the Treaty of Ryswick, he left everything to his chosen successor,

King Louis XIV's grandson, Philippe, Duke of Anjou. King William and his allies, the Emperor of Austria, the Dutch and the German Protestant princes, saw no alternative but to fight all over again for what they had won in the previous war.

Another Irish friend of Mr Congreve was Mr Robin Fitzgerald, who had been at Trinity College, Dublin, with him. Mr Fitzgerald came from a line of distinguished ancestors, Norman, English and Irish, and studied law at the Inner Temple. He returned to Ireland at about the same time as Mr Keally, like him became a lawyer and a member of the Irish Parliament, and married Mr Keally's sister Ellen. Mr Fitzgerald also suffered from gout and grew very fat. My master, Mr Keally and Mr Mein often teased him, but he had a very easy, sunny temperament and seems to have been happy enough to be their butt. Mr Mein, however, was not so happy with Mr Fitzgerald's light-hearted approach to life when he returned to Ireland leaving a debt for which Mr Mein was the recognisance. Mr Mein had to disappear into the country to avoid arrest and feared losing his Custom House job. I believe Mr Fitzgerald did then settle the debt. Laughing Mr Mein grew so fat that my master, not very slim himself, could not share the same seat with him in a coach.

Mr Congreve's other particular friends in this group, Mr Amory and Mr Luther, were both from Trinity College, Dublin, and studying at the Middle Temple, and both returned to Ireland and became substantial property owners. Mr Luther, like Mr Keally and Mr Fitzgerald, was for a time a member of the Irish parliament. So most of these friends had left London by the time Mr Congreve made his first and only trip to the Continent; and gradually, as such youthful friendships will, when the parties move apart and embark on quite different careers, they faded into memories of the past and the intermittent exchange of letters. Mr Mein, however, remained in London, together with Mr and Mrs Porter, Mr Congreve's friends and landlords in Arundel Street and soon to be our landlords again in neighbouring Surrey Street. And in Howard Street, which joined Arundel Street to Surrey Street, lived Mrs Porter's sister, Bracey, and their mother.

Another of my master's Middle Temple friends was Mr Walter Moyle, a Cornishman. Unlike the others, he was also a regular of Will's Coffee House, where he and Mr Congreve conducted a kind of sword-play of witty exchanges, full of learned references to classical authors which must have left many of their companions goggling. Or at least I assume so, since although I never attended the coffee-house I often heard them at it when Mr Moyle visited our lodgings, and they left me goggling in spite of my classical learning. Mr Moyle returned at one point to his home territory in Cornwall, that remote corner of our island where the natives live by mining for tin, smuggling and wrecking ships, whose cargo they loot and whose unfortunate sailors, if any makes it to the shore, they murder. One of these Cornish savages, a woman, even murdered a well-known admiral, Sir Cloudesley Shovell, wrecked on the Scilly Islands, for the valuable ring on his finger. I doubt whether Mr Moyle threw away any of his learned quips on these terrible cut-throats, but I suppose he knew them well enough to go safely among them and to canvass for a seat in Parliament, which, dressed as a soldier, he said, rather than a poet, he won.

Mr Congreve associated with his poet friends in those early years chiefly at Will's Coffee House. He might occasionally dine with them at an 'ordinary,' but could not afford to do so frequently. He dined out frequently with his grander friends and otherwise I would fetch his meals in. His most important literary friendship in those early years was with Mr Dryden, although, because of the great difference in their ages and, to begin with, in their status, their relationship was more that of father and son. Almost from the time that Mr Dryden commissioned my master's renderings of Juvenal and Homer and helped to make his first play a success, he singled out Mr Congreve as his poetic heir, and Mr Congreve responded accordingly. Once, I remember, when Mr Dryden was returning from the country in a public coach, Mr Congreve and Captain Southerne rode out of London some miles to meet him and accompany him home. On another occasion when Mr Dryden quarrelled violently with Mr Tonson over a book he was publishing, Mr Congreve, who by then was lodging with Mr Tonson, sorted out their differences, calmed their tempers and made them friends again.

Some people gossiped that Mr Dryden began to resent his protégé's increasing success, but I did not see it that way. I saw a steady and natural reversal of their relative positions, as the ageing Mr Dryden looked to my master to see that his work was not forgotten and my master, always grateful for the way Mr Dryden had launched his career, fully accepted his role as the old man's standard-bearer. After the poor initial response to Mr Congreve's second play, *The Double-Dealer*, Mr Dryden continued to put the weight of his own great reputation behind the partly stalled wheels of my master's and openly declared:

> Maintain your Post: that's all the Fame you need;
> For 'tis impossible you should proceed. [He means 'become any more famous'.]
> Already I am worn with Cares and Age;
> And just abandoning th' Ungrateful Stage:
> Unprofitably kept at Heav'n's Expence,
> I live a Rent-charge on his Providence:
> But You, whom ev'ry Muse and Grace adorn,
> Whom I foresee to better Fortune born,
> Be kind to my Remains; and oh defend,
> Against your Judgment, your departed Friend!
> Let not th' insulting Foe my Fame pursue;
> But shade those Lawrels which descend to You:
> And take for Tribute what these Lines express:
> You merit more; nor cou'd my Love do less.

Mr Dryden lived to see all Mr Congreve's plays performed and his prophecy amply fulfilled. He died in the spring of the year 1700, very soon after the first performances of *The Way of the World* , which he was too ill to attend, but able to read. Although it took him nearly twenty years to get round to it, my master always knew that he must ensure, with Mr Tonson's assistance, the publication of a handsome collected edition of Mr Dryden's dramatic works. I don't believe there can be many such examples in the history of poets – who are often, I'm afraid, selfish and unreliable people – of such generosity being repaid with such unfailing loyalty and love as Mr Congreve felt for Mr Dryden.

It was Mr Dryden who introduced my master to Mr Addison, a brilliant young scholar from Oxford who contributed verses to a volume edited by Mr Dryden and published by Mr Tonson. Mr Addison was a tall, pale, ascetic young man, a couple of years younger than my master and like him a charming and witty friend, but equally disinclined to push himself forward in public. In fact, for all his learning and intelligence and the important posts he came to occupy, he was a very poor public speaker and did not show at his best as a Member of Parliament. In private, of course, there was no one like Mr Addison – not even Mr Vanbrugh – for attracting powerful patrons and he held, as I have already mentioned, some of the highest posts in the land. I have also pointed out that it was Mr Congreve who introduced Mr Addison to his first important patron, Mr Charles Montagu, the youngest member of the Whig Junto, and advised Mr Montagu not to let a person of Mr Addison's quality be swallowed up by the Church. Mr Montagu accordingly sent him on an extended tour of the Continent in order to gain experience and knowledge of our friends and enemies there.

Mr Addison was deeply impressed by the culture and politesse of Paris and its society, but considered the French 'the vainest nation in the world' and warned that they:

> are certainly the most implacable, and the most dangerous enemies of the British nation. Their form of government, their religion, their jealousy of the British power, as well as their prosecutions of commerce, and pursuits of universal Monarchy, will fix them for ever in their animosities and aversion towards us, and make them catch at all opportunities of subverting our constitution, destroying our religion, ruining our trade, and sinking the figure which we make

among the nations of Europe. As we are thus in a natural state of war, if I may so call it, with the French nation; it is our misfortune, that they are not only the most inveterate, but most formidable of our enemies; and have the greatest power, as well as the strongest inclination to ruin us.

All this remains only too true, even as I write, and even though we have recently driven off their latest attempt to invade our country and place the Catholic Jacobite Pretender, the so-called Bonnie Prince Charlie, on our throne. I suppose that since we consistently frustrate their attempts both to dominate Europe and monopolise the trade with other parts of the world, we must expect never to be at peace with them; however much we admire some aspects of their arts and manners and however much certain enlightened Frenchman, like Monsieur Voltaire, admire our constitution and envy our freedom from the arbitrary power of a despotic monarch.

I have strayed from Mr Congreve's friendships, although, of course, this contrast between our hard-won liberty (though endangered by Mr Walpole) and French tyranny is exactly what the interior of Lord Cobham's Temple of Friendship is intended to express. Mr Addison's schooling was in London at the Charterhouse, where he became close friends with another boy of the same age but a little ahead of him, Mr Richard Steele. He was born in Dublin, but his father died when he was very young and his mother sent him to live with an uncle and aunt in London, though he often spent the school holidays staying with Mr Addison's family in Lichfield, where Mr Addison's father was Dean of the Cathedral. They both went on to Oxford University, where Mr Addison excelled but Mr Steele was less successful and left to join the army. He did so as a private soldier, since he could not afford to buy a commission, and fought in Flanders for two years. But when Queen Mary died he wrote and published an elegy for her, as did Mr Congreve and several others. My master's, as I mentioned, was rewarded by King William, while Mr Steele's, shrewdly dedicated to Lord Cutts, a high-ranking officer, gained him a captain's commission in the Guards. Short and stumpy, with a broad coarse face, so that he always looked more like a soldier than the poet, famous author of journals and knight he became, he was ambitious and enterprising, but also rootless and insecure. In consequence he clung to his friends and was lavish with his praise for their successes. He admired no one more than Mr Addison and Mr Congreve and, in the dedication of a book of poems he edited, perhaps caught my master's particular gifts as a friend more exactly than anyone:

As much as I esteem you for your excellent Writings, by which you are an Honour to our Nation; I chuse rather, as one that has passed many happy Hours with you, to celebrate the easie Condescension of Mind, and Command of a pleasant Imagination, which give you the uncommon Praise of a Man of Wit, always to please and never to offend. No one, after a joyful Evening, can reflect upon an Expression of Mr *Congreve's*, that dwells upon him with Pain.

Captain Steele's own life, however, for all he achieved, was messy. It seemed to be a perpetual struggle: with a wife he loved but who ceased to be able to put up with his incessant difficulties and eventually retired to live without him in Wales; with five children (one of them illegitimate) whom he also loved deeply but who needed the attention he had no time to give them; and above all with debt and constant changes of address either to show the world and his creditors that he was still keeping his head above water, or simply to evade his creditors. He was imprisoned for debt on at least two occasions. I don't know whether this story is true, but if not it ought to be, for it perfectly encapsulates Captain Steele's up-and-down life as well as his open character and sense of humour. He had moved into new premises and held a grand dinner party for his distinguished friends, with a phalanx of footmen in livery to wait on them. One of the party wondered how he could afford such a large staff. 'They are the bailiffs,' he said. 'I can't keep them out of my house, so I thought I'd at least make them useful.'

Captain Steele wrote numerous pamphlets, one or two successful plays and, most famously, the journals called the *Tatler*, *Spectator* and *Guardian*, with the collaboration of Mr Addison and once, in the *Tatler*, Mr Congreve. Captain Steele was elected to Parliament as a Whig towards the end of the Tory period of government under Queen Anne, but was expelled for writing a pamphlet favouring the Hanoverian succession. However, that gained him his knighthood a year later, when George I became king, and Sir Richard Steele was soon afterwards re-elected to Parliament. He might have hoped, indeed expected, that when Mr Addison became such a powerful figure in the administration he would have found a lucrative post for his oldest friend and collaborator, but he did not. Their friendship ended in coldness, followed by open enmity, as each attacked the other in anonymous pamphlets for and against the Peerage Bill, which proposed to limit the number of peers. Sir Richard attacked it in a pamphlet called *The Plebeian,* while Mr Addison supported it on the government's behalf in a pamphlet called *The Old Whig.* Sir Richard's reply became personal: 'I am afraid he is so old a Whig that he has quite forgot his principles'. Mr Addison's reply mocked Sir Richard for his habit of seeking patronage from peers, reminding 'this Author of the Milk with which he nurses our Nobles'. Sir Richard called Mr Addison a hypocrite. It was another Broken Friendship.

Mr Congreve's later poetic friendships included two authors much younger than himself, Mr Alexander Pope and Lady Mary Wortley-Montagu. Both remained his friends until the end of his life and missed him dreadfully when he died, but the friendship of Mr Pope and Lady Mary for each other was another broken one. While Lady Mary was absent in Constantinople with her husband the ambassador, she corresponded warmly and frequently with Mr Pope and Mr Congreve. Indeed my master considered that Mr Pope had fallen violently in love with Lady Mary, albeit only on the pages of letters. When she and her husband returned and bought a house near Mr Pope's in Twickenham, beside the River Thames, their friendship seemed to continue on a more realistic basis. Mr Pope helped Lady Mary find her house and plan its garden, they collaborated over private concerts, and Mr Pope even persuaded Lady Mary to buy South Sea shares, as he had himself. That was not, of course, good advice, but neither of them was ruined when the bubble burst. It was later that something went wrong and their friendship turned to fierce enmity and personal insults. She drew attention to his 'obscure birth' and deformity, he said she thought of nothing but men and money and even accused her of having caught a sexual disease. My master, remaining the friend of both, never knew what had come between them, but guessed that Mr Pope must have made some unequivocal advance towards Lady Mary and that she, equally unequivocally, repulsed him, even perhaps laughed at him, since she was not a person to hide her feelings.

'He is not a very attractive man, is he?' I suggested.

'On the contrary,' said my master, 'he's a quite fascinating man.'

'Purely as a man, I mean, with all his physical disabilities.'

'I don't think those would deter a person of Lady Mary's intelligence and sensibility. She would see and did see, I'm sure, the rich furnishings behind the damaged facade.'

'Then what? She is too faithful to her husband?'

'She is not the sort of woman to be shocked by a declaration of love from another man. She must get a great many of them.'

'So?'

'She is, after all, the daughter of the Duke of Kingston, while Mr Pope is a person of comparatively humble birth.'

'But that never deters people—'

I was about to say 'in love' but broke off abruptly, considering that by then my master's relationship with the young Duchess of Marlborough was exactly what I was describing.

'In love, you were about to say. True. But I don't think Lady Mary was ever in love with Mr Pope, however much he was with her. A lady does not compromise herself or her distinguished family unless she really cannot help it.'

'But she must have known all along that Mr Pope adored her, and, as you say, was used to dealing with it. Why the sudden break?'

'She is a woman, Jeremy, a woman of unusual individuality and courage. She had suddenly had enough of a false relationship and probably told him so. She might have told him something much softer the next day if he had waited to hear it. But Mr Pope is always on the edge of becoming a nervous wreck and whatever she said to him drove him on to the rocks. Women, I think, rely on men not to take everything they say at face value, but to wait for further confirmation or modification. Mr Pope, however, is sometimes more like a woman than a man in his reactions. Lady Mary may have miscalculated.'

Lady Mary did not entirely spare even Mr Congreve from her war with Mr Pope, letting it be known that he despised Mr Pope's poems. That was not true. He may have found fault with one or other of them in her hearing, but then he often criticised her poems to her face. She asked him to do so, of course, which Mr Pope did not, but I know that my master regarded Mr Pope's work very highly indeed. He compared it to Mr Dryden's and added, 'But I'm not sure that Mr Pope is not the greater poet – or at least the more perfect maker of smooth and yet always surprising verses.'

Mr John Gay was also a late and close friend of both Mr Pope and Mr Congreve and no one could have been more pleased than my master when, just before he died, Mr Gay's strange low-life play with ballads, The Beggar's Opera, proved a success. Mr Gay's origins were almost as humble as mine: he was an orphan from a poor family in Devonshire, apprenticed to a silk-mercer in London until he began to write and publish poems and secured the patronage of the Duke and Duchess of Queensberry. My own favourite work of his, at least until I saw The Beggar's Opera, was his Trivia, or the Art of Walking the Streets of London, which, if I had ever thought of becoming an author before starting this book about my master, I would have been well qualified to write myself. Mr Gay was a gentle, simple man, entirely without pretensions or affectations, but with a sharp eye for those of others, and shared both Mr Congreve's ill-health and his delight in lazy ease and the pleasures of the table. They found each other altogether congenial. Mr Gay died only three years after Mr Congreve and my master would perhaps have preferred to his own more resounding epitaphs at Stowe and in Westminster Abbey Mr Gay's pert couplet inscribed by the faithful Queensberrys on *his* tomb in the Abbey:

Life is a jest, and all things show it:
I thought so once, and now I know it.

8

THE TEMPLE OF ANCIENT VIRTUE

In the immediate aftermath of his quarrel with Mr Walpole, Lord Cobham commissioned two temples from Mr Kent on the high ground above the Elysian Fields. They look down on the Temple of British Worthies – also Mr Kent's work – at the bottom of the slope, on the far side of the stream. The Temple of Modern Virtue is an untidy circle of bricks containing the headless statue of a fat man with a protuberant belly. I should guess that this was originally a figure of Silenus, the obese old man customarily depicted among the drunken followers of the god Bacchus, but in this context it probably represents Mr Walpole, also noted for his girth. The Temple of Ancient Virtue, on the other hand, is a large and elegant circular edifice, made of stone, with a dome, and surrounded with Ionic columns. Inside are four niches containing full-size statues of four great men from Ancient Greece: the Ionian poet Homer, the Athenian philosopher Socrates, the Spartan law-giver Lycurgus and the Theban general Epaminondas. Here, then, from four points and four periods of that ancient civilisation are the models we are to emulate in ours, whether in poetry, philosophy, the rule of law or victory over our enemies. The Temple of Ancient Virtue will thus do very well to stand for Mr Congreve's membership of the famous Kit-Cat Club, devoted to the same causes.

The Club had a modest beginning. It was simply a gathering once a week, usually on Thursdays, at the Cat and Fiddle tavern in Gray's Inn Lane, so that Mr Jacob Tonson, the bookseller, could keep in touch with his authors, listen to their ideas, hear of new talent he might recruit, and generally keep up with all the town gossip, especially as it might affect the book trade. Mr Tonson had been introduced to the place even before the Glorious Revolution by a distinguished lawyer, Mr John Somers from the Middle Temple, who frequently bought Mr Tonson's publications for his ambitious library. The tavern's proprietor, Christopher Cat, served particularly delicious pies and was always grateful for sheets of sturdy paper to bake them on, declaring that a piece of scratched-out verse on the paper enhanced the flavour, so the authors were encouraged to bring him their discarded manuscripts. For the authors themselves the occasion meant a generous helping of mutton pie for dinner, which not all of them could enjoy every day, and the chance perhaps to get something published. For Mr Tonson it was a useful way of increasing both the quality and quantity of his trade, for just as a few pigeons swooping on some dropped crumbs will attract more pigeons, so promising authors are apt to attract their rivals. I'm not sure whether Mr Dryden ever attended any of these earlier gatherings – he was certainly never a member of the Kit-Cat Club in its later form – but he was Mr Tonson's leading author and those young authors he approved of became Mr Tonson's authors too and therefore his guests at Kit Cat's tavern. My master, of course, both as Mr Dryden's favourite and, for some years, Mr Tonson's lodger, attended regularly, and after his early success with *The Old Bachelor* few authors of any standing would have turned down the chance to enjoy his company and conversation.

But how did such an informal meeting of poetic minds turn into a centre – *the* centre – for Whig political action? Towards the end of the Nineties I overheard a conversation between Mr Tonson and Mr Congreve.

'Why should we not invite one or two useful patrons to attend our meetings?' asked my master.

'Such as?'

'Montagu and Dorset, perhaps?'

'Such grandees? Government ministers. Would they want to sit down and eat humble pies with authors?'

'I don't notice that authors these days have a particularly humble opinion of themselves. Besides, Mr Somers, who buys so many books from you, often turns up to eat a pie with us and he is a government minister. And, after all, Montagu and Dorset are both poets as well as ministers. They might feel more flattered than condescending.'

'I will give it some thought,' said Mr Tonson.

He didn't have to think for long. He may not have foreseen what his Club would become, but he was not the man to miss an opportunity that would boost his trade. He was indeed as ambitious in his own line of bookselling as any author or for that matter politician in theirs. Mr Montagu, soon to be created Lord Halifax, and Lord Dorset were invited to attend the Thursday dinners at the Cat and Fiddle tavern and declared themselves honoured to accept.

But politicians, no less than authors and pigeons, are inclined to flock; and where Lords Halifax and Dorset and Mr Somers, soon to be Lord Somers, pecked at pies, more – including Mr Wharton, another member of the inner circle of ministers, the so-called Junto – were happy to follow. They were, of course, all birds of the same feather, that's to say Whigs. If Mr Dryden was never a Kit-Cat, it was no doubt because he was Catholic and Tory and had refused to swear allegiance to King William after the Glorious Revolution.

So gradually what had been a small, informal group of authors became a much more formal gathering of rich and powerful noblemen around a nucleus of authors. They did not come primarily for the mutton pies, which in any case were soon supplemented with cuts of beef as well as venison and other game from the lords' estates, as well as copious supplies of good wine, imported or smuggled, in spite of the restrictions of the war with France, under diplomatic passports or false labels. The politicians came principally to plot against the Tories and defend the new constitution, the Protestant succession and the war with France against Tory attempts to subvert, alter and end them. Mr Tonson remained the chairman of the meetings and always sat at the head of the table in a throne-like armchair, but he did not have to foot the large bills for the more exotic fare, the increased staff and the larger premises at the Fountain Tavern on the Strand, which were needed as the membership rose to nearly forty. Mr Congreve remarked jokingly to Mr Tonson that they really should invite King William to join the Club, since he was the best Whig of them all.

Alas, the words were hardly out of his mouth before the king was dead, thrown by his horse as it stumbled on a molehill. This was a setback for the Whigs, since his successor, Queen Anne, younger daughter of the deposed King James II, sympathised with the Tories and thought kindly of her exiled half-brother James, the Pretender. She would have preferred him as her successor rather than her more distant relations in Hanover, but he remained a Catholic and would not change his religion even for a throne. Fortunately for the Whigs, the queen's closest friend and adviser at this time was Sarah, Duchess of Marlborough, an ardent Whig, although the Duke of Marlborough, siding overtly with neither party, inclined to the Tories. He began to change his tune, as did Queen Anne's chief minister, Lord Godolphin, also inclined to be a Tory, over the war with France.

After the death of King William, the Duke of Marlborough became the commander-in-chief of the allied armies on the continent, and Lord Godolphin managed the war effort at home. But the Tories were vehemently opposed to the war, considering it to be chiefly King William's war to defend his Dutch homeland and objecting to its enormous expense and the taxes they had to pay for it, so that the Duke and Lord Godolphin soon found themselves closer to the Whigs. Neither was ever a member of the Kit-Cat Club, though Lord Godolphin's son, Francis, married to the Duke of Marlborough's eldest daughter, Lady Henrietta, did become a member and the Club would certainly have been delighted to admit either or both if they had wished it.

I myself once attended a Kit-Cat dinner, in the capacity of a waiter. Many of the guests supplied their own footmen to help out the tavern's own servants and on this occasion Mr Tonson had heard that there was likely to be a shortage due to sickness – it was a winter day early in the year 1703 – so I offered my services.

'Are you qualified for this?' asked my master. 'These are very grand people and used to being served like the earls and dukes they are.'

'I have often observed waiters in action,' I said. 'It does not seem to require any great expertise.'

'If you drop a plate or spill the wine I shall be permanently shamed and probably have to resign from the Club. Some of my fellow members are very extreme to mark lapses of etiquette.'

'I thought you told me that they all liked to appear friends of equal status, however exalted their rank.'

'Quite so. Which means that anyone who betrays signs of lower status through too much deference, or manners which are either over- or under-scrupulous, is liable to be picked on for censure or worse still mockery.'

'And this would apply even to someone whose servant was found wanting?'

'Servants inevitably reflect their masters.'

'Then how can the servant of such a perfect gentleman as Mr Congreve go wrong?'

'You twist my words. I mean that any error of yours would reflect on me.'

'But would they know that this particular clumsy clown was your servant?'

'They would want to know.'

'It sounds a daunting experience.'

'So it is, for those who are not born and bred gentlemen, even if they have managed to acquire a title. It's safer, of course, to be merely a poet, when some allowance is made for eccentricity and wit. Mr Tonson, I'm afraid, for all he started the thing and remains its high priest, is sometimes the subject of mockery when people have drunk too much.'

'For his lowly origin – for being a tradesman and the son of a barber?'

'For that, yes, and for his ungainly manner of walking – you know there's something wrong with his right leg and he's often called "two left legs" – and for his tradesman's accent.'

'Surely he could cease inviting people with such bad manners?'

'He might have done in the past, but if he expelled some rude lord, the rest would probably resign in sympathy. He simply pretends not to hear their raillery, which of course makes them think he is not very bright and has missed the point. A far cry from the truth, of course, since among so many clever men he is surely one of the cleverest.'

'Are you telling me that you'd rather I didn't serve at this dinner?'

'No, just warning you that it's no ordinary dinner. You will need to have your wits about you.'

'Don't I always?'

'You are a treasure, Jeremy, but your greatest fault is over-confidence. That and drinking too much, which augments the former.'

'I will touch no liquor.'

'That would be wise. Afterwards, when you are clearing up the debris, you can make up for lost time with the unfinished bottles.'

'You will make your own way home?'

'What are you suggesting? That I shall be quite incapable myself?'

'There have been occasions...'

'Have I ever failed to reach my own door?'

'No, sir. Though there was one night when I opened it and you fell at my feet.'

'I don't recall that.'

'No, sir, nor did you the next day.'

'Your memory is a great gift, Jeremy. But sometimes you should give it a rest.'

I did no such thing when it came to the Kit-Cat dinner. This was a unique opportunity to observe some of the greatest in the land at their leisure, although it soon became clear, after the preliminaries were over, that eating, drinking and conversing were only a cover for serious business. The preliminaries consisted, so far as we servants were concerned, in relieving the lords and gentlemen of their outer wrappings, their cloaks, hats, swords, sticks and gloves. This process was supervised by an elderly Scotchman, in charge of the tavern's staff, who had some method of identifying each person's belongings as they were carried into another room. I asked him how he did it.

'You're an inquisitive bugger,' he said.

'When I see a clever man,' I said, 'I always try to learn something from him.'

'A sycophant, too, are you? A right sly-boots. Which gentleman dragged you out of a drain?'

'I serve Mr Congreve.'

'Mr Congreve, is it? Now he *is* a gentleman. What would he want with a nosey young snipe like you?'

I shrugged, not wishing to provoke him further, but the name of my master seemed enough to allay his suspicion of me and he led me into the room where the cloaks and other gear were taken. Every person's belongings were hung on separate pegs and every peg labelled with the owner's name. The Scotchman only had to murmur each guest's name to one of his staff for the items to be carried to the right peg. I suppose in a way it is what I am doing with Mr Congreve's life – hanging up the different parts of his outer garments on various hooks in the hope that the shape and style of the clothes may somehow give my reader a notion of the person that wore them. Perhaps it was that cloak-room which first gave me the idea.

'Can all your staff read the labels, then?' I asked.

He pointed to a thin, pale youth by the door. 'If they can't, young Tom will guide them. His father was a schoolmaster who drank too much to keep his job and threw himself into the river. The mother's dead too. Five children to fend for themselves, but at least he taught this one to read before filling his own pockets with stones.'

The members had all assembled by this time, greeted each other with bows or claps on the shoulder, washed their hands in bowls of water brought by the servitors, and were lining up, still standing and chattering, behind the chairs at the long table. Mr Tonson, at the end of the table, knocked with his knife-handle and everyone fell silent and bowed their heads as the senior duke recited a Grace in English. I was a little surprised at that, since at Oxford the Grace was always in Latin, but reflected that although many of these gentlemen probably knew Latin as well as I did, they would make a sharp distinction between the classical Latin of the Roman poets and the Christian form of it associated with the Catholic Church. For this was a company of Whigs, some still adhering to the Church of England, some Dissenters, some Deists or atheists, but all absolutely at one in detesting Catholics and fearing their return to power.

The table was already crammed with eatables, the famous pies down the centre, joints of beef and venison, roast birds, boiled fishes and bowls of root vegetables around them. Considering that it was still winter it was amazing to see such a spread of perishable flesh, but I remembered that many of these noblemen kept ice-houses on their estates. We servants stepped forward to pull out the chairs and the gentlemen sat down to their feast. One gentleman, however, too eager to sit down, had grasped the back of his chair to pull it out for himself and broken off its decorative knob. There was much laughter at his expense, though Mr Tonson looked annoyed. The gentleman himself seemed quite unfazed and threw the knob over the table towards the fireplace. Under cover of the great noise of laughter and ribald comment, I asked my now friendly Scotchman who this was.

'Who would you think?' he replied. 'One of the newest members and not one you'd have thought they'd have wanted in this company. He's killed at least two men in duels and was mixed up in the murder of an actor many years ago, though he always seems to escape punishment.'

'Lord Mohun?'

'The same. A nasty piece of work, if you ask me.'

He looked innocent enough, a youngish fellow in his late twenties, fattish, with a long fleshy face, thick pouting lips, pudgy fingers and the usual nose-in-the-air arrogant expression of his class. But the thought of how he had contributed to the death of kind Mr Mountfort made my hand tremble with anger as I poured wine into his glass and a drop fell on the table. He didn't seem to notice. I would have liked to empty the whole flask into his wig.

I asked Mr Congreve the next day how they came to invite Lord Mohun to be a Kit-Cat.

'He's a friend of the Duke of Marlborough, fought under him in Flanders, and he's one of several such military people recruited recently, in the hope that the duke himself might be persuaded to join. The others, I'm glad to say, do us more credit: Stanhope, Berkeley, Lord Shannon, Lord Cornwallis. And of course my friend Sir Richard Temple has been with us almost from the beginning.'

I had noticed a handsome young man with a strong nose and soldierly look sitting next to my master at the dinner and asked if that was Sir Richard – later to be Lord Cobham.

'Which one? I was sitting between two soldiers, both very handsome. The fair one on my left was Temple, the dark one on the right was Stanhope, just back from taking a conspicuous part in our victory over the Spanish at Vigo Bay and about to join the duke's army in Flanders.'

'You prefer to sit with soldiers than poets?'

'That depends on the poets and the soldiers. In fact both Temple and Stanhope are highly cultured men and Stanhope is a notable scholar of Greek.'

'And who was the older man, with the beaky nose, sitting next to Stanhope? He seemed to be more interested in the food and wine than conversation. He looked French.'

'He *is* French. Mr Charles Dartiquenave, a Huguenot refugee. I'm not quite sure why he was made a member, perhaps because

he knows so much about food and wine. I was glad Stanhope
sat between us, since personally I find Darty tiresome. He never
stops making puns, drying up the conversation every time he
speaks. Swift is a friend of his and has the same irritating habit.
Imagine being caught between them at dinner!'

'But Dr Swift is not a Kit-Cat, is he?'

'Dr Swift is a Tory.'

When they had all had enough of the main feast, the dishes
were cleared away and most of the diners rose from their seats
and moved about, greeting friends who had been sitting far
away and eventually settling down in different places with fresh
companions. Mr Congreve was now sitting between two old
and older friends, Dr Samuel Garth, the eminent physician
and author of the long satirical poem *The Dispensary*, and Mr
Arthur Maynwaring, later one of the chief propagandists for the
Whigs. But the group sitting nearest to where I stood against
the wall, with the other servitors, was political – the diminutive
Lord Halifax, Lord Somers and Lord Wharton – and this was
the closest I ever came to the famous Whig Junto. I could not
hear much of what they said, but they were certainly down to
business. Their problem was, it seemed, that the Tories, led by the
Speaker of the House of Commons, Mr Harley, had just won
the election and that, in spite of the Duke of Marlborough's
capture of two Flemish cities, the war was not going well. Our
Dutch allies were constantly spoiling his plans for daring attacks
with their nervous caution. Little did any of us know then that
the following year, with the great victory of Blenheim, the
Duke of Marlborough would at last achieve what King William
had hardly dreamed of, the first of a series of French defeats
which would eventually destroy all King Louis XIV's hopes of
dominating Europe. As the duke himself said, capturing cities
counted little compared to winning battles.

The animated discussion in front of me suddenly ended
when, after we had removed the sweetmeats, Mr Tonson threw
down his napkin. We brought in bowls of water, the guests
washed their hands, we placed a bottle of wine beside every

place, and Mr Tonson rose to call for the toasts. Kit-Cat dinners were, of course, entirely male, but the members were some of them married, many of them keepers of mistresses, and most of them as fond of the fair sex as they were of food and wine. So at this point in their gathering they always made toasts to ladies. The gentlemen called out the names of ladies, married or not, whom they wished to honour, they all voted by raising their hands, Mr Tonson counted the votes and announced the winners. Afterwards a glass was engraved with the lady's name and a brief verse improvised in her praise.

On one earlier occasion, Mr Congreve told me, the Earl of Kingston asked for a toast to his beautiful eight-year-old daughter, Lady Mary Pierrepont. The other members were dubious and said they could not toast someone they had never seen. The earl then immediately sent for his daughter, though it was well into night-time and she must have been in bed. When she finally arrived, summarily woken and dressed for the occasion, and stood wondering and surely terrified in the doorway, they all with one accord raised their glasses and agreed that they had never toasted any lady who deserved it more. And this little girl, the only female ever to be seen at a Kit-Cat dinner, grew up to marry Lord Halifax's nephew, Mr Wortley Montagu, and become my master's friend and Mr Pope's love-hate. On a later occasion, at the time of her retirement from the stage, the Kit-Cats were about to toast Bracey, 'this incomparable woman who in spite of her profession is famous for her virtue', when Lord Halifax intervened and suggested that they would do better to make her a gift of 200 guineas. They all agreed, but not on the sum. Their contributions amounted in the end to 800 guineas and Mr Congreve was asked to deliver it to her. Their relationship was then in its last stages and the task perhaps a little embarrassing to him, but I don't think she threw the money in his face.

The toasts on this occasion were to ladies I had not heard of, and when they were over the gentlemen settled down again to steady drinking, while we servitors, feeling now rather hungry and dry, stood solemnly against the walls, stepping forward frequently to replace the bottles as they emptied. How many bottles, I wondered, does it take to put a Kit-Cat under the table? I never discovered, for however much they drank, they all retained their seats and were even able eventually to rise to their feet and leave without falling over. But just as, when they arrived, they had removed their outer clothes, so now, when the chatter and laughter became louder and their faces redder, these important men from the very summit of our society threw off a protective layer of dignity and reserve and reverted to being more simply themselves. Many were still young and yet to succeed to their fathers' titles or to win their own in the years ahead, but I learnt that night what I had not realised before: that although birth, upbringing, education and social status make a gentleman very different from a person like myself, a nobleman is not different from a gentleman. Few of their titles go back more than a generation or two and merely signify that he or his father or grandfather performed some service, often trivial, for the monarch personally or his government. I no longer considered it strange that my master should mix equally in such company, when I saw with my own eyes that this age of innovation was also creating a new kind of nobility, in which character, intelligence and achievement counted more than birthright. Perhaps this was just what our grandfathers tried to bring about during those chaotic times of the Civil War and Cromwell's Republic, but then it was all by force, intimidation and religious fanaticism, whereas now it seemed the natural thing in a more enlightened world.

Of course wealth counts too and noblemen, being more in need of it than the rest of us, who do not have estates or carriages or great houses or appearances to keep up, are accustomed to seek it out in the shape of government appointments or mercenary marriages. But merchants are better at acquiring and especially heaping up wealth than noblemen, and sharp-eyed, quick-minded young gentlemen of the Kit-Cat kind make even the grandest titles seem only decorative ribbons. I saw my master, as he was leaving the dinner, exchange a word with a man of about his own age, a dark-complexioned man I almost seemed to recognise.

'Who is that?' I asked my Scotch mentor.

'The Duke of Richmond and Lennox,' he said.

'A double duke? What has he done to be so honoured?'

The Scotchman smiled.

'A very good question,' he said. 'Himself has done nothing at all. His mother was a French whore who went to bed with King Charles.'

'I might have guessed,' I said. 'He looks so like his father's pictures.'

'He's a friendly young fellow, for all that,' said the Scotchman. 'Drinks too much, but very likeable.'

And shortly afterwards I saw him pocket a gold coin given him by this king's son who did nothing at all except drink too much.

'Yes, I like him too,' my master said afterwards when I told him what the Scotchman had said. 'I think he feels that to be a Kit-Cat is a greater honour than to be a duke, in that it's an honour earned by himself. But the sad truth is that it's only the dukedom and voting regularly with the Whigs in the House of Lords that makes him a Kit-Cat.'

So what began with mutton pies and hungry authors and always remained a jovial feast was at the same time a response to that yet-undreamed-of Temple of Ancient Virtue at Stowe. Here at the Kit-Cat Club were gathered some of the most ambitious, most cultivated and imaginative men of our age, those with ribbons and those still to receive them. Many of them were at various times Members of Parliament, their elections paid for by the richest among them, such as Lord Wharton and the Duke of Newcastle. But ironically enough the most successful of all those young gentlemen at consolidating the changes begun by King William's Revolution was Mr Walpole himself, Lord Cobham's friend and later enemy, whose headless statue occupies the Temple of Modern Virtue. Six years younger than my master,

Mr Walpole was not yet a Kit-Cat when I served at that dinner in the year 1703, though he joined it about a year later, at the same time as Mr Addison. Mr Walpole, more interested in real power than ribbons, did not accept a peerage until he retired, but remained in the House of Commons for forty years and led the country for twenty years as our first Prime Minister. Suppose that Lord Cobham had built his two temples before their quarrel! Mr Walpole's statue, head and all, might then have stood with those of the other luminaries of the new Britannia, many of them Kit-Cats – Lords Halifax and Somers, General Stanhope, Mr Addison, Sir Richard Steele, Mr Congreve and Sir John Vanbrugh – in a Temple of Modern Virtue as elegant and exemplary as the Temple of Ancient Virtue. As it was, the Kit-Cats' monument was a set of half-length portraits by Sir Godfrey Kneller, which hung in Mr Tonson's house at Barn Elms and included Mr Tonson's own portrait. That pleased me, and considering what Mr Tonson did for our literature with his handsome editions – of Milton and Shakespeare and his own contemporaries, notably Mr Dryden and Mr Congreve – as well as his creation of the Kit-Cat Club, he too surely deserved a statue in a Temple of Modern Virtue.

9

THE GOTHIC TEMPLE

Mr Congreve, whose taste generally was for classical models and the most polished forms of literature, surprised me with his liking for popular ballads. He made a collection of the broadsheets which were sold on the streets and even composed some himself. One of his earlier ballads was 'Buxom Joan of Deptford' which he used in his play *Love for Love* as a song for the ribald sailor Ben. Another was written in the year 1708, after the Duke of Marlborough had won his third great battle against the French at Oudenarde. The news reached us in London a few days later and my master immediately sat down to express his joy in a ballad called 'Jack French-Man's Defeat', to be sung to the tune of 'There was a Fair Maid in the North-Country':

Ye Commons and Peers,
Pray lend me your Ears,
I'll sing you a Song if I can;
How *Louis le Grand*
Was put to a Stand,
By the Arms of our Gracious Queen *Anne.*

How his Army so great
Had a total Defeat,
Not far from the River of *Dender;*

Where his Grand-Children twain
For fear of being Slain,
Gallop'd off with the Popish Pretender.

He contrasts this cowardice on the part of Louis XIV's grandsons
and James II's son with the courage of the Elector of Hanover's
son – the future King George II – who was leading his father's
dragoons in the Duke of Marlborough's army of many nations:

Not so did Behave
The Young *Hannover* Brave
In this Bloody Field I assure ye;
When his War Horse was shot
Yet he matter'd it not,
But charg'd still on Foot like a Fury.

Later in the ballad he mocks the French monarch's futile shuffling
of his defeated marshals:

O *Louis* Perplex'd,
What General's next?
Thou hast hitherto chang'd 'em in Vain:
He has Beat 'em all round,
If no New ones are found,
He shall Beat the Old over again.

Marshal Tallard was defeated at Blenheim and replaced by
Marshal Villeroi, who was defeated at Ramillies and replaced
by Marshal Vendome. Vendome was defeated at Oudenarde and
replaced by Marshal Villars, who was defeated in Marlborough's
last and bloodiest victory at Malplaquet. Meanwhile Marshal
Tallard, captured after the battle of Blenheim, was still a prisoner
in Nottingham Castle.

We'll let *Tallard* out
If he'll take t'other Bout;

And much he's Improv'd let me tell ye
With *Nottingham* Ale,
At every Meal,
And good Pudding and Beef in his Belly.

The ballad was published anonymously as a broadsheet which proved very popular, and it was published the next year by Mr Tonson in one of his *Poetical Miscellanies* together with a translation into Latin by Mr Congreve's Irish friend Mr Keally.

Now that I copy out these extracts so many decades later, their boastfulness jars a little, but it seemed mild enough at the time, when we all began to realise that the constant threat from France was at last being lifted. Earlier that same year the Pretender sailed with French troops to Scotland to lead an invasion of the newly united kingdoms. Our former king, James II, had died. King Louis, in contravention of his undertaking in the Treaty of Rysbrick not to do so, now recognised the Pretender as King James III. The invasion failed miserably and the Pretender returned to France, but there seemed no end then to these attempts by our powerful and more populous neighbour across the Channel to saddle us again with a tyrannical, Papist monarchy.

Yet the irony was that the new sense of safety created by the Duke of Marlborough's military victories on the Continent brought political defeat at home for him and his close colleague the Earl of Godolphin and their Whig supporters. Once the immediate fear of the French was removed with their fourth defeat at Malplaquet, the country wanted an end to the war. The Tories, some of whom still believed in the Stuarts' divine right to rule and that it had been wrong to replace King James with King William, had always disliked the war, both for the heavy land tax they had to pay towards it and because they regarded it as the usurping Dutchman's war, even now that King William himself was dead and Queen Anne was on the throne.

Ten years earlier the puritanical Mr Collier had appeared out of nowhere to express a sudden shift in public opinion against too much licence in the theatre. Now another clergyman, a

High Church Tory called the Reverend Dr Sacheverell, was permitted by the Tory Lord Mayor of London to deliver two rabble-rousing sermons from the pulpit of St Paul's Cathedral. Dr Sacheverell called down 'fire and brimstone' on the Whig government and by implication on all those who had tamely accepted the overthrow of their anointed sovereign and the new constitution devised by the Whigs after their Glorious Revolution. The Tories were delighted and the capricious populace, having rejoiced at the duke's victories, now turned to blaming him, the government and the war for food-shortages, high prices and an influx of European refugees taking their jobs. The printed copies of Dr Sacheverell's sermon sold in their thousands.

The Whigs were highly alarmed and meeting for a particularly sumptuous Kit-Cat dinner laid on by their latest member, a wealthy financier called Sir Henry Furnese, discussed how they should respond. The Duke of Marlborough himself was present as a guest. He was not a member of the Club, though the members would have liked to make him one, and Mr Congreve told me that he did not take part in the discussion. He did, however, approach my master with his customary affable charm.

'I believe that ballad on Oudenarde was yours.'

'It was.'

'I would not have recognised the hand myself. Such a very different mode from your elegy for my poor son, Blandford.'

'As joy is from sorrow.'

'I am much obliged to you for both. Not forgetting your ode on the battle of Ramillies addressed to Her Majesty.'

'Neither I nor any Englishman can ever sufficiently express our obligation to you, Sir, for your genius in the field.'

'Genius? I don't know. It's mostly hard work and catching opportunity by the tail. I daresay that could be said of poets too.'

'True, but we don't have cannonballs falling around us and only obstinate words not men with swords and matchlocks to tussle with.'

'Critics, however, armed with sharp reproofs.'

'Which we may sometimes deserve. Much worse are the sneers of the envious.'

'How right you are! Envy is worse than cannonballs for striking a man down.'

The duke's presence must have strongly influenced the general feeling among the Kit-Cats that Dr Sacheverell should be impeached. What he was really saying, after all, was that the duke, who had played a crucial part in the Revolution by changing sides from James to William, had betrayed his king and that William's successor, Queen Anne herself, had no right to be queen.

'So will they try Dr Sacheverell?' I asked.

'It was not decided there and then,' said my master, 'but I'm very much afraid that they will.'

'What else can they do?'

'Let him alone. If we try him, we give him more publicity. Just what he wants.'

'But if you let him alone, he will preach more sermons and make the situation worse.'

'Better sermons than stones. If we make him a martyr there will be riots. Better confine his views to churches and pamphlets than let him air them in a law court and look like a victim.'

My master was right. Dr Sacheverell's trial, which took place the following winter, led swiftly to a change of government and the most unhappy years of Mr Congreve's life.

I am setting this low point of his story against the Gothic Temple in Lord Cobham's grounds at Stowe because, although he never saw it, I am almost sure Mr Congreve would have considered it an unfortunate discrepancy among all the other classically inspired buildings. The inspiration for it, I think, came originally from Sir John Vanbrugh, who liked to mingle the Gothic with the classical in his buildings, though the Temple was designed by Mr Gibbs and built many years after Sir John's death. This nod to our Saxon ancestors was part of the Whig programme: the idea that we owed our English liberty to the Saxons, whose democratic inclinations still persisted after the Norman Conquest in trial by jury, parliamentary representation and the imposition on a tyrannical monarch of *Magna Carta*.

Mr Gibbs's Gothic Temple is a two-storey triangular confection, something between a house and a priory, with a square church tower on one corner and two small cupolas on the others, flanking facades with Gothic windows and crenellated rooflines. It is built of orange ironstone and stands high on the hill to the east of the house: an intrusive oddity only too visible from most parts of the grounds. Once it was built, Lord Cobham had the seven stone statues of Saxon gods, carved by the famous Flemish sculptor Mr Rysbrack, moved from the western side of the grounds to form a semi-circle round the Gothic Temple. These statues depicted the gods who gave their names to our days of the week: Sunna, Mona, Tiw, Woden, Thunor, Friga and Seatern. Mr Congreve, so far as I know, did not divulge his opinion of these statues to Lord Cobham, but he did to me one day when we were walking round them:

'What do you feel about your Saxon ancestors, Jeremy?'

'Mine? What ancestors could I have, sir?'

'Oh come! You could not be here at all without ancestors. According to the Bible you are descended from Adam and Eve. But whether that's true or not, every person ever born must have had two parents and each of them two parents and so on back to some original two, and who knows how *they* got here, unless they were Adam and Eve or apes. But we need not go back so far. You and I, Englishmen as we are, are most likely descended from the people who worshipped these gods?'

'Then we must be cousins, sir. At some remove.'

'Granted, so long as you keep the remove in mind!'

He walked slowly round the figures, inspecting them carefully both front and back, then stood back surveying them all from the front.

'Now which of these curious deities do you think is your tutelary god, Jeremy?

'I am at a loss, sir. They look more minatory than tutelary.'

'What day of the week were you born on?'

'How should I know? They never told me the day, the month, or even the year.'

'No need to feel sorry for yourself, Jeremy. That gives you a free choice. I don't think it could be Seatern – "Saturday's child works hard for its living". You have a very easy life. I'm sure it can't be one-eyed Woden – "Wednesday's child is full of woe". When you're not brooding on your obscure origin, you are a cheerful companion.'

'Thank you, sir.'

'What about Mona – "Monday's child is fair of face"?'

'You are too kind, sir. But which is yours?'

'Oh, mine is Sunna – "The child that is born on the Sabbath day is bonny and blithe and good and gay".'

How well that fitted him in his best days, even if those I am about to describe made him temporarily more of a Wednesday's child!

'These figures are very well executed,' he went on, 'but hardly in a style the Saxons would have recognised. This style, though artfully coarsened, is derived from Greek and Roman statuary by way of the Renaissance and Signor Bernini. Besides, the Saxons who founded our democracy, notably Alfred the Great, soon became ardent Christians. I find this particular fancy of Lord Cobham's a little far-fetched.'

Dr Sacheverell's trial took the best part of a month and the streets round Westminster Hall, where it was held, were filled with tumultuous crowds of his supporters. Several Kit-Cat Members of Parliament spoke for the prosecution. Mr Walpole, newly promoted Secretary at War, attacked the Tories who stood behind Dr Sacheverell: 'To recommend themselves to the queen they condemn the Revolution without which she never had been queen.' Lieutenant-General Stanhope accused Dr Sacheverell of being a Jacobite in disguise, fomenting sedition, making out that those who had taken the oaths to King William and Queen Mary were heretics and rebels.

That night Tory mobs went wild through the London streets, looting Dissenters' shops, burning Dissenters' chapels and attacking the houses of two Kit-Cat Dissenters: Lord Wharton, seen as a prime mover in the trial, and Sir Henry Furnese, hated for his great wealth and support for the Whigs. Woe betide anyone out on the street who could not persuade these wretches that he loved Dr Sacheverell and loathed the Whigs! We all, in the Porters' house, kept fast within doors. It was worse than the Great Storm, for that at least had no quarrel with anyone in particular, whereas this human storm would have gladly discovered Mr Congreve, that well-known Kit-Cat, and likely torn him to pieces or thrown him in the river.

My master, huddled by the fireside – it was late February – reminded only too sharply once again of what he had endured twenty years before from Lord Tyrconnell's soldiers in Ireland, refused to go to bed and kept a sword and pistol by his chair.

'If they break down the door,' he said, 'I do not wish to meet them in my night clothes.'

'Mr Porter has a fine, strong outer door,' I said. 'I don't think they would get past it too easily and besides these hooligans will hardly know your address.'

But I sat up with him and read him, at his request, since he was nearly blind with cataracts, rolling iambics from Mr Milton's *Paradise Lost* and crystal-clear arguments from Mr Locke's *Concerning Human Understanding*, antidotes certainly to the madness on the streets. Until, dawn breaking and the distant noise of shouting and mayhem dying away, we both slept for a few hours.

Dr Sacheverell's trial continued with his own defence, in which he denied sedition and prayed for his prosecutors to be delivered from sin and error. That was followed by the prosecution's response, and finally the lords' debate over the verdict. They pronounced him guilty, though only by seventeen votes. The Duke of Shrewsbury, the man my master had so admired when he met him at Boughton House, was one of those who voted 'not guilty'. I asked Mr Congreve if this did not make him alter his opinion of the duke.

'Not at all,' he said. 'On the contrary. Shrewsbury voted as I would have done.'

'But surely Dr Sacheverell *is* guilty of sedition?'

'Certainly, but Shrewsbury understood very well that a guilty verdict would only make Sacheverell still more popular with the mob. He did not vote in favour of Sacheverell, but in favour of stifling the man's malice, of letting the whole affair die away and be sooner forgotten. My opinion of Shrewsbury as a wise man is entirely confirmed.'

After such a narrow margin for the verdict, the sentence was light. Dr Sacheverell was not imprisoned or fined, but only banned from giving sermons for three years, while his previous sermons and speeches were to be confiscated and destroyed. The Whigs were the real losers and the Kit-Cats in their anger expelled one of their most distinguished members, the Duke of Somerset, who had absented himself on the grounds of illness from the verdict on Sacheverell and was thought to be making up to the triumphant Tories. The Duke of Shrewsbury was not a Kit-Cat or he would surely have been expelled too.

Led now by that Mr Harley, whom I had encountered on the back stairs of Boughton House and who was soon to replace Lord Godolphin as Lord Treasurer and become Earl of Oxford, the Tories won a large majority in the autumn election of that year 1710. Mr Harley himself, known as Robin the Trickster, was a moderate Tory, prepared to work with other political moderates such as the Duke of Shrewsbury, who was now appointed Lord Chamberlain of the queen's household. The queen herself, shaking off the influence of her close friend the Duchess of Marlborough, was more in sympathy with the Tories than the Whigs. But such a decisive vote made moderation unnecessary and by the following year, as the Tories began negotiations towards ending the war, the Duke of Marlborough was dismissed as captain-general of the army in Flanders and, disgracefully accused of peculation, went into exile.

My master now feared for his own government post as a Commissioner of Wine Licences – I mention elsewhere how he had exchanged his previous office as a Commissioner for Hackney Carriages for this better one – and the small but essential salary that kept us in food and lodging. In addition, his loving relationship with Mrs Bracegirdle was under strain, as I shall explain in another place, and, as I mentioned, he was nearly blind from cataracts. The one good thing that winter was the publication of *The Works of William Congreve* in a handsome three-volume edition, and even that occasioned a quarrel between my master and his old friend Mr Tonson over the terms for future impressions.

'Mr Tonson drives a hard bargain,' Mr Congreve told me, 'and is a rich man in consequence. Old friend he may be, but he takes advantage of knowing that I hate to argue about money. However, at this time, with the prospect of a Tory government and the likelihood that they will sack all the Whigs in government posts, I must scrabble for scraps.'

Mr Tonson offered a 'gentlemen's agreement', but Mr Congreve insisted on a written one.

'Are you saying you don't consider me a gentleman?' asked Mr Tonson angrily.

'No. I'm saying that in this matter neither you nor I appear as gentlemen, but as a poor poet and a not so poor publisher.'

'You are behaving more like a lawyer,' said Mr Tonson.

'Which I might once have been and relied for my living on other men's folly, instead of on my own and your foolish love of literature.'

Mr Tonson smiled, my master smiled back.

'Look at you!' said Mr Congreve. 'You've published a fine edition of *Paradise Lost*, and now this very year you publish the first proper critical edition of Will Shakespeare's plays and the works of his humble admirer Will Congreve. Who do you think you are if you are not the leading publisher of this age and perhaps of many ages to come? And we have a new law of copyright to discourage pirates. Are Mr Milton and Mr Shakespeare going to ask you for written agreements? No, they are safely lodged where they need neither food nor clothing nor anything but your generous fillip to their reputations. But what about that miserable latter-day poet Will Congreve, still struggling to stay alive? Will you enhance his reputation while seeing him join his friend Captain Steele in a debtor's prison?'

Mr Tonson could not help laughing.

'What nonsense!' he said.

'I know,' said Mr Congreve, also laughing, 'but you must admit that there's something in it.'

Sighing ostentatiously, looking as if every word gave him pain, Mr Tonson wrote out and signed two copies of a document promising Mr Congreve twenty guineas each time the book was reprinted, as well as to keep him informed of how many copies of the first impression had been sold. Telling me all this, Mr Congreve flourished his copy of the document and declared, 'Congratulate me, Jeremy! This was my Blenheim.'

But it was only a brief gleam of light in a darkening sky. Lord Wharton, the leading Whig and Dissident, whose satirical song 'Lilliburlero' had 'whistled King James off his throne', lost his post as Lord Lieutenant of Ireland. My master's particular patron, Lord Halifax, former Chancellor of the Exchequer and Lord Treasurer, was out of office, though he remained on friendly terms with the new Lord Treasurer, Mr Harley. Mr Walpole was still a Member of Parliament but lost his post as Secretary at War. Ralph, Duke of Montagu, our host at Boughton House, had died a year or two earlier and been succeeded by his son John. But he, a new member of the Kit-Cat Club, who had served under the Duke of Marlborough in Flanders and married the duke's youngest daughter, Mary, could expect nothing from a Tory government. Nor could Major-General Sir Richard Temple – not yet Lord Cobham – another officer under the Duke of Marlborough. Lieutenant-General Stanhope, who had made one of the key speeches for the prosecution of Dr Sacheverell, had been taken prisoner fighting the French in Spain. Captain Steele was sacked from his post as editor of the government newspaper, the *London Gazette*, though he had now started a paper of his own, *Tatler*, and would soon follow that with another, the *Spectator*, with Mr Addison's collaboration. Mr Addison had retained his seat as a Member of Parliament in the election, but having lost his post as Lord Wharton's Chief Secretary for Ireland, had time on his hands.

Not all Mr Congreve's friends, however, were Whigs, and the Tory victory brought bright hopes of preferment, perhaps a bishopric, to the Reverend Dr Jonathan Swift. He was particularly valued by the Tories as a propagandist for their views, and was a regular visitor to the homes and offices of both Mr Harley, the Lord Treasurer, and the other Tory leader, Mr Henry St John, Secretary of State, soon to be created Viscount Bolingbroke. Dr Swift often dropped in to see Mr Congreve at this time, assuring him that he was doing all he could to persuade Mr Harley to look kindly on him and not to deprive him of his living. Lord Halifax too spoke up for him and told my master that Mr Harley had seemed sympathetic. But when a summons came for the five Commissioners for Licensing Wines to attend the Treasury, Mr Congreve went there with foreboding.

Three of his fellow commissioners were indeed dismissed, but Mr Congreve was called into Mr Harley's room for a private interview. The Lord Treasurer told him that he admired his work, did not mean to inconvenience such a fine poet and, as long as he (Mr Harley) had the power, would always look after Mr Congreve's interests. He even quoted from Virgil's *Aeneid*. My master returned home in high spirits, repeating Mr Harley's quotation in Latin:

'"*Non obtusa adeo gestamus pectora Poeni, Nec tam aversus equos Tyria Sol jangit ab urbe.*" Do you understand that, Jeremy?'

'I can construe the Latin, sir: "We Phoenicians do not have such hard hearts, nor does the Sun yoke his steeds so far from our Tyrian city." But I find the meaning somewhat elusive.'

'Isn't it curious and perhaps hopeful that the Tory leader should call his party Carthaginians?'

'Carthaginians?'

'Phoenicians, Tyrians. The Carthaginians were originally Phoenicians from the city of Tyre.'

'And why is that hopeful, sir?'

'Because in the great wars between the Carthaginians and the Romans, the Carthaginians were the losers.'

'I don't suppose he had thought of that.'

'No, he was clearly thinking more of the sun-god, Phoebus Apollo, patron of the arts, inferring that the Tories too are friendly to the arts. The *Aeneid*, after all, is the story of a much earlier period when the Romans and Carthaginians were not enemies. The hero Aeneas lands at Carthage and makes love to its queen, Dido, before sailing on to Italy to found Rome.'

'Didn't Aeneas abandon Dido?'

'He did.'

'Causing her to take her own life?'

'Yes.'

'So the Carthaginians must have been very angry with these future Romans even at that earlier period.'

'Are you just showing off your erudition, Dr Fetch, or what are you getting at?'

'Perhaps Mr Harley was just showing off his erudition.'

'Most likely. But still, I take it as a fortunate omen.'

Later, as my master was dining, Dr Swift called. He had heard the good news from Mr Harley himself.

'Am I to thank you for this relief?' asked my master, as I brought in another glass for the visitor and poured wine for them.

'Certainly,' said Dr Swift. 'But I need no thanks. It's a service that any friend would do for another, to use his own influence in high places for the other's benefit. A very good day's work I call it, to have made a worthy man easy. I have been trying to do the same for Addison, with less success. He is not so easily contented with a small office as you are.'

'I thank you nonetheless. My "small office" is in Andrew Marvell's words "world enough and time" for me. Ease and quiet is all I seek. Mr Addison, I think, will be quite comfortable financially even after the loss of his lucrative post under Wharton – he had the foresight to buy himself another permanent post in Ireland. But he will still be very discontented, since it is the exercise of power he enjoys more than its perquisites.'

There was something about Dr Swift's company that always made my master speak in a more studied manner than he did with other friends. Dr Swift's puddingy face did not show much expression, but his sharp sky-blue eyes seemed always to be searching one's own face to find out the truth or pretence of what was said to him. At this time, however, when all was going well with him and he felt that he was at last a person of real importance in this new era of Tory dominance, he took on, to my thinking, an unpleasantly patronising air.

'Addison must fend for himself,' he said. 'And will no doubt do so, one way or another. I can do nothing for poor Steele, whom the Lord Treasurer considers to be quite unreliable as a man and politically hostile. Harley is a most reasonable person and will work with any Whig who can put aside his prejudices for the good of the country. And I must say that the country is fortunate to have found such a man to lead it and that I feel most privileged to be his friend, welcome at any time to call on him, dine with him and give him my advice.'

'Will you have something to eat now? Jeremy can fetch you a dish.'

'No, I dined with Mr Harley, who is apt to keep me late, but on this occasion I told him I must visit my old friend Congreve to share his relief.'

'Please tell him how grateful I am.'

'I shall, of course, and say how cheerful I find you, in spite of your poor health and the worry you must have had about your future. Well, that is lifted now and you must try to do something about your eyes. Is there any treatment?'

'I believe so, though the cataracts must ripen further before they can be removed.'

'And the gout?'

'Nothing much to be done for that. I have learnt to live with it.'

'Oh, dear! How old are you now, Will?'

'Forty-one.'

'Younger than me by a year or two, but who would guess it? How unfortunate you are and what a lottery life is, where health is concerned! But I do admire your cheerfulness.'

My master was always extraordinarily patient with Dr Swift's visits, but I don't think he welcomed them. Their friendship was too unbalanced, their political allegiances inimical and although Dr Swift professed to admire Mr Congreve's plays, Mr Congreve had not liked Dr Swift's then most successful work, *The Tale of a Tub*. There might also have been a religious barrier, since Dr Swift was a Church of England clergyman and my master had little time for any brand of organised religion. But I hope I am not libelling the reverend doctor if I say that if he was at all religious he concealed it well.

Dr Swift's friendship with the Tory leaders gained him the deanery of St Patrick's Cathedral in Dublin, but this was not, I'm sure, anything like what he had expected in the way of preferment, and with the fall of the Tory government at Queen Anne's death and the long years of Whig power that followed, he could hope for nothing more. He spent most of the rest of his life in Ireland, pouring his bitter personal and political frustration at last into *Gulliver's Travels*. My master was nearing his end when it was published, but he read it slowly, sometimes with his magnifying glass, sometimes asking me or his loving duchess, Lady Henrietta, to read it aloud.

'This is more than I ever expected from that unhappy man,' he said when he had finished it. 'I cannot say I like it. Satire, like sulphurous spa water, grapples with the bitter bile and eases the digestion, but has an unpleasant taste. I must always prefer comedy which, like good wine, warms the heart and lifts the spirit. Nonetheless, this book is astonishing, a masterpiece of invention and imagination. It will stand beside *Don Quixote* as something absolutely unique in the history of literature. For this alone, Swift will be remembered long after the rest of us are forgotten.'

Dr Swift outlived my master by some seventeen years, but, growing severely deaf and increasingly senile, can hardly have enjoyed for long what he had sought all his life, the fame and homage to his genius brought him by that book.

Mr Congreve's remark to the Duke of Marlborough about the sneers of the envious might have been due to what I know lingered poisonously in his memory. Mr Matthew Prior, one of several Kit-Cat poets who had composed elegies for Queen Mary's death, had dismissed Mr Congreve's as 'only for Hanging the Rooms, and painting a dismal scene' and compared it unfavourably to Mr Prior's school-friend George Stepney's. Mr Prior, as I have described elsewhere, shifted his allegiance to the Tories in the year 1701, after he had voted in the House of Commons for the impeachment of three members of the Whig Junto, including another former school-friend, Mr Charles Montagu. Mr Prior had been expelled from the Kit-Cat Club, but the Tory election victory brought him back into the sunshine. He now became the Tory government's principal negotiator for peace terms with the French, both in France and at his own house in London. He and Dr Swift both joined a new Tory club, 'The Brothers' Club', founded by Mr St John and meeting on Thursdays, the same day of the week as the Kit-Cat; and, while Dr Swift produced a highly popular tract, *The Conduct of the Allies and of the Late Ministry*, attacking the war and its commander-in-chief, the Duke of Marlborough, Mr Prior played a leading part in what became the Treaty of Utrecht. The Tory majority easily passed it through the House of Commons, but the House of Lords still had a small majority of Whigs. Queen Anne was persuaded to create twelve new lords to force the Treaty through, and so the war with France ended in the spring of the year 1713.

Mr Congreve viewed all these events with deepening gloom.

'Surely it's good that the war is over?' I said.

'It would have been better if Marlborough had been allowed to push the French right back into their own country. As it is they retain many fortified towns in Flanders.'

'But the Pretender is expelled from France, we keep Gibraltar and Minorca and gain Hudson's Bay in North America, as well as trading rights with Spanish America.'

'You see, Jeremy, you take the common view. You are pleased with the peace and therefore with the Tories who made it. That's the real danger. What else will the Tories set about now? They have driven the Duke of Marlborough into exile, they have imprisoned Mr Walpole in the Tower, both on false charges. They will reverse the Act of Settlement and make the Pretender king instead of the House of Hanover. They will persecute Dissenters, they will fill every office with Tories.'

'Not yours, sir. You have Mr Harley's protection.'

'Mr Harley – Lord Oxford – is a moderate man. He will be ousted by that Jacobite Mr St John – we must learn to call him Lord Bolingbroke. We have lost everything, Jeremy, everything we have gained since King James ran away and King William came in.'

He was nearly right. His own office was again threatened the following year and Lord Bolingbroke's plans to make the Pretender king, with the sympathy if not the direct agreement of the queen herself, were only frustrated by the Pretender's refusal to turn Protestant. Mr Congreve believed that even so Lord Bolingbroke would make him king and told me at a later time, when the clouds were lifted, that the Kit-Cats in desperation had laid their own plans to prevent him. The Duke of Marlborough's quartermaster, Lord Cadogan, was to seize the Tower of London and the Duke himself would lead all the British troops on the continent to England.

Would we have suffered another civil war? As it was, the dying queen saved us by giving the Lord Treasurer's white staff to the wise Duke of Shrewsbury. Lord Bolingbroke fled the country, Mr Harley (Lord Oxford) was imprisoned, King George came to reign over us, the Whigs returned to power, and Mr Congreve, as I explain elsewhere, was made Secretary of Jamaica with a much enhanced salary. My own wages rose a little too, although Mr Congreve said he did not wish to be too generous.

'I don't want you taking on the airs of some nobleman's major-domo, Jeremy, and concluding that higher wages mean less work.'

I refrained from pointing out that his new office seemed to mean precisely that on his account. But I did wonder how I would have managed if I had been in Mr Prior's shoes and risen to be our ambassador in Paris, in spite of the queen's view that his origins were too humble for such promotion. Of course my own origins were even humbler than his and my education much less complete than his at Westminster School and Cambridge, but would I have been so disloyal to my old friends and patrons? Does one require to be born a gentleman to overcome his baser instincts? No, I don't think we common people have a monopoly of those. In any case, Mr Prior, imprisoned after the queen's death and dependent thereafter on the hospitality of Lord Oxford's son, Lord Edward Harley, did not prosper in the end. But even my master had to admit that, for all his personal faults, Mr Prior was a fine poet. His books were on the shelves of Mr Congreve's library and he subscribed to the deluxe edition of Mr Prior's last publication, *Poems on Several Occasions*.

So I end this bleak chapter in the shadow of that unsightly Gothic Temple at Stowe with thankfulness to God or Providence or whatever power or chance rules our destiny. Our country now returned to peace and prosperity under the Whigs, with only occasional alarms from the frustrated Jacobites. Kind Mr Harley, Earl of Oxford, was at first impeached and imprisoned, but later acquitted and freed to devote himself to his collection of manuscripts. Even Lord Bolingbroke, having joined the Pretender and become disillusioned with him, was allowed to return to England. Political executions seem to belong to the dark days of the past, and security and prosperity to breed gentler manners. Perhaps we shall all be gentlemen one day in the future, but I doubt if my master would agree. He would say that for a man of my origins I was unusually privileged and that my comfortable life had made me sentimental.

Mr Congreve's ripened cataracts were cut away by a skilful French surgeon, though his sight improved only a little and his gout could never be cured. But, thanks to the return of the Whigs, his new office and the loving care of his duchess, which I shall describe in another place, he was once more himself, once more Sunday's child.

10

THE TEMPLE OF VENUS

Both Mr Congreve and Sir John Vanbrugh urged Lord Cobham to include a Temple of Venus in his plans for Stowe. Sir John may even have made a sketch of it. But they were both dead before His Lordship got round to it. The design is Mr Kent's, three classical pavilions joined in a gentle curve by arcades, and it is sited in the south-west corner of the grounds on the far side of the Eleven-Acre Lake, below and in view of Sir John's Rotondo with its golden statue of the callipygian goddess herself. But for all its name, I doubt whether this temple was ever intended for sexual orgies. Lord Cobham was married, though he had no children, and was never a person to countenance excess or wild behaviour. His Temple of Bacchus and his Temple of Venus were, I'm sure, intended as references to the civilisation of Ancient Rome, to the pleasures of drinking and the love of women, rather than invitations to drunkenness or licentiousness.

I am well aware that if Mr Congreve's spirit still hovers and may tolerate, however reluctantly, what I have revealed of his life up to now, it can feel nothing but anger and anguish at my attempt to describe his relationships with the two ladies he loved. Yet neither was ever at all secret. All the world knew that Mr Congreve doted on Mrs Anne Bracegirdle and that Henrietta, Duchess of Marlborough, doted on him.

Every heroine in every play he wrote was played by Bracey and in his musical masque *The Judgment of Paris* he gave her the role of Venus. He even meant her to sing the title role in his opera *Semele*, if that had opened the new theatre in the Haymarket as he planned. Who could doubt what she meant to him? He could hardly have made it clearer if he had stepped on to the stage himself and announced it to the audience, which could in any case see him night after night watching her from the box next to the stage with his hat tipped over his eyes. Yet, so far as I know, he spoke of it only to her and occasionally, as if I were merely an extension of himself, to me. He was not the man, unlike most of the lovesick gentlemen in his plays, to discuss his amours with his friends. It was another example, I'm inclined to think, of the division between Author Congreve and Social Congreve which I've already touched on in connection with Monsieur Voltaire's visit. AC could express his passion for Bracey in all those parts and poems, but SC, the gentleman, was not prepared to talk about it.

He first saw her acting in other authors' plays during those months before *The Old Bachelor* was ready, when he was given free access to the Drury Lane Theatre, so that by the time she was cast as Araminta and he was helping Mr Betterton and Captain Southerne to direct the play, he was certainly in love with her. I did not quite realise this at the time, since his shining eyes, jaunty spirits and the energy he gave off were as much attributable to the production of his first play as to his feelings for one of the performers. But after the play's extraordinary success and as he began working towards his next play, *The Double-Dealer*, and writing the part of Cynthia especially for her, I could no longer miss the symptoms of a man besotted. He had discovered that she was the sister of our landlord Mr Porter's wife and that she lived with her mother in Howard Street, just round the corner from our lodgings in Arundel Street. He was soon visiting Howard Street and attending every new performance she gave in the theatre. If he had not been so eager to woo her with that role in *The Double-Dealer*, I wonder if he would ever have got round to finishing it.

But what of Bracey herself? Did she love him in return? To begin with, perhaps not. She was so used, after all, to men falling for her in the theatre and making advances to her at the stage door, that she must have thought Mr Congreve was just another suitor trying his luck. She treated him, during the rehearsals for *The Old Bachelor* and its subsequent run, with the polite affection that any leading actress would show towards an author who clearly appreciated her talent. They were both so very young and inexperienced. Yes, she had plenty of experience of fending off would-be lovers, but none of being in love herself, while he had no experience whatever either of the emotion that had suddenly swept over him or of how to convey what he felt to her in a manner that might win her. Once he had discovered her address, he became a regular visitor, but complained to me that he was afraid he was giving the wrong impression there.

'In what way?' I asked.

'Her mother is a charming and well-informed person,' he said, 'and of course she is always present. I find myself conversing more with her than with Bracey, who is not a chatterbox – far from it.'

'Well, it must be helpful to make a good impression on the mother.'

'Not if the mother thinks I have come more to see her than her daughter.'

I did not permit myself to smile – or only inwardly. Mr Congreve's experience of women at that age had been confined mainly to his own mother and I suspect that his relationship with Mrs Katherine Leveson in Staffordshire had been more that of son to mother, or at least elder sister, than of lover.

But how could I assist him? I was no older than he was and *my* only experience of relationships with women had been a few clumsy scuffles with chambermaids in Oxford or servant-girls at London taverns. How did gentlemen make love to ladies? Although Bracey was only an actress, she came from a respectable family – her deceased father had been, I fancy, a reasonably well-to-do tradesman in Wolverhampton – and she had spent much of her childhood in the equally respectable family of Mr and Mrs Betterton. And off the stage she was an entirely different person from the vivacious, dark-eyed, teasing actress with 'the begging face', as Mr Congreve himself described her in his epilogue to *Love for Love*. Off the stage she was a serious, polite, even shy young lady. I didn't know how gentlemen made love to ladies, nor did he. I thought it quite ironic that his first play was full of racy young ladies and highly experienced young gentlemen pursuers, but the character nearest to himself was really the old bachelor, Heartwell, who was secretly in love with a woman but had no idea how to make out with her and pretended to have no interest in ladies at all. Of course Mr Congreve's seeming knowledge of the manoeuvres of ladies and gentlemen in love came mainly from reading and seeing other plays, touched up and refreshed by his own wit and imagination. He could write lovers with the best, but faced with the real thing he was quite at a loss.

His problem was solved – perhaps it often is – by the woman. Bracey, I'm sure, admired this clever, ambitious, gentle young author of her own age from the start. But when she saw that he was truly in love with her and that he was not the least like the cynical characters in his first play or the sort of insinuating wolves who came to the stage door in pursuit of her, she began to love him in return. This happened soon after the performances of *The Double-Dealer* in the winter of the year 1693. Not that the course of their mutual love ran easily at first. He saw her only in the theatre or at her house, chaperoned by her mother, or at the Porters', chaperoned by her sister, Mrs Frances Porter. In both cases, if he flirted at all, it was with the mother or the sister, who, the one as an older widow, the other as a married woman, could safely indulge in this traditional sport between the sexes without consequences, though they were both fond of Mr Congreve and must have been fully aware of where his real interest lay.

Once it was clear that Bracey returned Mr Congreve's love, the next question was how far their mutual love should carry them. Much of Bracey's popularity depended on her unusual reputation for chastity, and the parts he wrote for her – Cynthia, Angelica, Millamant and Almeria – were all chaste ladies who ended the plays with marriage to their gentlemanly suitors – Mellefont, Valentine, Mirabell and Osmyn – versions, as most people agreed, of himself. Did he propose marriage to her, did she accept, did they marry in secret, as some believed? I can say for sure that they did not.

Perhaps the most famous passage in all his plays is the pre-marriage contract agreed between Mirabell and Millamant in *The Way of the World*. She states her conditions and he responds with his in a scene which makes everyone laugh, but gives at the same time an entirely realistic picture of the sort of strains which make so many marriages the pitiful outcome of a love affair. After seeing Bracey and Mr Verbruggen play that scene, in which Millamant concludes that 'if I continue to endure you a little longer, I may by degrees dwindle into a wife', while Mirabell hopes that he 'may not be beyond measure enlarged into a husband', I asked Mr Congreve if he thought Mirabell and Millamant would have a happy marriage.

'We do not ask that question, Jeremy,' he said. 'They are fictional characters. Their existence closes with the prospect of their marriage.'

'However, sir,' I said, 'the play does depend on their very much wanting to be married. We must take it, surely, that they will be happy with each other ever after, or else feel that we have watched nothing but a prologue to disappointment, a sad mistake on the part of those two attractive and spirited lovers.'

'Take it how you will!' he said, annoyed.

'I am not criticising the play,' I said. 'Only wondering if you think marriage can ever be a good outcome for two people in love.'

'Sometimes, yes,' he said, 'if the couple want children and the children are born and survive, when their original love can be expanded and spread to their little copies. And sometimes if the couple are intelligent and successful enough – equally so – in their approach to the life around them, to remain close friends and colleagues once the first passion has faded. But chance plays a great part in the outcome. It is a game of cards. Clever partners at cards can make even poor hands work for them, but most people are not clever or confident enough to stave off defeat if chance is against them.'

No, Bracey and Mr Congreve did not marry. Apart from any damage being married might have done to Bracey's stage persona as a coy maiden, their social status was too far apart. Mr Congreve might be a poet, but he was also a gentleman from an old and proud family. A gentleman might make an actress his mistress, but did not marry her. And even if he had cared or dared to ignore this convention, marriage would have entailed a complete alteration in his way of life. His income was meagre and he would have had to seek out more lucrative government posts in order to set up a proper gentleman's household with at least a cook, a housemaid and a personal maid for his wife, even if he did not keep a carriage and groom. He had no liking or talent for conducting business and no ambition for worldly power of the kind Mr Addison and Mr Vanbrugh sought and found. In the next century, though that was after he had parted with Bracey, he would have before him the discouraging example of Captain Steele's perpetual struggle as a poet and journalist to maintain a family and remain solvent.

But two people who are as much in love with each other as Mr Congreve and Bracey cannot be long content with looking into one another's eyes, touching hands, exchanging the customary actors' kisses. The goddess Venus and her mischievous son Cupid, if I may adopt my master's frequent recourse to classical references, are inexorable. Even the general public could hardly mistake the meaning of that poem, *Cynthia*, which Mr Congreve published in June of the year 1694, a mere six months after Bracey had played the role of Cynthia in *The Double-Dealer*.

I know what 'tis to Wish, and Hope, and all in vain,
And meet, for humble Love, unkind Disdain;
Anger, and Hate, I have been forc'd to bear,

Nay Jealousie – and I have felt Despair.
These Pains, for you, I have been forc'd to prove,
For cruel you, when I began to Love.
'Till warm Compassion took at length my part,
And melted to my Wish your yielding Heart.
O the dear Hour, in which you did resign!
When round my Neck your willing Arms did twine,
And, in a Kiss, you said your Heart was mine.
[...]
Now, when a mutual Flame you have reveal'd,
And the dear Union of our Souls is seal'd,
When all my Joys compleat in you I find,
Shall I not share the Sorrows of your Mind?
[...]
Lean on my Breast, and let me fold thee fast,
Lock'd in these Arms, think all thy Sorrows past;
Or, what remain, think lighter made by me;
So I should think, were I so held by thee.

Unequivocal, is it not? I myself knew that they were true
lovers, man and mistress, earlier than that, in the spring, when
they solved the problem of meeting only in the presence of
her mother or sister or the other actors by hiring horses and
riding out into the country around Islington. I even knew how
thoroughly she had fallen in love with him, for, like Waitwell
in *The Way of the World* – still several years in the future – I
had my Foible, the maid Susan who served Bracey and her
mother in their Howard Street lodging. Indeed, we four –
brown-eyed Bracey and Mr Congreve, green-eyed Susan and
I – might have furnished the high and low characters for a
comedy. Susan would bring notes from Bracey to our house
and I would take notes from my master to hers and we would
hand them to each other at our doors with a sly smile and a
kiss and pass them on with solemn, straight faces to our master
and mistress respectively, as if we had no notion of where they
came from.

Did we read these notes? Of course we did. Are servants to share their employers' scruples when they do not share their social dignity? Not that the earliest notes were very revealing: they were full of endearments, but little else except the time of assignation at the stable where they hired the horses. One note, however, later that spring, from her to him, gave us more to think about:

> Dearest Heart, the King's Head was a ride too far. Your mare is saddle-sore and begs to be excused another ride till Thursday. I shall not skip so lightly as I like on to the stage this evening. Ever your loving Cynthia, even so.

And his reply:

> Sweet Cynthia, your stallion stamps in his stable. Will it ever be Thursday? Must I be mewed up beyond Wednesday? I shall see you at least this evening, skipping, I'm sure, as my heart is now and my heat unabated when I think of seeing and enjoying again what Actaeon died for.

I hesitate to insult my reader's intelligence by glossing that reference to the young hunter who, chancing to spy the goddess Diana and her attendants bathing naked in a pool, was transformed into a stag and torn to pieces by his own hounds. Well, I apologise. Of course you knew without my telling you.

But Thursday it remained and I was so injudicious as to bring out his riding clothes that day without being asked.

'Do you read my letters, Jeremy?' he said.

'Your letters?'

'My letters from Howard Street, brought by that girl you are always fumbling in the hall.'

So, you see, masters spy on their servants as closely as vice versa.

'Oh, sir,' I said, 'we all have our secrets.'

'Very well, but I do not wish you to read mine.'

'No, sir.'

So in future he sealed his notes to Bracey and must have told her to do the same. But at least when they were out riding – towards or at the King's Head or wherever – Susan and I could also ride out an hour or so at my master's lodgings. Bracey's mother was a kind person and if she knew how Bracey's maid spent her time off, she never complained. It was a very happy time for all four lovers in that comedy.

I recall another occasion when his clothing proved an embarrassment, this time to him rather than me. I was dressing him one morning, but could not find his steinkirk – a very ample linen cravat of the kind worn at that time.

'Your steinkirk, sir?' I said. 'It doesn't seem to be with your other clothes as usual.'

'Look under the chair!' he said.

'I have already done so.'

But as I stooped to look again, out of the corner of my eye I saw him hastily retrieve it from the bed, where it lay on the pillow. He saw that I had seen him and blushed.

'Strange!' he said, handing it to me. 'It seems to have walked.'

'Without legs,' I said. 'Slid like a snake.'

No more was said as I tied it for him and tucked it into his waistcoat, noticing as I did so that it had an unusually sweet scent. I mentioned this curious incident later to Susan and she laughed.

'Oh, I know what that was about,' she said. 'Yesterday Mrs Anne forgot to take her mask.'

Bracey, whose face was so well known, always wore male dress and a mask when she went riding with Mr Congreve. The combination struck me as inconsistent, since the lady's mask would contradict the impression conveyed by the male clothes.

'So?'

'She told me that she wanted to abandon their ride when she realised she had forgotten the mask. But he whipped off his steinkirk and wrapped it round her face.'

'She must have looked like a Moroccan pirate.'

'Where did you say he found it?'

'On his pillow.'

'Oh, I will tell her that. That he slept the night with his steinkirk on his pillow as if it kept the shape and touch of her face.'

'It certainly kept her scent.'

'How sweet lovers are!'

'Or how silly.'

'And which are we?'

'You are sweet and I am silly.'

But nothing is quite perfect and lovers' fires can spark and spit and turn to smoke. There were times when my master was grumpy and did not send me to Howard Street nor Susan come to our door. What were 'the Sorrows of your Mind' that he speaks of in his poem to Cynthia? Surely not connected with the theatre, where she remained a star, or with his slow, extreme concentration on writing plays and polishing his lines, which, if they took his mind and time away from seeing and touching her in the flesh while he wrote them, were also, in their oblique way, such ardent and crafted love letters to her as few if any women can ever have received?

The sorrows he refers to must have been, I believe, his failure even to consider marrying her, for although marriage may end in tears, it also makes love sure, at least to begin with, and socially acceptable. In their case it would have removed the need for secrecy and for meeting in out-of-the-way places; and I do think that women, even unusually independent women like Bracey, look for something more settled and domestic beyond the first transports of love. Perhaps she would have liked to have children. My green-eyed Susan, I know, wanted all that and if the two major players in our four-part comedy had set up house together, she and I could have become domestic too. As it was, she left me and her mistress at last for a well-to-do wigmaker and has at least four surviving children. Do I regret that? I don't think so, any more than Mr Congreve. Some men are born fathers, some need heirs to their estates, others, like my own father, are born to sow seed and take no interest in the harvest. But, after all, towards the end of his life Mr Congreve did father a child and how he loved her! Perhaps I do regret that I had none – or none that I know of.

Sorrows or not, the love of Mr Congreve and Bracey and consequently of Susan and me lasted several years. He wrote no more plays after *The Way of the World*, with that famous dialogue between Mirabell and Millamant, and I wonder if she did not take that to be almost a declaration that he might consider marriage himself. If not, it was perhaps a little insensitive on his part to close his career as a playwright by making his and her dramatic counterparts argue the case so cogently. But although there were no more plays, there was his musical masque, *The Judgment of Paris*, in the spring of the year 1701 and, courting her still in his oblique, authorial way, he gave her the part of Venus. You will know the story, of course. Paris, the son of King Priam of Troy, is guarding a flock of sheep, when the god Mercury descends, hands him a golden apple and tells him he must give it to whichever of three goddesses he judges to be the most beautiful: Juno, Minerva or Venus. The goddesses descend and, not relying on their beauty alone, offer him bribes: respectively imperial power, glory in war, and the love of the most beautiful woman on earth. Paris, a simple, sensual lad, goes for the last – Helen, queen of Sparta, as it turns out – and gives the apple to Venus. Mr Congreve wrote these lines for him to sing to her:

> All Loves Darts are in thy Eyes,
> And Harmony falls from thy Tongue;
> Forbear, O Goddess of Desire,
> Thus my ravish'd Soul to move,
> Forbear to fan the raging Fire,
> And be propitious to my Love.

No diminution there of the author's love for the actress.

The masque was quite short and was set by different composers in competition for a first prize of £100. The idea,

I think, was Lord Halifax's, and was paid for by him and other members of the Kit-Cat Club, and administered by Mr Tonson. Four composers responded to the advertisement for competitors, each composition was to be performed on a different day and finally all four together on the same day, when the audience would choose the winner. There were prizes also of £50 for the runner-up and £30 for whoever came third.

The performances took place not in either of the two regular theatres, Drury Lane and Lincoln's Inn Fields, but in the old Dorset Garden Theatre, beside the river at Blackfriars, and they were not open to any comers, but only to those who had been invited, members of the Kit-Cat Club and their friends and relations mostly, a very distinguished and privileged audience. There was no place, of course, for anyone of the servant class, but Susan and I were allowed in as ushers.

The theatre, designed by Sir Christopher Wren for Sir William Davenant's company, was larger and grander than either of the others and had once been the scene of Mr Betterton's early triumphs until the companies merged in the eighties and Drury Lane became the only theatre in use. For this new venture carpenters had altered the front of the stage to make it concave and lined it with tin to improve the acoustic. The boxes and pit were all thrown into one and the stage was hung with innumerable candles in sconces to augment the usual candelabra. I had never been inside this theatre before and marvelled at the elaborate proscenium with its intricate wooden carvings by Mr Grinling Gibbons. There were also statues of two ladies in ancient Greek costume representing the Muses of Tragedy and Comedy.

Including the soloists, the chorus and the musicians, there were, Mr Congreve told me, no less than eighty-five performers on the stage. But perhaps the most extraordinary part of all this sumptuous scene was that White's chocolate-house had brought all its staff and appurtenances into the area between the pit and the stage, where the musicians usually performed, and were serving cold drinks, wine, ratafia and of course chocolate, quite free of charge, to anyone who asked. We ushers were too busy showing ladies and gentlemen to their seats to stop for refreshment before the show, but afterwards we too could help ourselves. And all this was to be laid on four times more, including the final judgement day for all four composers.

The performances themselves did not much differ except in the music, since the cast was always the same, with the same movements and gestures, wearing the same fine costumes. Ah, but that first performance with Mr John Eccles' music was therefore the most startling, for, you see, Paris tells the god Mercury that he cannot properly judge the goddesses' beauty with all their clothes on. We drew in our breath, yes, all of us simultaneously, dukes and duchesses, earls and countesses, knights and ladies and gentlemen, and humble ushers. Would they dare, these three beautiful actresses, Mrs Hodgson as Juno, Mrs Bowman as Minerva, Bracey as Venus, to undress on the stage? And they did – demurely, not entirely, permitting glimpses only of their lovely naked breasts. Silence – you never heard such silence from such a huge audience, such stillness, except for the distant cry of a waterman on the river outside and Mr Eccles' music. For who had ever seen such a sight before in a respectable theatre in front of the grandest people? Of course, both Susan and Mr Congreve had often seen Bracey's breasts, but surely no one else in the world had except her mother. I asked my master next day if the actresses had objected to exposing themselves like that.

'They were a little reluctant, yes, but after all they are actresses, ready to enter into the parts they play.'

'But not usually to show intimate parts of themselves.'

'True, but the story requires it and they did so in character, with the proud modesty of goddesses showing themselves to a mere mortal.'

'And upwards of seven hundred other mortals.'

'Jeremy, you have had this difficulty before. You must try to understand the difference between art and life. The theatre holds a mirror to life. What you see is reflection not reality.'

'But it seems to me that in such a case the reality obscures the reflection.'

'You have the same literal mind as Mr Collier.'

'Well, I do wonder how Mr Collier would take it.'

'Mr Collier was not invited, nor will be, nor any of his kind.'

Two things occurred to me after this conversation: first, that Mr Congreve could have chosen some other classical story for his masque; and secondly, that perhaps he was, as Mr Vanbrugh put it, still conducting his cockfight with Mr Collier in defence of the liberty of the stage.

The outcome of this competition – and I may say that the competition to be invited to the subsequent performances became almost frenzied – was that an almost unknown composer, Mr John Weldon, an organist from Oxford, won the first prize. Mr Eccles won second prize, Mr Daniel Purcell (brother of the more famous Mr Henry Purcell) won third prize and poor Mr Godfrey Finger came last and almost immediately returned in disgust to his native Germany. The outcome for the love of Bracey and Mr Congreve was more uncertain. Susan told me that Bracey was not happy to have exposed her bosom to the gaze of the town on eight separate occasions – four on the same day, when all four compositions were played in succession. She had accepted that her profession as an actress required her to meet the demands of the text, but she felt that her author and lover had exceeded his rights in sharing her charms with the public. Where now were the mutual terms of polite engagement agreed between Millamant and Mirabell?

Furthermore, if Mr Congreve had so blatantly acknowledged his passion for his Venus, had he not also made her all the more desirable to other men? She was besieged with new suitors, many of them, considering that those audiences had been drawn exclusively from the highest classes in the land, much grander, richer and more open-handed than a poor gentleman poet who could barely afford the cost of hiring two horses and a room in an inn for the day. They had been lovers now for seven years and it may be that, even without the strains created by *The Judgment of Paris*, their ardent relationship was beginning to cool.

One winter day that same year my master became very short-tempered with me.

'You are getting lazy and incompetent,' he said, after complaining about the way I had cleaned his shoes.

'I'm sorry, sir,' I said.

'You seem to think you have got too big for my boots.'

'They were very scuffed, sir, and I did my best to amend them, but I will try again.'

'Do so! And try to remember that you are my valet as well as my friend.'

'I am grateful, sir, that you think of me as such. May I ask, as the friend, if there is anything I can do to help beyond improving the shine of your shoes?'

'Nothing.'

He shut himself in his study and I assumed that his ill temper was caused by the recent falling-off of the audiences for Mr Betterton's company, in which he had a share. He must have read my thoughts for he emerged a few minutes later to say:

'You may imagine that I'm put out because the company is not doing well. Not at all. I expected nothing else. They do not perform, as Drury Lane does, for monkeys.'

'Certainly not,' I said, continuing to work on the shoes.

'Hm,' he said and went inside the study again, closing the door, but a moment or two later, opened it again.

'More coal!' he said.

I fetched it, made up the fire and was about to go out.

'I have a rival,' he said.

'A rival? Who could that be? Mr Farquhar? I wouldn't say he was much of a threat. His plays are popular, but quite light and superficial.'

He looked at me in silence for a while, then, as I moved towards the door, said, 'A rival for Bracey.'

'There are rivals for Mrs Bracegirdle all over town,' I said.

'Not serious rivals.'

'How serious?'

'Very. Lord Scarsdale.'

The third Earl of Scarsdale had married a cousin of Mr Congreve, on his mother's side of the family, but the earl's wife had since died.

'Scarsdale is infatuated with her,' he said. 'He calls on her nearly every day, he sends her expensive presents.'

'How does she respond?'

'How should I know?'

'I should think you might guess by the way she responds to you.'

'I find no change in that.'

'Then you have nothing to worry about.'

'She accepts his visits and his presents.'

'He visits Howard Street?'

'Yes. And her dressing room at the theatre. Frequently.'

'You must occasionally meet him by accident.'

'Of course.'

'And sometimes find yourselves both in her presence at the same time.'

'Yes. What are you getting at?'

'You can surely tell which of you she prefers?'

'She behaves in her best ladylike manner to both of us.'

'Have you spoken to Lord Scarsdale and asked him his intentions?'

'His intentions are perfectly clear. And I am not her father.'

'Is he hoping to marry her?'

'I'm afraid he may be.'

'But you are not?'

'You know perfectly well, Jeremy, that I'm in no position to marry anybody.'

'Then if she fancies herself as the Countess of Scarsdale, I'm afraid you will have to give way.'

'Give way! What is the matter with you, Jeremy? You have become a useless friend as well as a useless servant. Perhaps Scarsdale has offered you a job at twice the salary?'

'No, sir, and I would not accept it if he did. You do me wrong, sir, to suggest such a thing.'

'Then what advice can you give me other than this odious "give way"?'

'Only to love her all the more and to show her that you do.'

So things continued for a while, Mr Congreve visiting and riding with Bracey, Lord Scarsdale visiting, but not, according to Susan, riding with her. Susan's view was that her mistress still preferred Mr Congreve, but that Lord Scarsdale's attentions allowed her to hope that my master would at last propose marriage.

'Does Lord Scarsdale offer to marry her?' I asked.

'He has not so far, I think,' she said, 'but she believes he will.'

'And would she accept?'

'I think she might, if no other offer came her way. She is not as young as she was and sometimes worries about how long her career can continue as a young heroine.'

'She could move, I suppose, into the sort of roles Mrs Barry takes?'

'She doesn't think so. She considers that her speciality is youth and vivacity and that she could not find the weight and dignity of Mrs Barry's roles.'

I do not know, nor did Susan, whether Lord Scarsdale ever did offer to marry Bracey. If he did, she must have temporised or even refused him. He continued to solicit her love and my master continued to see him as a rival until his own love for her dwindled, as Henrietta, Lady Godolphin – later the young Duchess of Marlborough – entered his life. Lord Scarsdale died in the year 1707, leaving Bracey £1000 in his will, and no doubt on the strength of that Bracey retired from the stage, soon afterwards also receiving the £800 donated by the Kit-Cat Club, as I have already mentioned. By then she and her mother were living with the Porters in Surrey Street, having moved there after the Great Storm of November 1703, which severely damaged the roof of their lodging in Howard Street.

That hurricane did huge damage all over the country, where fallen trees blocked the roads, but especially in the cities, where windows were smashed, walls and trees in the parks blown down

and the lead sheets protecting the roofs of churches were, as my
master put it, 'rolled up as they were before they were laid on'
and sometimes lifted away on to other houses, breaking their
roofs. Yet our lodging was spared, except that the small window
in my room was blown in. Mr Collier took the opportunity
to publish a paper describing the storm as a warning of 'the
Punishment of Sodom, and that God should destroy us with Fire
and Brimstone' if the English went on attending theatres. Mr
Dennis, the critic, replied that if so, it was unjust of God to allow
this same storm to do so much damage around the Baltic Sea.

We ourselves moved into lodgings in the Porters' new house
in Surrey Street in the summer of the year 1706, so that although
by then Mr Congreve and Bracey had ceased to be active lovers,
they remained friends and even closer neighbours than before.
My Susan married her wigmaker at about that time and Bracey's
new French maid was a sharp-tempered person who already had
a lover from her own Huguenot community, so I got no further
inside information about Bracey.

But before I close this chapter of Mr Congreve's life, I must
go back a year to the opening of the new Queen's Theatre in
the Haymarket, that unsuccessful venture on which my master
collaborated with Mr Vanbrugh. My master had not wanted the
theatre to be used for operas – it was intended to be an altogether
grander and more modern venue for Mr Betterton's company
than the old tennis-court theatre in Lincoln's Inn Fields. But
Mr Vanbrugh had made it too grand, with its lofty ceiling and
vast columns, so that it was much better suited to singers than
actors. Before becoming immersed in the business of building
and raising the money for the theatre from his fellow Kit-Cats,
Mr Congreve had started to follow up on his success with *The
Judgment of Paris* by writing a full opera. He therefore set about
completing it for the opening. His favourite musician, Mr John
Eccles, composed the music and the principal part of Semele
was to be played, of course, by Bracey. This was another classical
story and somewhat less well known than that of Paris and the
three goddesses, so you will forgive me if I tell you that Semele,

the beautiful daughter of Cadmus, king of Thebes, is loved by
Jupiter, king of the gods. He carries her off to live with him on
Mount Olympus and all is perfectly delightful:

> Endless pleasure, endless love,
> Semele enjoys above;
> On her bosom Jove reclining,
> Useless now his thunder lies;
> To her arms his bolts resigning,
> And his lightning to her eyes.

Yet her pleasure is not, after all, endless:

> I love and am lov'd, yet more I desire;
> Ah, how foolish a Thing is Fruition!
> As one Passion cools, some other takes Fire,
> And I'm still in a longing Condition.
> Whate'er I possess
> Soon seems an Excess,
> For something untry'd I petition;
> Tho' daily I prove
> The Pleasures of Love,
> I die for the Joys of Ambition.

And in lines which I think are a fair summary of the male view
of women, she pleads with Jupiter:

> With my Frailty don't upbraid me,
> I am Woman as you made me.
> Causeless doubting or despairing,
> Rashly trusting, idly fearing,
> If obtaining
> Still complaining,
> If consenting
> Still repenting,
> Most complying

When denying,
And to be follow'd, only flying.
With my frailty don't upbraid me,
I am Woman as you made me.

She now wants to be immortal and queen of the gods. But Jupiter's jealous wife Juno is plotting to destroy her. Disguised as Semele's sister Ino, she visits Semele and hands her a magic mirror which makes her look like a goddess. Semele gazes into the mirror and sings:

O Ecstasy of Happiness!
Celestial Graces
I discover in each Feature!
Myself I shall adore,
If I persist in gazing;
No Object sure before
Was ever half so pleasing.

Juno persuades Semele to demand that Jupiter show himself in his full glory. Knowing what will happen if he does, Jupiter demurs, but she nags away at him and at last he gives way, with the inevitable consequence: Semele is burnt to a cinder.

Does an author's work always reflect, however opaquely, the author's own life? It certainly reflects his prepossessions, even when the subject has not been chosen by him in the first place. But no one asked Mr Congreve to tell the story of Semele any more than they did *The Judgment of Paris*. One must conclude that he chose both stories in order to give the best parts to Bracey. I don't know that my master consciously saw Semele's fatal claims on Jupiter as reflections of Bracey's on him, but I'm sure that at some level of his thinking they were. And I'm even more sure that *she* saw them that way. Perhaps she was also afraid that he would again ask her to unveil her charms to the public. There were several reasons why Mr Congreve's only opera *Semele* was never performed in his lifetime, but the main one was undoubtedly that Bracey would not take the role. Her excuse was that, in spite of Mr Dryden's view that she was a better singer than many professionals, she was an actress who sang, not an opera-singer and such a demanding role was beyond her. When there was a question of the opera being performed a couple of years later, she again excused herself and indeed that was the very year of her final retirement from the stage.

Semele was performed at last, in 1744, six years after my master's death, with music by Mr George Handel. The text was somewhat altered, with some additions and subtractions, and seemed to me, when I attended a performance, more of a comic opera than the tragedy my master intended. Whatever his personal feelings towards Bracey were, behind its ostensible story, he surely intended it, like the ancient Greek tragedies, to show the flaws of humanity and their touching vulnerability in the face of the inexorable laws of nature: love, change and death. I may, incidentally, have confused some of Mr Handel's alterations with the original, but I hope I have not misinterpreted either Mr Congreve's conscious or unconscious intentions, since I believe it was one of his finest creations.

Well, I have told the story of Mr Congreve's great love for Mrs Bracegirdle, expressed in every major work he wrote, and I will end with his farewell to her, when he believed that she had finally succumbed to the enticements of his cousin Lord Scarsdale:

> False tho' you've been to me and Love,
> I nere can take revenge,
> (So much your wondrous beautys move)
> Tho' I resent your change.

> In hours of bliss we oft have met,
> They could not always last;
> And tho' the present I regret,
> I still am Grateful for the past.

But think not, Iris, tho' my breast
A gen'rous flame has warm'd
You ere again could make me blest,
Or charm as once you charm'd.

Who may your future favours own
May future change forgive;
In Love, the first deceit alone
Is what you never can retrieve.

I think that sentiment somewhat unfair, since whether or not
Bracey succumbed to Lord Scarsdale, Mr Congreve himself had
undoubtedly by then succumbed to his new love for Henrietta,
Lady Godolphin, which I shall try next to relate, but in another
chapter, since this one has grown longer than I anticipated.

11

THE LADIES' TEMPLE

The Ladies' Temple at Stowe has only recently been completed. Designed by Mr Gibbs, it is sited on the upper ground, east of the Elysian Fields, directly facing the Temple of Friendship in the distance, on the far side of the Octagon Lake. The Ladies' Temple, a sturdy four-square building set above two broad flights of steps, is Lady Cobham's and her female friends' answer to Lord Cobham's and his male friends' Temple of Friendship and the two parties can perhaps wave to each other from the doors of their respective temples but scarcely hear each other even if they shouted. Since they can enjoy as much of each others' presence and conversation as they wish inside the house, this separation in the landscape, where they can say what they like about the other sex without being overheard, is evidently a most attractive alternative. I wonder whether it was Lord Cobham or his lady who first thought of it. The interior of the Ladies' Temple is tastefully decorated by the Venetian artist Francesco Sleter with murals depicting the particular interests of ladies: music and art, shellwork and needlework. The decorations on the inside of the Temple of Friendship, you may recall, are all about patriotism and politics.

Having filled the Temple of Venus with the love of Mr Congreve and Bracey, this new Temple for Ladies would seem a suitable place to install my memories of the love between my master and a lady as much his social superior as he was Bracey's. Henrietta, Lady Godolphin succeeded her father, the great Duke of Marlborough, as Duchess of Marlborough in her own right by a special Act of Parliament. Bracey was Mr Congreve's Venus, but Lady Henrietta was his 'learned Minerva', for so he meant to designate her on the foundation stone of the Queen's Theatre in Haymarket. As it turned out, she was suffering from smallpox at the time, so it was her younger sister, Anne, Countess of Sunderland, who received the honour, not as Minerva but under her nickname 'Little Whig', since the theatre was paid for by the Whigs of the Kit-Cat Club and her husband, the third earl, soon to be Secretary of State for the South, was a leading member of the party as of the Club.

Lady Henrietta, as I will take leave to call her, since her titles as Countess of Godolphin and then as Duchess of Marlborough will prove too cumbersome, was eleven years younger than Mr Congreve. I have explained elsewhere how the Duke of Marlborough and the first Earl of Godolphin worked as a partnership to prosecute the war against France, the duke as Captain-General of the Allied army in the field and the earl as Lord Treasurer in Parliament and Whitehall. Their greatest work together, which was to bring our country triumphantly through the war with France and establish Britain as one of the leading powers in Europe, was done after the untimely death of King William and in spite of the constant Tory opposition to the war. They depended, of course, also on the influence of the old Duchess of Marlborough (Lady Henrietta's mother Sarah) with Queen Anne.

The duke and the earl were already close friends in the Nineties and they sealed their friendship in the year 1698 with the marriage of the Duke's eldest daughter, Lady Henrietta, to Lord Godolphin's son Francis. Our upper classes being accustomed to arrange dynastic marriages at quite a tender age, she was then still only sixteen years old and her husband nineteen. She bore her husband two daughters and two sons, though only one of the daughters and neither of the sons survived her. The Marlboroughs were not lucky with their sons, for Lady Henrietta's only brother, Lord Blandford, who was said to be a most admirable young man and should have inherited his father's title and estates, died of smallpox at the age of sixteen early in the year 1703, a year and a half before the duke won his great victory of Blenheim.

It was this young man's death which first brought Mr Congreve and Lady Henrietta together. He wrote a long and elaborate elegy for Lord Blandford, in the style of a classical pastoral. It was entitled *The Tears of Amaryllis for Amyntas*, and, before it was published, he sent a copy of the manuscript to Lord Godolphin, to whom as the young man's godfather the poem was dedicated. It was not one of his best works, but to a grieving family such a tribute from a poet of Mr Congreve's renown is valued more for the sympathy it conveys than its artistic quality. Some people naturally assumed that my master, whose finances were then at a very low point, was seeking some sort of reward, perhaps a more lucrative government post than his existing job as a Commissioner for Hackney Carriages, which brought in only £100 a year. Neither the duke nor the Earl of Godolphin were members of the Kit-Cat Club, nor even Whigs, and my master did not know them personally. It may be that he did have a notion of finding new patrons, but when I entered his study to make up the fire, found him at his desk and asked what he was writing, he looked up at me with tears in his eyes.

'The Duke of Marlborough's only son has died,' he said. 'What a catastrophe for that great man! Fate with one hand enables him to drive the French out of town after town in Flanders, and with the other strikes down the heir to all his glory. I feel for him as if it were my own son. I can't write him a letter – I don't know him. But perhaps I can publish some verses which might give him a little comfort.'

Lord Godolphin responded by inviting my master to dinner at Godolphin House, next to St James's Palace, where he was introduced to Lord Godolphin's son Francis and his wife, Lady Henrietta, who also lived there. Lady Henrietta, then aged twenty-one, a vivacious fair-haired beauty with blue eyes and a high forehead, paid particular attention to Mr Congreve, whose works she knew and admired. Her love of music, poetry and wit was well known, but whether she already felt more than admiration for his gifts at that first meeting I cannot say. However, I'm sure that he, whose love for Bracey was already dwindling as she saw more of Lord Scarsdale, fell at least half in love with Lady Henrietta at that dinner, for he returned home quite dazed with the experience.

'A good dinner, sir?' I asked him, as I opened the door and took his cloak.

'Dinner? Oh, yes, I think so.'

'Very grand company, I'm sure.'

'Oh, yes.'

'How did you find your host, my Lord Treasurer?'

'Most kind and condescending. Not a great talker, a dark, quite slight man, very contained. But he liked my verses, he said, and would send them to the Duke of Marlborough in Flanders, who would surely be most grateful for my thoughts for his family.'

'Did you meet other members of the family?'

'I did.'

'Lord Godolphin's son?'

'Oh, yes, a pleasant, easy-mannered fellow, but, of course, I already knew him a little from the Kit-Cat Club.'

'And his lady?'

'I was placed next to her.'

I think I heard him sigh. He was quite silent for a moment or two and then, speaking more to himself than me, said in a low voice, 'I talked far too much.'

'I'm sure she appreciated that. She is said to prefer wits to lords.'

'I don't know that I was very witty. Just voluble. I've no idea what I was talking about. A lot of nonsense, I'm afraid. Beautiful ladies have that effect on me.'

They met again from time to time after that, as Mr Congreve was occasionally invited to social occasions connected with the

Godolphins and, like most people except the more intransigent Tories, hero-worshipped the Duke of Marlborough for his succession of decisive victories over the French. In the year 1706 he was stirred to write a Pindaric Ode to Queen Anne celebrating the victory of Ramillies:

> Go on, Great Chief, in ANNA's cause proceed;
> Nor sheath the Terrors of thy Sword,
> 'Till *Europe* thou hast freed,
> And Universal Peace restor'd.
> This mighty Work when thou shalt End,
> Equal Rewards attend,
> Of Value far above
> Thy Trophies and thy Spoils;
> Rewards even worthy of thy Toils,
> Thy QUEEN's just Favour, and thy COUNTRY's Love.

I believe I have already mentioned in another chapter that he prefaced it with a long, scholarly introduction explaining the true nature of a Pindaric Ode, as originally invented by the ancient Greek poet Pindar. But although the queen was the ostensible dedicatee of this poem and received it graciously when he presented it to her, I was not deceived. He aimed, above all, to please his military hero's daughter, the 'learned Minerva' who had captured his heart and who would certainly appreciate his scholarly introduction better than Her Majesty.

He followed it up two years later with another Pindaric Ode, from which I have already quoted some lines. This one was addressed to Lord Godolphin, dwelling on his love for horse racing, but ended with a joint tribute to him and Lady Henrietta's father:

> Thus, thou GODOLPHIN, dost with MARLBRO strive,
> From whose joint Toils we Rest derive;
> Triumph in Wars abroad his Arm assures,
> Sweet Peace at home thy Care secures.

By then it was evident that his admiration for Lady Henrietta was returned, for he was visiting Godolphin House several times a week and they played cards together.

In January of the year 1707 there appeared a new magazine devoted to literature, *The Muses Mercury*, edited by various distinguished writers, Dr Garth, Mr Dennis, Mr Steele, Mr Nahum Tate and Mr Dryden's son. The first number announced Mr Congreve's completion of his opera *Semele* – unfortunately never to be performed in his lifetime – and the November edition in that same year contained the poem 'To Maria' under his initials, W.C.:

> Tho' all the boist'rous Waves of Fortune Rowl,
> And in united Torrents drench my Soul;
> Yet when my bright Meridian Star appears,
> She'll scatter all my Doubts, and dissipate my Fears,
> Tho' the Foundation of the World should shake,
> And all the enormous Frame of Nature break;
> Nay, tho' the Heavens should fall, or Earth shou'd rise,
> With strange convulsions, far above the Skies;
> Impossibles should come to pass, yet I
> Would with Maria live, or with her die.

Now who was this Maria? I knew of no such person in his life, so it was clearly a pseudonym and although the world at that early stage of his new attraction might be deceived, I was not. He did not show me the poem, but did not object when I took his copy of the magazine into my room and read it. Serving the dinner I had brought in for him that day, I complimented him on the poem.

'You liked it?'

'Very much. "Impossibles should come to pass": that's very strong.'

'Thank you, Jeremy.'

'Might I ask about Maria?'

'A name that came into my head and fits the last line.'

'Of course.'

And here, since he was so pleased by my praise, I became rash. 'The name that came into my head when I read it was that famous queen of King Charles the First.' (Henrietta Maria, in case my reader has forgotten.)

Mr Congreve went very red.

'Maria is a very common name,' he said.

'Indeed.'

Silence.

'All right, Jeremy, I will eat my dinner now before it gets cold.'

I left the room. But when I returned to take away his plate and bring him some fruit, he said, 'You do get some very far-fetched ideas into that teeming noddle of yours. Surely most people will not associate "Maria" with a long-dead queen?'

'Oh, I don't think so, sir. Why should they? Just a fancy of mine, not knowing of any other Marias.'

'You are an inveterate tease, Jeremy. I don't know why I put up with you.'

'I hope, sir, it's because you can trust me not to air my far-fetched ideas outside this room.'

'Hm.'

But if, as his friendship with Lady Henrietta became common knowledge, he wrote any other verses to her, he kept them from me and was not foolish enough to publish them.

On the first of May in that same year, 1707, Parliament passed the Act of Union with Scotland, whose government had beggared themselves and their kingdom with a disastrous attempt to found an empire of their own in a tropical jungle near Panama. The Whig Junto, assisted by Mr Addison, saw some advantage from being able to present a united Protestant front against Catholic Jacobite invasion, while the impoverished Scots had their government's debts paid and could look to more favourable trading relations with their rich neighbour. Our own leading merchants were consequently no more enthusiastic about the Union than most ordinary Scots, who were violently against it. Lady Henrietta told my master, however, that her father was pleased, since it would now be much easier to raise soldiers from Scotland for the war with France and he valued Scottish soldiers above all others for their courage and steadfastness.

Mr Congreve had gone to play cards with Lady Henrietta on this occasion, taking with him as a small present for her a newly published pack illustrated with elaborate engravings of her father's and his allies' victories. The Ten of Diamonds, for instance, showed a panorama of the battle of Ramillies with, in the foreground, the Duke of Marlborough swinging one leg over his horse just as the soldier holding the horse's head has his head taken off by a cannonball, a thing that really happened and increased the Duke's reputation for being invulnerable. The Ace of Hearts showed Queen Anne riding high on a chariot drawn by two horses and trampling down the Pope and the king of France. Most of the suit of spades was devoted to ridiculing King Louis, the Queen of Spades being a picture of him with his mistress Madame Maintenon, who is driving a small flock of turkeys. Underneath is this scurrilous verse:

At first dishonest when I Turkeys fed
Little I thought t'enjoy a Monarcks bed
But now ye dotards glutted wth a baudy Reign
I may to Turkey keeping go again.

My master told me that before settling to their bidding in the game of three-handed ombre with one of Lady Henrietta's attendant ladies, they were laughing over this card and others when her mother, Duchess Sarah, entered the room in a great rage. Her close relationship with and domination of the queen had begun to sour, as Mrs Abigail Hill, the cousin she had given a lowly place in the royal household, began to oust her in the queen's affection. The queen, she said, had taken £2000 out of the privy purse, which Duchess Sarah controlled, as a dowry for Mrs Hill, who was to marry Colonel Sam Masham, groom of the bedchamber to the queen's husband, Prince George of Denmark. But as soon as she had got over spluttering about her cousin's 'insolence and ingratitude', she turned a frosty eye on Mr Congreve.

'You here again!' she said.

My master rose to bow to her, but Lady Henrietta simply ignored her.

'I suppose when the queen prefers her own sex, all morals are out of the window,' said Duchess Sarah.

Lady Henrietta said nothing. Her lady attendant looked fixedly at the table. Mr Congreve, still standing, inclined his head, signifying, he told me, either agreement or disagreement without, as the lawyers say, prejudice.

'At least the queen has no daughters to shame her,' said the duchess.

'Will you deal, Mr Congreve?' said Lady Henrietta.

'With these cards?' asked my master, sitting down.

'Of course. We can enjoy Father's triumphs as we play.'

'We must first remove the eights, nines and tens,' he said, beginning to do so.

Duchess Sarah turned on her heel and left the room, slamming the door.

'Oh dear!' said Lady Henrietta. 'She could not think of an exit line. What line would you give her, Mr Congreve?'

'If I had my way I would send Mrs Abigail Hill back to keeping turkeys.'

With the death of his famous father five years later, Lady Henrietta's husband Francis became the second Earl and she the Countess of Godolphin. My master left it to Mr Maynwaring to propose her as a toast at a Kit–Cat dinner and compose the verse to be inscribed on a glass:

Godolphin's easy and unpractised Air
Gains without Art and governs without Care
Her conquering Race with various Fate surprise
Who 'scape their Arms are captive to their Eyes.

After his first Pindaric Ode Mr Congreve did at last receive a better post. He ceased to be a Commissioner for Hackney Carriages and became a Commissioner for Wine Licences, at twice the salary. The office was again conveniently near our lodgings, the more so that my master was now beginning to suffer more often and more painfully from gout, as well as losing his sight. He very much regretted that he had often to refuse invitations from Lady Henrietta, who was especially fond of country dancing, to partner her.

'My dancing days, which never really began, are over,' he said to me. 'It would look too like Beauty and the Beast if I were to stumble round the floor with my poor sight, painful feet and round belly.'

'But isn't Beauty fond of the Beast?'

He looked at me angrily. 'What are you saying, Jeremy?'

'I mean in the tale.'

'I hope that's what you meant.'

But Lady Henrietta didn't seem to mind that her tame poet was so often an invalid. Indeed, I wonder whether she didn't like him all the better for it, as somebody she could care for as well as admire for his genius. She began to accompany him to the spas he visited for his health, Tunbridge Wells, Epsom and Bath, and so I became acquainted with her myself, as well as with her travelling staff of several maids, a housekeeper, grooms and footmen. Our progress to these watering-places was no longer hugger-mugger in a public coach, but in a procession of several coaches emblazoned with the arms of Godolphin.

Among all these attendants I soon made friends with one of the maids called Polly, a high-spirited girl much my junior in age but who rated herself far above me in station, considering that she served a countess, whereas I was the solitary servant of a poor gentleman, 'a hanger-on,' as she expressed it, 'of a hanger-on'. Nevertheless, she said, she 'liked my face and thought I was honest', which most of the footmen in such a large and wealthy establishment she believed were not. My likeable face and honest manner also won me the favour of the formidable housekeeper, Mrs Ann Jellet, to whom Polly and the other maids were nervously subservient, so that what I lost in Polly's eyes by my master's lowly status on the upper floor, I gained by my own charms on the lower.

What, I wondered, when Mr Congreve first became a frequent visitor to Godolphin House, was Lord Godolphin's view of this regular addition to his dinner table and his wife's tea- and card-parties? He and Mr Congreve were, as he remarked, fellow Kit-Cats, but they were hardly more than acquaintances and Lord Godolphin was certainly more interested in horses and horse racing, as his famous father was, than wit and poetry. Like his father, too, he was a reserved and mild-mannered man. But that quiet self-containment in his father the Lord Treasurer had masked a sharp intelligence and stern determination – who but he had held the ship of state steady at home while abroad the Duke of Marlborough chased the French back inside their own borders? In the son, who held only minor court offices, it masked nothing but his personal feelings. Polly told me that he was a kind master, thoughtful for his servants, devoted to his only surviving daughter, another Lady Henrietta, married to the Duke of Newcastle, but slow.

'Slow?'

'Slow, you know, not quick-witted.'

'A bit dim?'

'No, not exactly stupid. You know, dozy. He always looks half asleep.'

'Doesn't that irritate your mistress? She's always on the go.'

'Oh, I think she took his measure long ago. And I'm sure he took hers. They go their own ways.'

'Do they quarrel?'

'Not really. She sometimes shouts a bit at him, but he doesn't seem to mind. Blinks, you know, sighs, smiles, pats her shoulder or her hand, walks off. I think he's a bit deaf, or maybe he just pretends to be. He's a comfortable sort of man, he doesn't want trouble or strife. They tell me he's very good with his horses, his thoroughbred racers, I mean, which can be quite nervy and difficult to handle. He calms them down.'

'Pats them and smiles.'

'Something like that, I daresay. I've never seen it myself. Horses terrify me, even the ordinary kind.'

'Does *she* terrify you? Lady Henrietta?'

'Heavens, no! She's a dear. Excitable, always in a rush, quite brusque sometimes if you don't fetch what she wants or find what she's lost immediately, but not terrifying, no, far from it. Demanding, yes, but she has the right, doesn't she?'

'The right?'

'She's a grand lady – one of the grandest – and her father won all those battles and saved us from the French. Didn't he have the right to send his soldiers into danger? Doesn't she have the right to expect the best service from her servants?'

'And the right to bestow her favour on other men besides her husband?'

'I don't know what you insinuate with that "favour". She likes sprightly conversation. Don't we all? You think Mr Congreve goes to bed with her? Not as far as I know. He's not very agile, is he, physically? He keeps her amused.'

I believe this was true, at the time, though the town believed otherwise and so did Lady Henrietta's mother, the old Duchess Sarah, whose previously close relationship with her eldest daughter became even more strained and finally broke as my master's grew more intimate. Polly told me that she had called Lady Henrietta 'Congreve's Moll'. Not that he was by any means the sole cause of her displeasure. She thought her daughter had fallen into bad company: not only poets, musicians and theatre people, whose morals were never to be trusted, but also titled hostesses with bad reputations. Duchess Sarah, as we have seen in her dealings with Sir John Vanbrugh, was a person whose need to control everyone around her eventually brought most of her relationships to grief. She lost all influence with Queen Anne on that account and she was on bad terms not only with Lady Henrietta, but also her sister, Lady Mary, married to the second Duke of Montagu.

Duchess Sarah had been generous enough, before she quarrelled with Lady Henrietta, to give her a small lodge in Windsor Park and furnish it herself. Later she wanted to take it back and give it to Lady Henrietta's ne'er-do-well son Lord Blandford, but Lord Godolphin gently dissuaded her. This I learnt not from Polly, but my master, who had it from Lady Henrietta herself. And here I will say a word or two about that son, who was another cause of trouble in that troubled family. You might not imagine that the greatest people, with their dukedoms, their wealth, their property and their hosts of attendants, could be in any way pitiable, but it is so. Of course, like the rest of us, they suffer sickness, the loss of children and loved ones, and their own death. But what they avoid by not being poor or hungry or living in cramped and leaky houses, they inflict on themselves from pride, frustrated ambition, over-indulgence in rich foods and wines, gambling, envy, jealousy, cheating servants and, worst of all, the pointlessness of a life lived to no purpose except to maintain the luxury and ease they were born to and pass it on, whether diminished or augmented, to their heirs.

But if the heir chance to be a Marquis of Blandford – not, I mean, Lady Henrietta's promising brother, the Lord Blandford who died as a student at Cambridge, but the next Lord Blandford, Lady Henrietta's son – then surely all purpose is lost, all future for that unfortunate family becomes a dark corridor. And at the end of that corridor – what? A mortifying sort of looking-glass perhaps, a mirror for monkeys.

This second Lord Blandford was a wastrel and a spendthrift, a young man whose customary tour of the great cities of Europe did not improve his mind or add to his knowledge or widen his interest in culture, but gave him new foreign opportunities for dissipation. His sister Mary called him 'Lord Worthless'. He did not often care to visit his native country, where his worthlessness would be more obvious, and he was kept in funds by his grandmother, Duchess Sarah, as a way of getting back at her daughter. But he did not treat his grandmother any better than his mother, except when he wanted money. Duchess Sarah was one of the guests at a dinner he gave in his house on one of his rare visits to London, but he kept them all waiting for two hours while he dined elsewhere with another lady.

'I wish I was nearer to you, so that I could beat you,' said Duchess Sarah.

'Then I am very glad you are not,' he said, quite unrepentant, and soon abandoned his guests again and went to the theatre.

He married, against the wishes of his family, a Dutch woman from Utrecht, and luckily died before he could inherit and drag his grandfather's hard-earned dukedom into the dirt.

I hope I am not turning moralist in my old age, but whenever we heard of the antics of this youth, I did feel for the family of which my master and I had become almost part. On the other hand, I also thought I understood what made him behave so piggishly. Born to such an inheritance, knowing himself to be weak and inadequate, altogether puny in the mirror of both his grandfathers' achievements, what was he to do except throw himself away? The poor fellow surely despised himself.

Lord Godolphin, I believe, loved his wife and despaired of his son and must have been wounded by the town's view that my master had supplanted him in the affections of Lady Henrietta. I could not, of course, talk about this with Mr Congreve, but I did once venture to ask him why Lord Godolphin never accompanied his wife to the spas.

'Why should he? His health is excellent.'

'Well, but Lady Henrietta's is not.'

'What do you mean?'

'I mean, one might expect him to want to be there to look after her, if she needs to drink the waters.'

'She does not need to drink the waters.'

'But she does.'

'Only as a prophylactic, as a way of avoiding ill health. Ladies, you know, worry more about these things than men.'

'Lord Godolphin seems to be a very obliging man.'

'He is, but what are you implying?'

'That he's content for his wife to spend all this money and time on remedies which she doesn't really need.'

'You are fishing, Jeremy.'

'Fishing, sir?'

'You are trying to discover whether Lady Godolphin visits spas, not to drink the waters, but to get away from her husband.'

'No, sir.'

'Yes, sir.'

'If you say so, sir. Is that the reason?'

'The reason, Jeremy, as you very well know, is that my poor health requires me to visit spas and that Lady Godolphin is so kind as to enjoy my company and go with me.'

I bowed my head and was silent.

'Are you satisfied, Jeremy?'

'I am very happy that it should be so. I also enjoy our excursions.'

'Of course you do. We are both lucky men.'

But I could not think that Lord Godolphin was.

I happened one winter's day to be handing my master out of his hackney carriage on one of his visits to Godolphin House, as Lord Godolphin was emerging from the house and lost his footing on the icy steps. I left Mr Congreve, ran up the steps and helped Lord Godolphin to his feet.

'Thank you,' he said. 'You are a very prompt and obliging fellow. You work for Mr Congreve?'

'I do, my lord.'

'Is he a good master?'

'Very good. I have been with him ever since his first great success in the theatre.'

'And when was that?'

'Ninety-three, my lord.'

'Good Heavens! I was still a boy then. And he cannot have been much older.'

'His genius flowered early.'

'And withered early too, I fear. He does not write much now, does he?'

'Verses, my lord, from time to time. But no more plays.'

'Then he has little to occupy him?'

'He is a Commissioner for Licensing Wines, but, no, that doesn't take a lot of his time.'

I was wondering how I might slide over the fact that most of his time now was devoted to attending Lady Henrietta, but fortunately my master came up the steps and greeted Lord Godolphin with a bow and a lift of his hat. Lord Godolphin responded with a brief 'Mr Congreve!' and made his way gingerly down the steps.

It was soon after this encounter that my master was offered the post of Secretary of Jamaica, with a very substantial salary. Since Queen Anne had just died and the Whigs had returned to power, Mr Congreve took this as recognition by his friends in the party of his value to them, although he was afraid that it meant he would have to go to that distant island in the Caribbean and was not sure he could face such a radical displacement. It occurred to me, however, that this might be Lord Godolphin's doing and that he might be very well pleased to put the Atlantic Ocean between Mr Congreve and Lady Henrietta.

As it turned out, my master was relieved to be granted a special warranty by the Secretary of State for the South – his friend Mr Addison – allowing him to appoint a deputy on the island. So that although he had to share his salary – which still amounted to about £700 a year – he need not leave London. Lady Henrietta, I heard from Polly, was equally relieved, but I don't think Lord Godolphin can have been, whether or not he had had a hand in the appointment.

The Secretaryship of Jamaica caused Mr Congreve some trouble a year or two later, since the deputy he was advised to choose, a Mr Samuel Page, was a keen supporter of Jamaica's Assembly, which was at odds with the newly appointed Governor, Lord Archibald Hamilton, youngest brother of the fourth Duke of Hamilton. Lord Archibald opposed Mr Page's nomination, but Mr Congreve insisted. The Governor then persuaded the island's Council to remove Mr Page for being incompetent. Mr

Page, supported by the Assembly, came secretly to London and told the Board of Trade that the Governor was conspiring with Spanish pirates. Lord Archibald was arrested and brought to London to answer Mr Page's accusation, where he contrived to exonerate himself and bring further accusations against Mr Page. All this was far beyond Mr Congreve's knowledge or, unless he had actually gone to Jamaica himself to investigate, any way of knowing which of the parties, if either, was in the right. He and Mr Page met briefly, but had little to say to one another. Mr Congreve was suffering from a long and painful fit of gout at the time and their worlds and interests, except for the Secretary's salary and the deputy's share of it, were far apart. However, having chosen Mr Page, my master stood by him, although Lord Archibald, previously a distinguished captain in the Royal Navy, clearly had more powerful friends, including the Duke of Marlborough who had influenced his appointment as Governor.

We had just travelled to Ashley in Surrey, so that Mr Congreve could recuperate from his illness at his friend Viscount Shannon's house, when a letter came from the Board of Trade commanding Mr Congreve's attendance to speak for his deputy. He replied that he was not well enough to make the journey, but had already spoken for Mr Page to both the Secretaries of State. And there the matter ended as far as we were concerned. The Board of Trade seems to have lost patience with the whole imbroglio: Lord Archibald was replaced as Governor and Mr Page as deputy Secretary. Mr Congreve, however, was confirmed as Secretary for Jamaica for his lifetime, so that from then on, not changing his modest way of life, he was able to put money in the bank as well as raise my wages.

The Duke of Marlborough died in June of the year 1722. Lady Henrietta, her sister, the Duchess of Montagu, and Lady Henrietta's daughter, the Duchess of Newcastle, all sat with him in his room in Cumberland Lodge, a large house in Windsor Park, on the evening before his death. Duchess Sarah was also there, of course, and when she entered the room the sisters curtsied but did not speak to her. Lady Henrietta's daughter left after saying goodbye to her grandfather, but the sisters remained until the early hours of the morning in the drawing room. My master told me that Duchess Sarah had given instructions to the servants not to serve them with anything to eat or drink and had finally ordered them out of the house. Such was the miserably contentious end of one of the greatest Englishmen, though he had not been entirely in his right mind for some years previously and, having suffered a series of strokes, was perhaps not conscious of this last breaking point between his wife and daughters.

His Will, doubtless the work of Duchess Sarah, left most of his estate to his grandson, Lord Worthless Blandford, and Duchess Sarah herself, who added insult to injury by telling her friends that Lady Henrietta was upset by the Will and wanted to dispute it. Lady Henrietta herself told my master that, on the contrary, she had no quarrel with the Will, since 'covetousness has seemed so very odious in some other people' – her father was notorious for it and she probably also included her mother – 'that I am sometimes frightened I might have the seeds of it in my own blood.'

The duke's death led to a new phase in Mr Congreve's relationship with Lady Henrietta, now Duchess of Marlborough in her own right. It was as if, having lost her father, broken with her mother, ceased to be merely the Countess of Godolphin and acquired her father's title, she saw herself as a new and independent person. She was now over forty years old, so perhaps her age too had something to do with it. My master and I travelled to Bath that summer, by public coach. I was surprised at this and asked him if Lady Henrietta was no longer going to accompany him to take the waters.

'She has arrangements to make,' he said, 'but I think she may follow us in due course.'

He knew perfectly well that she would, for as soon as we reached Bath, we too had arrangements to make. We set about finding and eventually took the lease of a whole suite of rooms in one of the best locations. My master offered no explanation for this unheard-of extravagance and when I raised my eyebrows, said, 'Mind your own business, Jeremy, and wait for Act Two!'

Sure enough, after several days, Lady Henrietta and all her equipage arrived, drawing up as if by chance – but he must have given her the address in a letter I had posted for him – at this same house and asking for a lease of the very rooms we had already taken. The landlady, crestfallen to think that she had let her rooms to a nobody when she might have had the new Duchess of Marlborough, asked me to ask my master if he really needed the whole suite. Of course he didn't. He gallantly gave up all the rooms but one to the great lady and that one happened to be at the end of the corridor, immediately opposite the master bedroom, which was now to be the duchess's own chamber.

'Oh, sir!' I said. 'What a fine plot you've constructed here! I look forward to Act Three.'

'Jeremy,' he said, 'I want no more of your leaping eyebrows or your theatrical metaphors. Keep your wit to please your Polly!'

Polly and I had rooms in the attic and we – the whole ménage – stayed for the rest of the season, well into the autumn. My master had not seemed so blithe or agile for many years and I do not think it was due to any medical treatment he received or nasty mineral water he drank. As for the beautiful Lady Henrietta, always laughing at Mr Congreve's low-voiced witticisms, smiling sweetly at the people in the street who bowed and curtsied to her, she looked radiantly happy and more like a girl of twenty than a woman of over forty. Polly told me she had never seen her in such high spirits. Mr Gay, the author of The Beggar's Opera, was also visiting Bath for his health at this time, and often joined Mr Congreve and Lady Henrietta for suppers, concerts and expeditions into the countryside. Mr Gay was a very ribald man and had all three of them almost choking with laughter. This was particularly hard for Lady Henrietta, Polly told me, since, dressed in mourning for her father's death, she had to try, in any public place, to restrain her good humour and look suitably serious. It was not that she did not miss her father and feel sorrow at losing him, but really the father she had known and loved had been gone for several years before he died.

The following year, after Christmas, Mr Congreve was invited to join Lady Henrietta at her little lodge in Windsor Park – the one her mother had given her and then tried to take back to give to Lord Blandford. Lady Henrietta was again in high spirits and, since the lodge was very private, did not have to pretend otherwise. Mr Congreve was less ebullient, he never relished the winter, and the lodge, in spite of roaring fires and surrounding trees, seemed to be exposed to every wind that blew. But I judged that he was not feeling discomfort from the weather so much as from his anomalous situation. Lord Godolphin was not staying in the lodge. It was as if he had surrendered his place as Lady Henrietta's husband to my master.

I was never entirely certain that my master had crossed the corridor in our Bath lodgings from his room to hers. I got no light on the matter from him, though Polly said that he had. But we all knew that he spent nights with Lady Henrietta in her chamber in the lodge and she at least made no attempt to hide the fact. Indeed, she behaved more than ever like a much younger woman, almost like a new bride on her honeymoon, touching him frequently, leaning close to him at meals, enquiring tenderly after his health each morning. When the sun shone they went riding together, without any attendant, on dark or wet days they played cards or sat by the fire, talking or reading books or magazines. She, I mean, was usually reading to him, since his sight was so poor. It was altogether a strange business to see this inveterate bachelor, my old master – he had just passed his fifty-third birthday – thus take on the role of a married man with an adoring wife, roles he had only allotted in his plays to those ridiculous characters Lord and Lady Froth in *The Double-Dealer*.

When we returned to London in the early spring, Mr Congreve was still a regular guest at Godolphin House, where Lord Godolphin himself was once more the husband in residence. But Polly told me that relations between him and Lady Henrietta were very strained. She ceased to go out to the theatre or to parties and, except for a few special guests, including Mr Congreve, there were few visitors to the house.

The reason was soon apparent: Lady Henrietta was pregnant. Some people said that she was too ashamed to appear in public. Others shook their heads and said she was keeping her bed in the hope of saving her own life and that of the child, but that it must end badly, since the mother was too old for child-bearing. Few people, fortunately, were aware that Lord Godolphin had not been with her at the lodge in Windsor Park, and those that were kept their counsel.

Since the pregnancy was common knowledge and my master continued to visit Godolphin House, I dared to ask him if Lady Henrietta was confined to her bed.

'No, certainly not,' he said.

'She is quite confident, then, that all will be well?'

'You know her character. She is a brave person. If she feels fear, she does not care to show it.'

'Takes after her father?'

He looked up from the desk at which he had been writing a letter and smiled at me. Our relationship ever since he had become such a close friend of Lady Henrietta had been much less open than in the past. I remained his faithful retainer, but more the servant than the friend. This off-hand remark of mine seemed to restore our former alliance.

'You are right, Jeremy, and I hadn't thought of that.'

With this encouragement, I dared to probe further. 'Lord Godolphin must be worried.'

'He is standing by her.'

'And if the child is born alive?'

'I believe he will recognise it.'

'He has told her so?'

'He has told me so. Whatever people may say about Lord Godolphin's intellect, whatever I have thought about it myself in the past, I can say that I have met very few men of his emotional intelligence. He could behave one way and ruin the lives of his wife, the child and himself. Most men might do that out of misplaced pride, anger, vindictiveness or mere conventionality. He must feel some or all of those things himself, but he chooses to put them aside. He loves her, you see, for her courage, her beauty, even for her waywardness and independence.'

'As you do, sir.'

'Very well, Jeremy!'

He returned to his letter, dismissing me, but before I could leave the room turned back.

'Lord Godolphin, I find, deserves the greatest respect. He is entirely without affectation. His seeming sleepiness and slowness are his method of controlling himself. He is the exact opposite of all the monkeys that infest our nation, a gentleman through and through.'

Lady Henrietta's child was born towards the end of November in the year 1723. She was named Mary and was always known as Lady Mary Godolphin, until, many years after Mr Congreve's death, and after her mother's too, she married the fourth Duke of Leeds. The bride was given away by her still-surviving father, Lord Godolphin.

12

THE PEBBLE ALCOVE

Not far from the Temple of Friendship is the Pebble Alcove, designed by Mr Kent. It is a substantial stone shelter, a semi-cylinder with an open, arched front framed in rough-cast stone, pillars in relief and a triangular pediment. The curving back wall inside is set with a mosaic of coloured pebbles: Lord Cobham's coat of arms, supported by a red and gold lion rampant and a rearing white horse, while dotted around it are various small motifs also made of pebbles: flowers, birds, a cow, a cat, a mermaid, a scorpion, a butterfly, a dragonfly, a star, a crescent moon, etc. I suspect that Mr Kent encouraged the ladies and gentlemen staying in the house at the time to set these playful little images at random into the white plaster. The motto, picked out in black pebbles under the coat of arms, is *Templa quam dilecta* ('How lovely the temples'), punning on Lord Cobham's family name and appropriate to this landscape so prodigally furnished with temples. The semi-circular ceiling is also decorated with pebbles, bands of leafy and linear patterns swirling out from a central boss above the coat of arms. Mr Kent, I think, never let his imagination fly so freely, unless it was in designing Mr Congreve's strange monkey-monument now sited on a little island in the lake, only a pebble's throw from the shore in front of the Pebble Alcove.

I go there quite often and sit on the curving bench inside the Alcove, looking out at my master's monument and calling up my memories of our life together. Sometimes I almost feel he is seated beside me, murmuring in his soft, smiling, slightly caustic voice, 'Must you, Jeremy? Didn't I warn you against turning author? Are you really up to this? Let the monkeys do their worst to my reputation! In Latin? Really! What a show-off you are, Dr Fetch! And I always thought you such a modest, pragmatic fellow. Why not just enjoy your retirement in this English Elysium and let the dead lie in ease and quiet?'

'Was that really all you wanted, sir?' I would like to reply. 'Ease and quiet? Your favourite phrase. And now the ease and quiet of non-existence? I don't think so. I think you meant to leave us with an enigmatic ghost, a person whose outward life looked plain and ordinary enough, but was the covering, like this sturdy alcove, for a more than ordinary burst of colour and energy, wit and invention, sufficient to spark and crackle long beyond its own time. And why was I born, if not to draw attention to your persistent ghost?'

One day, I think it was in the year 1741, I was sitting in the Alcove absorbed in recalling those early years of his great theatrical successes, when Lord Cobham himself came in and sat down at the other end of the bench. I stood up immediately, bowed and would have removed myself. We servants were all somewhat more intimidated by him than usual, since he had been heard only the day before administering a furious verbal whipping to his steward. Mr Roberts had been particularly close to him for many years, but had somehow presented faulty accounts, perhaps by mistake or perhaps after surreptitiously helping himself from them. At any rate, Lord Cobham had threatened him with dismissal.

'Please sit down, Jeremy!' said Lord Cobham. 'I did not wish to disturb you.'

'But, my lord—'

'I asked you to sit down,' he said, more peremptorily. 'I meant it.'

I did as I was told, but could not feel much at ease. We sat there for a long time in silence. After a while I glanced at my companion and was surprised to see that he had his head in hands. Does he still feel such sorrow for his old friend so long after his death? I wondered. The silence continued. I began to feel more and more uncomfortable and at last risked speaking.

'I believe, my lord, that Mr Congreve would have made a jest of our sorrow, but would have been touched none the less.'

'Congreve? Oh, yes, no doubt. How is your book progressing?'

'It is slow work, my lord, but I am pleased with it in parts.'

'Good. Good.'

Again silence, until he suddenly said, 'Did you not hear what happened today, Jeremy?'

'Today, my lord? I don't think so. I have been walking about the grounds or sitting here on my own all morning.'

'Roberts has killed himself.'

'Mr William Roberts, the steward?'

'I was too harsh with him. He had done wrong, but I have a bad temper.'

I was at a loss what to say. I hardly knew Mr Roberts and my only point of contact with Lord Cobham up to now had been our mutual regard for Mr Congreve. But Lord Cobham continued to look at me as if he expected some response.

'Suicide is an extreme measure to take, my lord. He must have blamed himself.'

'Would you do the same if I were to reprimand you?'

'I, my lord? I hope I should never give occasion for it.'

'But if you did and I spoke to you as severely as I did to Roberts?'

'Not I, my lord. I should be very cast down, of course, but I think I would value my life above my pride.'

'Yes, of course. I injured his pride and now he has injured mine. We are quits, I suppose.'

Not quite, I thought, since he is dead and you are not, but did not say so.

'Pride makes monkeys of us all,' he said, looking across to Mr Congreve's monument, 'as your former master understood so well. I daresay that when Walpole took exception to my voting against his Excise Bill and dismissed me from my regiment, my pride was as wounded as Roberts's was yesterday. Yet I did not do away with myself. Instead, I took revenge by turning these grounds into a demonstration of British liberty and a protest against his tyranny and corruption. And my silent revenge in stone has not been in vain. So many people from our own and other nations come here now to admire the place – and, I trust, share the sentiments it expresses – that I have had to build that inn up there behind us to accommodate them. What do you think? Am I quits with Walpole?'

'More than quits, my lord. Mr Walpole can hardly remain in power for ever. If people remember him at all in the future, it will doubtless be as the person Lord Cobham justly reprimanded here at Stowe.'

Lord Cobham rose, picked up his walking stick and said with a smile, 'You are a credit to your master, Jeremy.'

'Thank you, my lord.'

'Did he often reprimand you?'

'From time to time.'

'Justly?'

'Not invariably.'

'Severely?'

'I wouldn't say severely, my lord. He was a gentle man, seldom angry, but occasionally irritable. Considering how he suffered from the pains of gout, I could not blame him for that.'

Lord Cobham moved away, but turned towards me again. 'I am very sorry for Roberts's death, very sorry that I wounded his pride so fatally. But what's done is done.' And, tipping his hat to Mr Congreve's monument: 'Very foolish monkeys we are.'

Then he set off walking briskly in the direction of the Lake Pavilions.

Lord Cobham was not content with what he called his 'silent revenge in stone'. He was also indoctrinating a bevy of young men with his views on liberty and his opposition to Mr Walpole.

Most of these young men were his nephews (he had no children of his own), sons of his younger sisters Mrs Maria West, Mrs Hester Grenville and Lady Christian Lyttelton. 'The cubs', as he called them, all born in the early years of the century, were now in their twenties or thirties. Several were Members of Parliament, including Lord Cobham's destined heir, Mr Richard Grenville, and a close friend of his from their schooldays at Eton, Mr William Pitt, who together led the notorious 'Boy Patriots' or 'Patriot Band' which opposed Mr Walpole in the House of Commons.

I should explain that all these politicians were Whigs. Ever since the death of Queen Anne, the Tories, associated as some of them were with Jacobite conspiracies and rebellions, had been a minority in Parliament and excluded from power with the full support of our new Hanoverian kings, George I and George II, who owed their throne to the Whigs. And just as Mr Robert Walpole himself had risen to power by displacing his Whig predecessors, Lords Stanhope and Sunderland, after the South Sea Bubble debacle, so the 'Patriot Band' aimed to displace Mr Walpole without loosening the Whigs' grip on power.

These young men often visited Stowe and brought new life and energy to the place, playing games of cricket in the summer, billiards and other indoor games in the winter, shooting pheasants and partridges in the autumn. Mr Pitt especially shone at cricket, turning that stately, tactical game into something more exciting and even dangerous by frequently hitting the hard ball into the trees around the church, and I think once nearly killing the vicar as he walked through the churchyard. This was no longer the rotund, good-living, former military chaplain, Mr Conway Rand, who had died a few years after I came to Stowe and whose suitably substantial memorial stone now adorns the floor of the church's chancel, but his slimmer and more austere successor Mr Henry Gabell.

A year or so after my encounter with Lord Cobham in the Pebble Alcove, I was seated there again, this time wondering what I should say of Mr Congreve's middle years, when I heard a great noise of shouting from the direction of the Temple of Friendship. Evidently some celebration was going on and, having already heard rumours, I had half guessed what it might be when the shouting grew louder and nearer. A minute or two later a dozen at least of the cubs in full cry came round the corner, bottles in their hands and at their lips, carrying their uncle on a chair raised to the level of their shoulders. Lord Cobham, flushed and clearly a little uncertain of his safety, noticed me as I rose from my seat and bowed.

'Jeremy!' he called out above the din from his retinue. 'You were right!'

'My lord?'

'That he couldn't last for ever.'

'Mr Walpole, then...?'

'Cock Robin's out!' shouted the cubs. 'Finished! Resigned! Who killed Cock Robin? We killed Cock Robin! Victory to the Patriots! Victory to Stowe! Victory to Lord Cobham!'

I followed them at a distance as they progressed from temple to temple, gathering visitors to the grounds as they went. Arriving finally at the house, they set their uncle in his chair down at the top of the steps in front of the great portico and sang 'For he's a jolly good fellow' and 'Rule Britannia! Britannia rule the waves, Britons never never never shall be slaves'. This catchy song from Mr Arne's masque *Alfred* had been first heard two years earlier at a garden party given at his country mansion, Cliveden, by the Prince of Wales. He was a friend of Lord Cobham, sometimes visited Stowe, and was an enthusiastic patron of the arts, especially music – he himself played the viola and cello – as well as of cricket matches, in which he also took part himself. Always at odds with his father King George II, who ruled in close association with Mr Walpole, Prince Frederick supported Mr Walpole's opponents and, being much the same age as the cubs, could almost be counted a Patriot Boy himself.

Mr Walpole's downfall, apparently, had been caused by a most trivial matter, a dispute in the House of Commons about a by-election in the town of Chippenham. Mr Walpole had made the motion one of 'no confidence', had lost the vote and so had no alternative but to resign. Perhaps he had had enough of government after forty years in and out of it, though he now entered the House of Lords as Earl of Orford and continued to exert some influence on politics, especially through his friendship with the king.

But we had entered a new era and Stowe itself, now that its most immediate purpose had been fulfilled, might almost seem to have sunk back into history. Lord Cobham, however, although he was nearly seventy years old, was galvanised by his nephew and heir, Mr Richard Grenville, and his ambitious head gardener, young Mr Brown, into building on an even grander scale than before – notably his own lofty monument and the mighty Grecian Temple – and refashioning the landscape around them.

I have strayed far beyond Mr Congreve's lifetime and cannot expect to enjoy much more of my own as we approach the middle of this eighteenth century. If I should outlive Lord Cobham I am not sure how I shall be treated by Mr Grenville. He is perfectly polite on the few occasions we meet and his father as well as his uncle was a friend of my master, for we visited his estate at Wotton, but I once heard him say to Mr Pitt, after I had stood aside to let them pass in a corridor, 'That old fellow is one of my uncle's more eccentric pensioners. He's writing a life of uncle's friend Congreve. In Latin. Can you imagine?'

'A labour of love, I suppose,' Mr Pitt was kind enough to say.

'Love's labour's lost, I should think,' said Mr Grenville.

He may be right. But Mr Pitt is right too, for whether or not I ever finish my manuscript and whatever may become of it, I take pleasure in working on it and it lends purpose to my life. And, after all, but for this labour of love I might still be one of Lord Cobham's footmen, eating in the servants' hall, instead of his assistant archivist, eating on ordinary occasions at his own table.

Mr Congreve's last years, in spite of his worsening health, were made happy not only by the love of Lady Henrietta but even more by his love for their daughter Mary. How he adored her and how she, once she had begun to walk and talk, loved to be with him! So far as she knew, he was not her father. Lord Godolphin had accepted that name and to do him credit, behaved to her like a father, though he was often absent. My master, so often present in Lady Henrietta's little lodge in Windsor Park or in lodgings at Bath, was her Uncle Will. She would sit on his knee while he told her stories or he would act out little scenes with her dolls, or they would carry on domestic dramas together in her dolls' house. Lady Henrietta was not jealous of the attention he gave to Mary, but sat and watched them with delight. I came in once bringing them cups of chocolate and found him down on the carpet pretending to be a lion and growling at her. Lady Henrietta was teasing him: 'You sound more like a dog than a lion.'

Growl, growl! 'Coming to bite your head off, Mary!'

'No, you're not. You're not really a lion,' said the child.

'What am I then?' *Growl, growl*!

'You sound like a DOG and you're really Uncle Will,' she said, laughing so much that Lady Henrietta and Mr Congreve began to laugh too and I had to put my tray down quickly on a table as my own shoulders started to shake.

'Oh dear!' he said. 'And I did think I was a lion. Well, we live and learn. Chocolate is that, Jeremy? I suppose that proves I'm not a lion. Lions must get very hoarse with all that roaring, but nobody ever brings them chocolate.'

He dragged himself to a chair and with difficulty got into it to drink his chocolate. Mary followed him and climbed up on the arm of the chair beside him, nearly upsetting his cup.

'Clumsy little monster!' he said.

'I'm not a monster. You're the monster.'

'But you told me I was really Uncle Will.'

She laid her head on his shoulder.

'Nice monster!' she said.

'You should have been a father,' said Lady Henrietta.

'But never could find a wife,' he said.

'Poor Uncle Will! Wouldn't anyone have you?'

'Not anyone that I would have.'

'I would have you,' said the child.

'Would you, my darling? But I'm afraid you are still too young,' he said.

'But when I grow up.'

'Then I shall be too old,' he said.

Mary looked sad.

'But you are very old now,' she said. 'I don't mind you being old.'

'Cheer up, Mary!' said Lady Henrietta. 'You have him now and so do I. We don't need to marry him to have him, do we?'

I wish Mr Congreve had lived long enough to see his darling married to Thomas Osborne, the fourth Duke of Leeds. That was in the year 1740, when he was twenty-seven and she was seventeen. It was not just a dynastic marriage between the Godolphins and the Osbornes. Lady Mary and her Duke were in love with each other and at their very fashionable wedding in June she wore the magnificent diamond necklace and earrings which her mother had bought with the money Mr Congreve left her in his Will.

Lady Henrietta too was dead by the time of Lady Mary's marriage, but it must have been the deep love she had experienced as a child from both her parents that caused her to remain, even after she had lost them, such a loving and much loved young woman. When somebody once asked Lady Henrietta why her little daughter was not allowed out of doors on a fine day, she replied, 'Miss is not well, somewhat feverish, and if she went out, perhaps might fancy the sun or the moon – things she can't have. But everything that is under them she may and shall have.'

She was ten years old when her mother died, but Lord Godolphin lived on and took care of her. Her much older sister, the Duchess of Newcastle, who also loved her dearly, would have liked to, but her husband forbade it, although they had no children of their own. Even her termagant grandmother, old Duchess Sarah, was fond of her, gave her more diamonds for her wedding and said that if anything made her wish to go on living it was to be able to see more of those two young married lovers. I find my eyes full of tears when I think of how the love of Mr Congreve and Lady Henrietta for each other was crowned and perpetuated like this, though they could not know it.

My master and Lady Henrietta, Duchess of Marlborough in her own right since her father's death in the year 1722, were often together, but not as often as they would have liked. There was always some cover to their relationship, even if no one was deceived: he was a guest at her little lodge in Windsor Park or he was taking the waters at Bath and so it happened was she. Our excursions to Bath became more prolonged, but we still made visits to Stowe and to Lord Shannon's house at Ashley in Surrey, which was not too far from Mr Congreve's friends at Twickenham, Mr Pope and Lady Mary Wortley Montagu. Lady Henrietta was, I think, a little jealous of this Lady Mary, who almost worshipped my master, and did not like them to meet. But when Lady Mary began to promote inoculations for smallpox, which she had learnt about during her time as our ambassador's wife in Constantinople, Lady Henrietta trusted her so far as to have her little daughter Mary inoculated. This was against the advice of many doctors, most of her friends and the view of Christian theologians that inoculation was contrary to the divine purpose of disease, namely to punish the wicked or test the faith of the innocent, as God had tested Job's faith with a plague of boils. Lady Henrietta had, as I once remarked to my master, inherited her father the great duke's calculating courage.

When we were not at Bath or visiting friends, we still lived in our lodgings in Mr Porter's house in Surrey Street. Mrs Bracegirdle's mother had died, but Bracey herself, retired from the stage, still lived there with the Porters, her sister and brother-in-law. I was amused and intrigued by her relationship with Mr Congreve. They remained friends of a sort, wary friends, friends who knew each other inside-out. They were almost like an old married couple, except that they no longer shared a bed or saw each other every day, and were studiously polite to each other, with an underlying hint of contention. There were dinners, of course, with the Porters from time to time, when they both attended and I was one of the servers.

I remember particularly an occasion when they had all been to see Sir Richard Steele's new play *The Conscious Lovers* the day before. Captain Steele had been expelled from Parliament by the Tories for his fierce attacks on them in print, but reinstated and knighted after the death of Queen Anne and the return of the Whigs to power, and was now the manager of Drury Lane Theatre. There were other friends of the Porters present at the dinner who had not seen the play and asked Mr Congreve for his opinion of it.

'A travesty of a play originally written by Terence,' he said.

'You are too harsh,' said Bracey. 'I liked it and so did the audience.'

'It was well acted, especially by Mrs Oldfield,' said my master, smiling provocatively. The rise of Mrs Oldfield's star was generally thought to be the cause of Bracey's retirement.

'She did well enough,' said Bracey. 'But Booth and Wilkes were admirable and so was Colley Cibber's direction.'

'It's certainly a play perfectly suited to Cibber's taste and talent,' said Mr Congreve.

'So you consider it worth seeing?' asked one of the other guests.

'If you like sentimental tosh, served up with lashings of moralistic cant.'

He was seldom so crushingly critical even among close friends. Was it Bracey he wanted to wound or was he still tilting at the long shadow Mr Collier had cast over the theatre?

'Mr Congreve is a fervent admirer of Terence,' said Bracey, 'so his opinion of Sir Richard's adaptation may be a little prejudiced.'

'I am also an admirer of Steele,' said Mr Congreve, 'but as a journalist not as a playwright.'

'Shouldn't admirers be more tender in their criticism?' asked Bracey.

'I am sacrificing my friend Steele in order to be tender to our friends here by advising them to seek better entertainment.'

'It's a pity that you've given up providing it yourself, if you are so dissatisfied with other people's work,' said Bracey.

'But when I did try to provide it I was frustrated by the desertion of the person for whom it was written.'

My master was referring to Bracey's refusal to take the part of Semele in his opera of that name. Bracey flushed and was momentarily silenced, and before she could reply Mr Porter intervened to break off this increasingly personal dispute:

'Well, we are caught between the opinions of a famous dramatist and a famous actress. Personally I tend to agree with the dramatist.'

'And I with the actress,' said Mrs Porter judiciously.

Conscious Lovers? I thought from my place beside the sideboard, but here we have two people all too conscious of being ex-lovers. I don't know whether the other guests, who looked bewildered, chose to see the play or not, but most theatregoers did, it was very successful, and Sir Richard's creditors as well as he himself must have been pleased.

Mr Congreve, however, was not pleased with that little storm in a dinner party. As we retired afterwards to our own apartment, I heard him muttering, 'Sorry, sorry, sorry!'

'Sir?'

'No business of yours, Jeremy.'

'Sorry, sir!'

'Don't be impudent! I can do without that ready repartee of yours.'

I said nothing, but as I followed him into his bedroom to help him undress, he added, 'I wish sometimes that I could do without my own.'

He did not so much mind, I'm sure, having tussled with Bracey as having spoken so dismissively of Sir Richard's play. He was very fond of Sir Richard, for the troubles of one sort or another he seemed to attract and for the robust way he struggled to overcome them.

'The gallant captain,' he said to me once after Sir Richard's latest release from debtors' prison, 'sometimes seems to steer his ship straight on to the rocks, but somehow veers off them and sets full sail again in a new direction.'

Sir Richard in return was one of Mr Congreve's keenest admirers and, when others had slighted *The Way of the World*, wrote the 'Commendatory Verses' which prefaced the second volume of *The Works of William Congreve*:

> You give us Torment, and you give us Ease,
> And vary our Afflictions as you please.
> Is not a Heart so kind as yours in Pain,
> To load your Friends with Cares you only feign;
> Your Friends in Grief, composed yourself, to leave?
> But 'tis the only Way you'll e'er deceive,
> Then still, great Sir, your moving Power employ,
> To lull our Sorrow, and correct our Joy.

Sir Richard's dedication of a book of *Poetical Miscellanies* to my master, which I quoted in a previous chapter, praised his character as wholeheartedly as his work:

> As much as I Esteem You for Your Excellent Writings, by which You are an Honour to our Nation; I chuse rather, as one that has passed many Happy Hours with You, to celebrate the easie Condescension of Mind, and Command of a pleasant Imagination, which give You the uncommon Praise of a Man of Wit, always to please and never to offend. No one, after a joyful Evening, can reflect upon an Expression of Mr *Congreve*'s, that dwells upon him with Pain.

Mr Congreve could not help but recall that passage after what he had said at the Porters' dinner party and reflect that he had not only contradicted it, but done so at its author's, his true friend's expense. But it was surely his nearly but not quite extinct relationship with Bracey that caused him to behave so uncharacteristically.

A year or two after the success of *The Conscious Lovers*, Sir Richard was struck down with paralysis. He retired to his estranged wife's property in Wales, where she had lived in retreat from his constant struggles with creditors and bailiffs. She was already dead, however, and he was cared for by his two surviving daughters. He died later in the same year as Mr Congreve, though he was a couple of years younger, and I should think he grieved for Mr Congreve as much as my master would have done for him.

Most of my master's friends were some years older than him and not many survived him. Lord Halifax, his early patron, with whom and Sir John Vanbrugh he had cooled himself in the fountain at Hampton Court, died only a year after returning to power as Lord Treasurer in the new reign of King George I. Sir John died a year or two before my master. The genial doctor and poet, Sir Samuel Garth, knighted by King George on the quayside at Greenwich at the same time as Sir John, died in the year 1719. Mr Addison, a little younger than Mr Congreve, died in that year too. Mr Congreve's school-friend Mr Keally was long dead. It occurs to me now that although I thought my master too young to die in his late fifties, only Sir John of all these friends lived to be any older.

Mr Congreve's father, Colonel Congreve, died in the year 1708, having retired six years before from his stewardship in Ireland to lodgings in London, not so very far from ours. He also had a house in the village of Northall, in Buckinghamshire. My master visited his parents frequently, both in London and the country. He was their only child, after all, and their chief pleasure was to see him, hear his gossip and admire him for the renown he had won for himself and their name. Not that they did not often criticise him for failing to add to his renown by writing more plays. They thought – or at least his father did – that he had become lazy and, if he pleaded his gout, his father would say that he too suffered from gout but it had not prevented him carrying out his duties at Lismore.

'He tells me I am too young to retire,' Mr Congreve complained to me, 'and I tell him that I have not retired, except from writing plays. He tells me that it looks like retirement. I reply that I have written an opera and several long poems. He says he doesn't consider that writing verse is a full-time occupation. Anyone can do it, he says, politicians, doctors, lawyers, even soldiers, in their spare time. "Do you do it?" I ask. "Of course not," he replies, "I don't have the talent or the skill and besides I'm old and retired."'

After his father's death, Mr Congreve made sure of seeing his mother, who had sold the house in Northall, at least once a week when he was in town. She had many friends visiting from Ireland, of course, and made new ones in London. She died in the spring of the year 1715 and my master, very distressed, arranged her funeral at St Clement Danes church in the Strand, as he had his father's seven years earlier.

Who remained? Lord Cobham, of course, and my master's other most regular host in the country, major-general Henry Boyle, Viscount Shannon, who had fought in the Battle of the Boyne and was a cousin of Colonel Congreve's employer in Ireland, the Earl of Cork; the poets Mr Pope and Mr Gay; the musician Mr John Eccles, some twenty years older than my master, but who lived well into his eighties; Dr Swift, who outlived Mr Congreve by many years but was usually over the sea in Ireland; and that clever and now very rich publisher, old Mr Tonson, though we saw him only once more after he retired in the year 1720 to the house and orchard he had bought far away in Herefordshire.

Mr Tonson left his nephew, also called Jacob, to manage his business and, before he left London, gave a grand farewell party for the Kit-Cats that summer at his house in Barn Elms. The guests, who travelled there on a decorated barge up the Thames, were led by the Duke of Newcastle. Although he was one of the youngest members of the Club, he had become its principal patron and even, when Mr Tonson was absent, its chairman. But this gathering was not confined to male Kit-Cats. The Duke of

Newcastle was accompanied by his Duchess (Lady Henrietta's daughter Lady Harriet), while the other guests included Sir John Vanbrugh and his new wife, Lord Cobham and his, Lord Shannon, Mr Walpole and many others. It was a mildly disturbing event, my master told me on his return, for the walls in Mr Tonson's house were covered with Sir Godfrey Kneller's portraits of the Kit-Cats and here were their originals, somewhat older and looking, he said, 'considerably more lived-in', drinking and dining beneath them.

'How did you feel about your own?' I asked.

'It was too chuffy when he painted it,' he said. 'I'm afraid I have grown more like it outwardly, though less so in spirit.'

'In spirit?'

'It depicts a very self-confident, not to say arrogant young man.'

'That was never you, sir.'

'Not self-confident or arrogant?'

'Never arrogant, sir. Self-confident, perhaps.'

'Was I ever self-confident?'

'You had gained your place in the world.'

'How can you say so? I had been lambasted by that reverend fanatic, Collier, my last play was no great success, our Haymarket theatre project had failed, my income was pitifully small. What had I to be confident about?'

'The best judges considered you to be our leading poet.'

'My friends, yes, they supported my good opinion of myself. And I suppose if one sits for a portrait at all one must consider oneself somebody worth being portrayed. But it was quite a shock, to see that preening young fellow.'

What could I say? Although he was fifty years old when we had this conversation, he had been nearly forty when the portrait was painted and I did not remember it being in any way 'preening'. Sir Godfrey had painted a successful gentleman-poet in his prime, and my master's reaction to it seemed to me to be another example of his ambivalent attitude to his reputation, his desire to keep the person separate from the work. Mr Giles

Jacob had expressed this well in his *Poetical Register*, published the previous year after a friendly interview with Mr Congreve at our lodgings:

> He does not show so much the Poet as the Gentleman; he is ambitious of few Praises, tho' he deserves numerous Encomiums; he is genteel and regular in Oeconomy, unaffected in Behaviour, pleasing and informing in his Conversation, and respectful to all.

But whatever the various emotions – pleasure, dismay, amusement – with which the living Kit-Cats viewed their younger selves on the walls of Mr Tonson's house, the chief emotion, Mr Congreve said, was sadness at seeing so many painted faces which were now all that existed of their owners. No one would miss the murderous Lord Mohun, dead in yet another duel. But four poets were gone: Mr Addison, Sir Samuel Garth, Mr Maynwaring and Mr Walsh. So were four leading Whig politicians who had devised and directed most of the great changes since the Glorious Revolution: old Lord Dorset, Lords Halifax, Somers and Wharton. Mr Stepney, ambassador to the Austrian Emperor and translator of the classics, was dead in his forties, and General Tidcomb in his seventies. He was another of the military Kit-Cats Mr Congreve found particularly sympathetic. Born before the Civil War, a friend and fellow-roisterer of Lord Dorset after the Restoration, Colonel Tidcomb, as he then was, had led a column of King James's deserting soldiers to join King William's invasion.

'So it was a somewhat melancholy occasion?' I suggested.

'Oh no, we enjoyed ourselves, ate and drank too much, laughed a lot at each other's sallies. But yes, tinged with melancholy. Old times, old faces staring down at us. The swansong of the Kit-Cats, I suppose. *Eheu! fugaces labuntur anni* (Alas! the fleeting years slide away). They slid for Horace, they slide for me and even for you, Jeremy. How old are you now?'

'I cannot say, sir. About your own age?'

'Fifty! No, Jeremy, you must be much younger. You lead such a comfortable life, never ill, never anxious. You sleep so soundly that if I need your help at night I have to shout like the victim of a footpad. You will outlast us all. It's by having no birthday, you see, that you escape the fleeting years. Yes, that's the answer. We should all forget our birthdays.'

He had certainly drunk well at Mr Tonson's party and paid for it next day with a serious attack of gout.

In those years after the end of the war with France, the succession of King George and the triumphant return of the Whigs, when Mr Congreve at last had a reliable income as Secretary for Jamaica (and after his mother's death inherited his parents' savings), he wrote a few poems, but none of the more public kind. Some of his old translations of Ovid's *Metamorphoses* were published in a splendid folio edition by Mr Tonson in the year 1717, together with other translations by his dead friends, Mr Dryden and Mr Maynwaring, and by the still living Sir Samuel Garth and Mr Addison, then at the height of his career as Secretary of State for the South. Mr Congreve, however, was chiefly occupied with the revised edition of his own collected *Works*. He also paid a debt that was long due, by editing Mr Dryden's *Dramatic Works*.

Published, of course, by Mr Tonson, these six volumes in duodecimo were dedicated to the Duke of Newcastle, who had undertaken to commission a monument to Mr Dryden in Westminster Abbey.

In some very Elegant, tho' very partial Verses [Mr Congreve wrote], which he did me the Honour to write to me, he recommended it to me to *be kind to his Remains* [...] You, my Lord, have furnish'd me with ample Means of acquitting my self, both of my Duty and Obligation to my *departed Friend*. What kinder Office lyes in me, to do to these, his most valuable and unperishable Remains, than to commit them to the Protection, and lodge them under the roof of a Patron, whose Hospitality has extended it self even to his Dust?

However, it was not, after all, the young Duke of Newcastle who commissioned Mr Dryden's monument, but some years later the old Duke of Buckingham. The Duke of Newcastle is still alive, as I write this, and was for many years Mr Walpole's chief colleague and perhaps, after Mr Walpole himself, the most powerful politician in the country, so I am chary of repeating my master's comments on his failure to erect Mr Dryden's monument. But no one will be able to read this manuscript until I am dead and anyway it is written in Latin, so here goes:

'The man is a flippertigibbet,' said Mr Congreve angrily as we came away from the unveiling ceremony, 'throws his promises about like his great wealth, but cannot be counted on for anything but his own advancement. It's bad enough having to write these lengthy toadying dedications to people who give something in return, but to have flattered this unreliable young fop makes me want to throw up.'

'At any rate,' I said, 'it will be a lasting shame to him to be praised so highly for something he has failed to do, knowing that his empty promise remains in print for all to read.'

'The fellow has no shame. It's I who feel shame for this futile sycophancy.'

'But you did it not for him, but Mr Dryden.'

'True. In amongst my bowings and scrapings to Newcastle I did at least smuggle in my love and respect for Dryden.'

'Who has got his monument, after all.'

'True. But no thanks to that jumped-up duke of vanity.'

My master's reputation for good temper and kind words was not false. It was usually only to me that he sometimes showed his real feelings. It was almost as if I were part of himself and indeed, as I write down my memories of him, it is almost as if he has become part of me.

Mr Congreve's cousin Colonel Ralph Congreve died towards the end of the year 1725, naming my master one of his executors, and it was this event, I think, which made my master finally decide to make his own Will, though he had had it in mind ever

since the birth of Lady Henrietta's daughter Mary two years
before. His Will left small legacies to Colonel Ralph's widow and
her daughter, and to his other military cousin, Colonel William
Congreve and his son, my master's godson; as well as to Lord
Cobham, Lord Shannon, Mrs Bracegirdle, her sister Mrs Porter
and his old fat friend Mr Charles Mein; and still smaller sums
to Mr Porter's servants and Lady Henrietta's housekeeper, Mrs
Ann Jellet. He left nothing to me. Why not? Firstly, he told me,
because he would arrange with Lord Cobham for me to go to
serve him at Stowe; and secondly because I knew where he kept
his secret store of gold coins, laid up in case his investments in
the Bank of England failed, and where the key was, and he hoped
I would empty the drawer into my own pocket before anyone
else entered the apartment. They would be worth, he reckoned,
rather more than any of his legacies. But if it appeared in the
Will that I was doing better than any of his friends or relations,
people might assume that our relationship was something more
than that of a gentleman and his manservant.

'Of course it is,' he added, 'but not in the way that ill-natured
people might imply, and although I shall be safely beyond their
power to hurt, you will not. I do not want you to suffer in any
way by my death.'

'Sir,' I said, 'your death would be the worst thing that could
happen to me. I thank you for taking such thought for me, but
there is nothing you can do to prevent me suffering except to
stay alive.'

'I will try to do so, Jeremy,' he said, 'for my own sake as well as
yours. I promise you I have no desire for oblivion, but one must
take precautions.'

His chief precaution was to leave the bulk of the money
he had invested – ten thousand pounds – to Lady Henrietta,
together with his library and his gold and silver plate engraved
with his Congreve coat of arms: three battleaxes, appropriate to
such a military family but hardly to himself, unless in his quarrel
with Mr Collier or his contempt for the Duke of Newcastle. To
her daughter, little Lady Mary, he left his enamelled miniature

portrait of her mother and his white brilliant diamond ring. And he named Lady Henrietta's husband, Lord Godolphin, as his sole executor. After his death, when this Will became public, there was no end of astonished disapproval of its contents. Why, everyone demanded, should he have left his relatively small fortune to one of the richest women in England? Surely Bracey and his Congreve relations deserved better? (Bracey, in fact, was not short of money and lived comfortably with her sister, and what had his Congreve relations ever done for him?) People were also shocked at his choice of executor. Was this a scene from one of his comedies? Was the husband not aware that Mr Congreve was his wife's lover? I knew the secret of the Will, of course, but pretended I didn't, and Lady Henrietta and Lord Godolphin, who must have discussed the matter with him in strict privacy, also knew but didn't tell. I will come back to this secret, in case you have not already guessed it for yourself.

In the summer of the year after making his Will, Mr Congreve came very near death. We were staying in Lady Henrietta's lodge in Windsor Park when he caught a cold – he was always particularly subject to colds – which turned to a fever. He became delirious and burning hot and after a day or two Lady Henrietta sent to London for Dr John Arbuthnot, who had been his physician for some years, recommended originally, I think, by Lady Henrietta herself. He was a Scot and a Tory, and had been a prominent member, with Dr Swift and Mr Harley, of the Brothers' Club and the Scriblerus Club which in the days of fierce contention between Whigs and Tories had been set up to counteract the Kit-Cat Club and spread Tory propaganda. Dr Arbuthnot wrote clever satirical pamphlets against the Whigs featuring a character called John Bull, supposedly a typical English Whig, honest and courageous, but none too clever, with a tendency to get drunk and lose his temper. Captain Steele in his *Spectator* had invented another such character, Sir Roger de Coverley, well-meaning but dim, a typical Tory from the country. So it was a case of clever people on both sides trying to portray each other as clodhoppers.

But Dr Arbuthnot was more than a Tory pamphleteer and more even than a doctor, though he had been physician to Queen Anne. He was a fellow of the Royal Society and his particular expertise was in mathematics, especially the branch of it concerned with probability. He stayed with us at the lodge for nearly three weeks. My master's gout, he said, had gone to his stomach and he could not promise to save his life. Lady Henrietta was distraught and nearly destroyed her own health by sitting up night and day to tend Mr Congreve. It was her housekeeper, Mrs Jellet, who finally persuaded her that she could not save the man she loved by driving herself to death.

Dr Arbuthnot impressed me greatly. He did not try to bleed my master too much, as most doctors would have done, more to show they were doing something than for any good it might do to the patient. He said that would only weaken the little strength he had left and preferred to try to lower the fever with mineral water and cordials, to feed him with thin broth, and above all, when his fever allowed, to talk to him. 'We must bring him back from his feverish dreams to this world,' he said. 'His own mind and body must fight to effect the cure – it is those we must support and encourage.' I was in the sickroom one day when Dr Arbuthnot was talking to my master in one of his lucid intervals and said that with the help of Providence he hoped to see him recover.

'You rely on Providence?' said Mr Congreve.

'Ay, I do.'

'I am never quite sure of its intentions. It seems to hand out rewards and punishments like lottery tickets.'

'Well, I have come to believe in Divine Providence,' said the doctor.

'On what grounds?' asked Mr Congreve.

'Probability. Consider the birth statistics! There are more males born than females, that is a long-established fact. And why should that be so, since it is against all probability? Because males die sooner than females. Therefore we may deduce that this is Divine Providence at work.'

'I am not wholly convinced,' said Mr Congreve. 'Males may be necessary to procreate the race, but their contribution is minimal and can be repeated up to almost any age. Females, on the other hand, cannot bear children beyond a certain age and have to continue caring for them.'

'Do you not see Divine Providence in that?'

'I see it in most things, if I choose to. Or, when I am less optimistic, mere natural causes and blind chance. I can understand that your theory of probability would work well in a game of cards, but life is not a game of cards.'

I remember him saying once that marriage was like a game of cards, but he regarded that, I suppose, as something less than life.

'Is it not?' said Dr Arbuthnot. 'To my mind life is very like a game of cards, although it's true that the rules are a tad more complicated and will only be understood one day by much greater mathematicians than I am.'

My master turned his head wearily towards me, sitting on a chair by the window, the other side of the bed from Dr Arbuthnot.

'Does the doctor's argument convince you, Jeremy?'

'If you will get better, sir,' I replied, 'I shall regard Dr Arbuthnot as an instrument of Divine Providence.'

Word of my master's illness had spread rapidly to his friends and there were letters nearly every day enquiring after his condition from Lord Cobham, Lord Shannon, Mr Pope, Dr Swift, the Porters and Lady Mary Wortley-Montagu. Very gradually, as autumn turned to winter, he began to improve and towards the end of November we were all able to return to London.

He lay fairly low at our lodgings through the winter and spring of the next year, and it was at this time Monsieur Voltaire visited us and was so shocked by his reception, as I described in my Prologue. But although death had spared Mr Congreve, it did not spare our house, for Mrs Frances Porter died, leaving us all very sad. She was a kind lady, less spirited than her sister Bracey, quieter and more retiring in manner, but firm and efficient in the management of the household. Mr Congreve was very fond of her and she of him. She made shirts from Holland linen for him, as well as on one occasion for Mr Keally in Ireland, so skilfully that she contrived eleven shirts out of a piece of Holland that should have produced only ten. This may sound a trivial thing to mention when speaking of someone's death, but it conveys something of her character and was the sort of accomplishment that my master particularly admired, whether in the famous or the obscure, in politicians, generals, poets, actors, musicians, tailors or housewives: a scrupulous, unshowy, hard-won proficiency. His lines to Sir Godfrey Kneller praising him for his portrait of an unnamed lady prove my point, and since the unnamed lady was none other than Lady Henrietta, he was especially well qualified to judge the portrait's accuracy:

> I yield, O *Kneller,* to superior Skill,
> Thy Pencil triumphs o'er the Poet's Quill:
> If yet my vanquish'd Muse exert her Lays,
> It is no more to Rival thee, but Praise.
> Oft have I try'd, with unavailing Care,
> To trace some Image of the much-lov'd Fair;
> But still my Numbers ineffectual prov'd,
> And rather shew'd how much, than whom, I lov'd:
> But thy unerring Hands, with matchless Art,
> Have shewn my Eyes th'Impression in my Heart;
> The bright Idea both exists and lives,
> Such vital Heat thy Genial Pencil gives:
> Whose daring Point, not to the Face confin'd,
> Can penetrate the Heart, and paint the Mind.

In the early summer we went to Bath, as did Lady Henrietta and her daughter, both of them overjoyed to have Uncle Will to themselves again.

'How nearly we lost you!' said Lady Henrietta, tears in her eyes, as they embraced in her lodging.

'Jeremy believes it was Divine Providence in the shape of Dr Arbuthnot,' said Mr Congreve.

'It certainly was,' said Lady Henrietta.

'I am deeply grateful to him, but I find it ironical that Divine Providence should take the form of a Tory to save the life of a Whig.'

'Do you really think that Providence cares a fig for your factious parties?'

Lady Henrietta, like her father, was neither quite Whig nor Tory, but perhaps inclined more to the Tories, since her mother the old Duchess, whom she scarcely ever met now, had always been a Whig.

'Well, we should not waste words on politics. I have had a near escape and might have been jostling at St Peter's Gate with King George and Sir Isaac Newton.'

Sir Isaac, the great philosopher, had died, aged 84, in March and King George I in June.

'I don't know,' he went on, 'whether kings remain kings in heaven – there must be quite a crowd of them by now and it would be tricky to sort out their precedence – but I'm sure Sir Isaac will be received with particular honour. He will be put in charge of hanging out the colours of the rainbow, though I wonder how he will get on without gravity.'

He was talking just for the sake of talking to her, while Lady Henrietta, I saw, was not really listening to what he said, but simply looking at him, smiling all the while, her eyes shining with tears of joy.

We were soon joined in Bath by Mr Gay. He was always a welcome companion to both Mr Congreve and Lady Henrietta, though on this occasion not quite as carefree as usual. He brought with him the manuscript of his *Beggar's Opera*, more play than opera, a burlesque piece set among thieves and bawds, whose dubious figures of authority, Lockit and Peachum, bore some resemblance to the Whig leaders, Mr Walpole and his brother-in-law Lord Townshend. Mr Pope and Dr Swift had helped him make some adjustments, but Mr Gay said they were not at all hopeful of it and he was afraid he might have written another 'dumpling'. He had not previously had much success with his plays. Mr Congreve carried the manuscript to his room and pored over it with his magnifying glass. When he emerged some hours later he was smiling broadly.

'Where is Mr Gay?' he asked.

'I don't know,' said Lady Henrietta. 'He sat in that chair there for a while wringing his hands and crossing and uncrossing his legs and looking like a man waiting to see his doctor or his lawyer on the most deadly business. Then he suddenly got up and went out.'

'He is pacing up and down the street,' I said, looking out of the window.

'Go and ask him to come in, if he will,' said Mr Congreve.

I fetched him in and he entered the room as if he were a schoolboy expecting to be caned, his steps slow, his head lowered, his hands trembling.

'John Gay!' said my master, slapping the manuscript. 'What have you done here? It's the most extraordinary piece of impudent invention. That ballad for Macheath, caught in prison between his Polly and his Lucy: "How happy could I be with either,/Were t'other dear charmer away!/But while ye thus tease me together,/To neither a word will I say." I love it. What music will you use for the ballads?'

'Just popular airs,' said Mr Gay, still sounding unlike his usual ebullient self, doubtful perhaps whether my master's enthusiasm was sincere. 'Mr Pepusch, the organist and teacher, has promised to choose and arrange them for me.'

'Well, it must be performed as soon as he has done so. My lease of life being so uncertain, I should hate to miss it.'

'I should hate to miss it myself,' said Mr Gay, whose health was also very poor. 'But do you think it will take with the public?' He sounded now more cheerful.

'It will either take mightily or be damned confoundedly. Who can second guess the fickle public? But if they damn it, they damn a masterpiece of a kind never created before.'

'Tell them to bring in bottles and glasses, Jeremy!' said Lady Henrietta. 'We must certainly celebrate such a masterpiece.'

So they celebrated and Mr Gay was finally convinced of my master's sincere approval and recovered his spirits. I may add that Mr Cibber turned it down for Drury Lane, but when *The Beggar's Opera* was put on by Mr Rich at his theatre in Lincoln's Inn Fields the next year, it ran for no less than sixty-three performances and, so the joke went round, 'made Gay rich and Rich gay'. But Mr Gay's anxiety and my master's encouragement reminded me of that time so long before when Mr Congreve gave the manuscript of *The Old Bachelor* to Mr Dryden with the same dread of what his verdict might be. *The Beggar's Opera* went all round the provincial theatres and is still being revived to this day, though Mr Gay had little time left to enjoy his success. He died in the year 1732, only three years after Mr Congreve.

That year of 1727 was really the last in which my master fully enjoyed his life and the company of his friend Mr Gay, his true lover Lady Henrietta and their little daughter, now nearly four years old. Lady Henrietta entertained her guest and his friend royally and provided carriages for excursions into the country. The two invalids drank the waters, entered them occasionally, and seemed to find their health improved, but I think it was more the warmth of each other's company and the salts of their lively conversation that worked a temporary cure. The days slid by – those seven mysterious Saxon gods – as they always do so inexorably, stealthily, raining or shining, cold or warm, the future becoming the present, the present lapsing into the past, just as these memories of my master's life slide now towards his and their conclusion.

We were in Bath again the following spring with Lady Henrietta and were joined in the summer by Mr Gay – now rich and successful Mr Gay – and Mr Tonson, who came as much to be with his author as for his own health. But Mr Congreve's condition had deteriorated again in the winter and he spent many days in bed. It was a pity that on one particular day when the sun was shining and he felt better, he chose to go out for a drive in an open chariot of the kind Sir John Vanbrugh had used to speed him around the country to his various building projects.

Sir John, so far as I know, never had a serious accident, but our driver was less lucky or less skilled. Passing some larger equipage in a narrow place, our wheel went into a ditch and the chariot overturned. Riding on the back, I was easily able to jump off, but Mr Congreve was badly bruised. He made light of it at the time as I and passers-by rushed to his assistance: 'Do you think Dr Arbuthnot would call this Divine Providence?' he asked me, as the chariot was righted and he was helped back into it. 'I wonder what I have done to provoke its malice.'

'Well, do not provoke it further, I beg you, sir!' I said. 'We must get you home and call a doctor.'

He continued to make light of his injuries in the face of Lady Henrietta's dismay, and the visible bruises gradually cleared up. We and Lady Henrietta, with her daughter and household, remained in Bath far beyond our usual period, well into the autumn, when most of the fashionable crowd had left, so that Mr Congreve could continue taking the waters and, Lady Henrietta hoped, be fully fit for the journey back to London. But my master did sometimes complain to me, though never to her, that he had an occasional violent pain in his side.

Perhaps to take his mind off that, he composed his last long poem and one of his best, and sent it off to Lord Cobham from Bath in August. It was entitled simply 'A Letter from Mr Congreve to the Right Honourable the LordViscount Cobham', and was headed with a quotation from his favourite poet Horace's letter to his friend Albius: '*Albi, nostrorum Sermonum candide Iudex*' (to Albius, candid judge of our conversations). I have already quoted from it at some length, but at this sorrowful penultimate point of my memories, take the liberty to repeat its brave buoyancy:

Defer not till to Morrow to be wise,
To Morrow's Sun to thee may never rise.
Or shou'd to Morrow chance to cheer thy Sight,
With her enliv'ning and unlookt-for Light,
How grateful will appear her dawning Rays!

As Favours unexpected doubly please.
Who thus can think and who such thoughts pursues,
Content may keep his Life, or calmly lose.

He was failing fast when we returned to London and winter came in, and soon after Christmas took to his bed. Friends visited and when he was awake he tried to converse with them as if he expected still to be seeing them again in better health in the spring. After Twelfth Night, when he had sunk still lower, Lady Henrietta visited nearly every day. She came in a plain carriage so as not to advertise her presence to the world, though the fashionable part of it knew very well what great lady it was that stepped hurriedly out of the carriage and into Mr Porter's house to sit with the dying poet in his humble lodging. In the last two days she sat with him day and night, until early on 19 January, a Sunday morning – the day of those born 'bonny and blithe and good and gay', but five days before his fifty-ninth birthday – he died in her arms and my presence.

'Mary?' I heard him ask her.

'Never fear!' she said. 'She will do well.'

She did not mean in general, let alone by that glorious marriage for love which neither of them would live to see. She was referring to Mr Congreve's Will and its secret, which was simply that her own Will – not so easily accessible to prying eyes as his – would pass everything that he left to Henrietta – his investments in the bank, the diamond necklace and earrings she bought with most of that money, his engraved plate and his library – to Mary. The executor of her Will would again be her husband, Lord Godolphin, truly, as my master had said, 'a gentleman through and through'.

People like to know the last words of the famous. Mr Congreve's were, '*We* have done well, my love.'

She buried him a week later, on the next Sunday evening, in Westminster Abbey. My master's corpse lay for three hours in state in the Jerusalem Chamber, where Lady Henrietta sat weeping with it – and I stood, equally desolate, in the shadow of the walls draped with black – silently acknowledging those who came to pay their respects. Then in the evening, between nine and ten o'clock it was carried into King Henry VII's Chapel and buried near the monument to her father-in-law, the first Earl of Godolphin, her father's friend and colleague during the years of war with France. The Chief Mourner was my master's cousin Colonel Congreve and the six pall-bearers were the Duke of Bridgewater (Lady Henrietta's brother-in-law), the Earl of Godolphin (her husband), Viscount Cobham, Lord Wilmington, the Honourable George Berkeley and Brigadier-General Churchill (Lady Henrietta's nephew). The first four were all Kit-Cats and Mr Berkeley was the son of one, Lord Berkeley. Not many plain gentlemen, as Mr Congreve liked to present himself, could boast of such distinguished attendants at their interment and I rather wished that Monsieur Voltaire, who thought his social status so modest, had been there to see it.

Unlike her errant son-in-law, the Duke of Newcastle, Lady Henrietta was quick to set up Mr Congreve's monument, topped by a portrait medallion carved after Sir Godfrey Kneller's painting by Mr Francis Bird. The epitaph reads:

MR WILLIAM CONGREVE,
Dyed *jan* the 19th 1728 Aged 56. And was buried near this place, To whose most Valuable Memory this Monument is Sett up by HENRIETTA, *Dutchess* of MARLBOROUGH, as a mark how dearly She remembers the Happiness and Honour She enjoyed in the Sincere Friendshipp of so worthy and Honest a Man, Whose Virtue Candour and Witt gained him the love and Esteem of the present Age and whose Writings will be the Admiration of the Future.

She evidently thought him two years younger than he really was. Old Duchess Sarah did not attend the funeral, but she must have read the epitaph, for she remarked that her daughter might have had happiness from her friendship with Mr Congreve, but hardly honour. As for the lurid stories circulating later, such as that Lady Henrietta sat at table with a wax effigy of Mr Congreve next to her and required her servants to put food in front of it, and other absurdities, they might suggest her intense sorrow, but not her intelligence or her character. She herself, when she died four years later, was buried in the same chamber in Westminster Abbey, near to her father-in-law and Mr Congreve.

His friends were deeply grieved by his loss. Lady Mary Wortley Montagu's poem 'To the Memory of Mr Congreve' begins:

> Farewell the best and loveliest of Mankind
> Where Nature with a happy hand had joyn'd
> The softest temper with the strongest mind,
> In pain could counsel and could charm when blind.
> In this Lewd Age when Honor is a Jest
> He found a refuge in his Congreve's breast,
> Superior there, unsully'd, and entire;
> And only could with the last breath expire.

Mr Pope said that the news of his friend's death 'quite strook me through', and Dr Swift's grief was so great that it made him almost regret he had ever had a friend, though he could not quite avoid moralising:

> He had the misfortune to squander away a very good con-
> stitution in his younger days, and I think a man of sense
> and merit like him, is bound in conscience to preserve his
> health for the sake of his friends, as well as of himself.

Mr Tonson was also saddened by his old friend's death, but not to the point of forgetting his business. He urged his nephew in London to buy my master's library and to republish his *Works*, since 'Let a mans worth be nevour so great after Death it gets strangely out of the minds of his Surviving acquaintance'. The fifth edition of the *Works of Mr William Congreve* duly appeared the year after his death, but the library, of course, now belonged to Lady Henrietta, so that she could pass it on to Mr Congreve's adored and only child.

I have done. This is my monument to the man I served and loved for more than half his life, a mirror for monkeys perhaps, or it may be that I am the monkey holding up the mirror, from the top of which my master's face stares at me in dismay. Lord Cobham is dying now and I feel that I am quite near doing so. Returning from the Pebble Alcove yesterday over the Palladian Bridge, I turned to look towards Mr Congreve's monument on the island and felt a great stitch in my chest which made me clutch at the parapet of the bridge. I soon recovered, but it makes me wonder, if Lord Cobham dies and I die too, what is to become of this bulky manuscript. I could leave it among the other papers in Lord Cobham's archive and let it take its chance, or I could try to find a publisher. But both Mr Tonson and his nephew are dead and I do not know who else to approach or whether there is any market these days for a book of this unscholarly kind in Latin. I begin to think now, when I have done all this work and it is far too late, that I should have written it in English.

But perhaps I will give it to Lord Cobham's new coachman, a friendly young man, who often drives to London, and ask him to take it to Mr Pitt. He is such a bold cricketer and I fancy a great man in the making, and was so kind as to call it a labour of love. He may know what to do with it. However my master might argue otherwise, I tend to think that he had a sneaking belief in Divine Providence, and so do I.

Jeremy Fetch, *Anno Domini MDCCXLIX*

Also Available

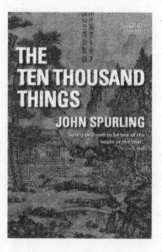

Winner of the Walter Scott Prize for Historical Fiction

In the turbulent final years of the Yuan Dynasty, Wang Meng is a low-level bureaucrat employed by the government of Mongol conquerors established by the Kublai Khan. Though he wonders about his own complicity with this regime he prefers not to dwell on his official duties, choosing instead to live the life of the mind. Wang is an extraordinarily gifted artist and his paintings are at once delicate and confident; in them one can see the wind blowing through the trees, the water rushing through rocky valleys, the infinite expanse of China's natural beauty.

But this is not a time for sitting still as Wang must soon travel through an empire in turmoil. In his wanderings he encounters master painters, a fierce female warrior known as the White Tigress who will recruit him as a military strategist, and an ugly young Buddhist monk who rises from beggary to extraordinary heights.

The Ten Thousand Things seamlessly fuses the epic and the intimate with the precision and depth that the real-life Wang Meng brought to his painting.

OUT NOW